PETALS
AND
STONES

JOANNE BURN

Legend Press Ltd, 107-111 Fleet Street, London, EC4A 2AB
info@legend-paperbooks.co.uk | www.legendpress.co.uk

Roger Keyes' poem 'Hokusai Says' on pages 193 and 194 is reproduced with the kind permission of Roger Keyes.

Print ISBN 978-1-78-719816-6
Ebook ISBN 978-1-78719815-9
Set in Times. Printing managed by Jellyfish Solutions Ltd
Cover design by Simon Levy | www.simonlevyassociates.co.uk

A lover of words, food and the wild outdoors, **Joanne Burn** lives in the Peak District where she works as a writing coach, and blogs about the the joys and challenges of the creative process. *Petals and Stones* is her debut novel.

Visit Joanne at
www.joanneburn.com

For Lance

Chapter One

2015

Holly's dark ringlets and olive skin meant the two of them were easily mistaken for mother and daughter. The shopkeeper – her elbows and heavy chest resting on the counter top, her long grey hair slicked behind her ears – seemed to make that assumption, exchanging knowing looks with Uma as Holly brushed her fingertips across the chocolate bars and packets of sweets.

'So lovely at this age…' the shopkeeper said, offering Uma the kind of smile that said *how lucky you are, how lovely she is, how proud you must be.* 'I always wanted a daughter but all I got was boys.'

If she had asked directly then Uma would have put her straight. But she didn't, and Uma let the untruth stand beside them like another customer waiting to be served. A deception of sorts, but nothing like an outright lie.

Outside, the snow blew into their eyes and mouths despite their generous layers of wool and fleece and all attempts to turn their faces from the bitter gusts. They walked, heads down, Uma squeezing Holly's hand through their gloves in silent encouragement.

'I'm cold, Auntie Uma,' Holly whimpered eventually, two streets from home.

'If we walk quickly, we'll be back in no time.'

Holly was slowing, resisting the tugging of Uma's hand, bowing her face towards the snow beneath her feet.

'We just need to keep going,' said Uma.

She thought of the log burner in the kitchen, the gentle warmth of the underfloor heating, the fairy lights she had strung around the place once the days had shortened. She imagined them sinking into plump cushions as they snuggled together to watch the television.

'Think how nice it will be, once we're home.'

The steps up to the house were buried, hardly discernible beneath the snow, and they kicked until they found the stone, making a game of it.

Inside the house, they stamped their feet, shedding their sodden clothes and scattering an icy slush across the hallway tiles.

'Your phone is ringing Auntie Uma.'

'Is it?' Uma said, straining to hear, faintly making out the sound. 'What brilliant ears you have!'

She ran to the kitchen and snatched up the handset. *You have new messages. Please wait to be connected to your messaging service.* Holly appeared in the kitchen, making straight for the wood burner, flopping onto the rug and lifting her feet towards the glass.

'Not too close.'

Voice text.

Uma sighed. They were an annoyance, these occasional, accidental text messages that came through to the landline – hard to decipher the robotic text translation and tedious to track down the mobile number in her contacts list to work out who it was from. Uma reached for a pad from the table and scribbled the number as it was given.

Message received today at 3.55pm: Missing you already Danny-boy. Why is it never enough? xxx

Motionless, she looked at the numbers on the paper.

To listen to the message again press one. To save it press two. To delete it press three.

Uma took the phone from her ear, looked down at the

keypad and carefully, heart quickening, pressed *one*. The message played again. *Missing you already Danny-boy.* Danny-boy? Who would address him so affectionately? His mother didn't call him Danny-boy. His sisters didn't call him Danny-boy. And why is *what* never enough?

A sense of unease, slow and cautious, seeped through her. She saved the message and replaced the phone in its cradle, staying where she was, looking through the window at the large garden that swept down towards the stream at the bottom. Everything familiar had been erased by white. Every shape and contour had been muffled beyond recognition by a thick blanket of snow. She became aware of Holly speaking, reaching up her little hands to pull on Uma's arm, taking her fingers, leading her towards the cupboards on the other side of the kitchen.

'I'm hungry Auntie Uma. I need a snack.'

She looked down at her Goddaughter. She was perfect – crazy ringlets, flawless skin, the tiniest scar from her lip operation. Her gaze rested on Uma, trusting her needs to be met.

'A snack,' Uma repeated, allowing herself to be manoeuvred. She took bread from the bread bin and cut it with a knife, dropping it into the toaster.

'Can I have chocolate spread?'

'Peanut butter would be better,' Uma said, her voice a whisper. 'Don't you think? You've got your sweeties too so I think peanut butter would be better. And some orange juice.'

Holly didn't argue, and fetched her special plate and cup. They were heavy crockery with pictures of Pooh and Piglet. Uma had bought them when she first agreed to have Holly after school once a week. She had been aware of her efforts to make it special, of her craving for the child to like her – to *really* like her. Pippa, Holly's mother, had laughed at the expensive crockery. *You want plastic*, she had said, picking up the plate and turning it over in her hands. *She'll throw this straight on the floor*. But somehow, even as a toddler, Holly had known not to throw things. And now, of course, she loved her Pooh and Piglet plate, and how grown up it felt to be trusted with something so lovely.

Uma put the snack in front of Holly and left the room. She sat on the bottom step of the stairs, the paper with the scribbled number on it trembling in her hands. She checked the number against her contacts list, but it wasn't recognised. She dialled it – no idea what she intended to say – but it rang out and went through to voicemail. She listened to the voice-text message again, as if she needed to, as if every word hadn't already become a song she had known forever, a song she couldn't prevent from repeating. *Missing you already Danny-boy*.

Her confusion was merging slowly, inescapably, with suspicion, and a looming certainty that she *knew* what this was. She was trying to turn away from it but it was everywhere she looked. Her face was hot, her mouth dry. And Daniel was having an affair. Her husband was doing *that thing* that people do.

Uma grabbed handfuls of her jumper, pulling the soft wool to cover her face, images of him kissing another woman, his hands against imaginary skin, running through her mind.

**

She made a cappuccino for Pippa without asking her if she wanted one. It gave her something to do with her hands, and an excuse to turn away from Pippa's scrutiny.

'Are you o*kay*?' Pippa asked, after the briefest of pauses. 'You sounded… *odd* when I called.'

'*Shattered*,' Uma said, shaking her head. 'I'm super busy with the new deli opening next week. It's a never-ending snagging list.' She cut the conversation short by flicking on the steamer and taking longer than necessary to froth a jug of milk.

'Holly was good as gold,' Uma said, when she'd finished. She sprinkled the cappuccino with chocolate and turned towards her friend, handing her the cup, avoiding her gaze. 'And I bought her fruit pastilles on the way home.'

Pippa shrugged. 'Godmother's prerogative I suppose.'

Uma forced a smile, shifting her attention to Holly who, belly-down on the rug, was colouring a picture in the firelight, her face obscured by a mass of curls, a halo of pencils encircling her.

'Not having a drink?' Pippa asked, spooning froth into her mouth.

'I've not long had one,' said Uma, thinking about the cold wine in the fridge, how much she wanted the house to herself and the chance to pour a glass.

'Where's Daniel?'

'Away. Work stuff.'

She heard the tone of her voice – brisk and defensive. She rolled up the sleeves of her shirt, one at a time, as if readying herself for a fight, folding the lemon-yellow fabric neatly, revealing her golden-brown forearms.

'What's up, hon?' Pippa queried.

'I told you,' Uma replied, unfolding the left sleeve, re-rolling it a little neater this time. 'I'm tired, that's all.'

Pippa's lack of response was heavy with scepticism and Uma bristled, conscious of her friend's ability to sense fragility and to needle until she excavated its cause. Cupping her coffee in one hand, Pippa dipped the spoon with the other, lifting it every so often to her pale lips.

'I'm not daft, Uma.' Her large hoop earrings swung blithely. She dropped the spoon in her coffee and ran splayed fingers through her long brown hair.

'Then leave it,' said Uma.

'But this is what you always do.'

'And *this* is what *you* do,' Uma reminded her. 'I don't want to talk about it.'

And there it was. Unintentional, but a confession that

11

there was, at least, *something* to talk about. A concession that Pippa was justified in her prying.

'Okay,' Pippa said. 'That's fine. We can talk about me. I've got a second date with Mr Salsa tonight. But, more importantly, do you like my new boots?'

Uma looked the long length of Pippa's legs as Pippa did a turn of the kitchen, strutting, swishing her hair like a bull-fighter's cape. They laughed, forgiving one another, and Uma leaned briefly against her friend as Pippa put an arm around her.

**

Uma flicked the outside light on, opening the front door. It was snowing still, but gently now, and Holly reached out to catch snowflakes on her open palms.

'Holly, sweetie,' cautioned Pippa. 'Concentrate on the steps.'

They turned at the gate, waving goodbye, and Pippa turned again after strapping Holly into the car.

'Let's get that night out sorted,' she called, giving Uma a thumbs up. Uma returned the gesture, nodding as enthusiastically as she could manage, her smile falling from her face as soon as she turned towards the house. Inside, she slumped against the door, eyes closed, summoning strength.

In the warm kitchen she poured herself a large glass of wine and fed several logs into the burner. After lighting candles on the mantelpiece she stretched out on the sofa, emptying her glass with slow sips, her mobile and the house phone like stones in her lap. Her mobile had buzzed with calls and text messages from friends and work colleagues all afternoon, and she had silenced them or deleted them or thumbed in speedy replies. Now it was the evening the messages were petering out, and she waited for the call that she knew would come. What would she say to him? Would he know by now about his lover's mistake? Daniel always called home early in the evening when he was away. And he texted goodnight sometime around 11pm. These small, careful acts had always made her feel that he was thinking of her. His phone his only company on the pillow beside him.

She took large mouthfuls of wine, teasing apart the fraying fabric of the recent past, unpicking the stitching of their marriage. She tried to remember whether Daniel had been behaving differently, whether there had been a shift in the ease of their dealings. They had always worked so smoothly together, and Uma found it hard to see what, if anything, had altered between them.

She replayed the moment he'd left for Devon on Tuesday morning, tiny flecks of swirling snow pattering the window panes. He'd come towards her at the kitchen table where she had been eating breakfast. His pale skin had been cleanly shaved. He'd paused, fiddling with his cufflinks, and perhaps they had exchanged a few words – she couldn't remember. What she did remember was that he had kissed her cheek. A fleeting, flutter of a kiss.

What must he have been thinking? She tried to imagine him keeping that most significant of secrets, and realised that perhaps it wouldn't have been such a difficult task. She thought about his need for privacy, his tendency to keep ideas to himself until they were fully formed, alive and kicking and ready for the world's scrutiny. She thought, too, of how she had always accommodated this.

Wishing she could resist, Uma listened to the message again and redialled the mystery mobile number. It had been switched off. She let the phone slip into her lap where it rang immediately and, despite expecting it, she felt strangely shocked that he was calling her. She imagined him – spare hand fidgeting with some small object that had been within easy reach, or running his fingers through his short black hair or brushing his hand across his cheek, rough with stubble by now. He was rarely still, restless even when relaxing, chewing his nails if there was nothing else to hand. She picked up the phone, heart pounding at the pulsing of his name on the screen, and forced herself to tap the little green icon to accept the call.

'Hey.'

'Hi.'

There was a flicker of emptiness, then a great black hole in their conversation, and Uma fell into it, unable to speak.

'Are you… *okay*?' he said eventually.

He knew. Uma could hear it in his voice. She didn't know what to say, how to start, what to ask.

'Uma…?'

'How long…?'

'Oh, Lord,' he whispered.

She understood those words for what they were, more prayer than blasphemy. She made a noise of disdain, after which neither of them spoke. She listened to the sound of him breathing, refusing to break the silence, unwilling to navigate on his behalf.

'I'm so sorry,' he said.

'Let's do this when you're home.'

'Then I'll come back tonight.'

'It's a six hour drive.'

'It doesn't matter.'

'It's gone ten. I don't want you waking me up at four in the morning.'

'I'll leave first thing.'

'Fine.'

'I… I love you.'

She hung up without replying and refilled her glass, not bothering to put the bottle back into the fridge. *Loves me?* She crossed her legs beneath her on the sofa, looking towards the fire, stroking her fingers over the old, familiar threadbare fabric. The very same sofa had kept vigil with the fire in her childhood home and sometimes, these days, staring into the glimmering heat and feeling the rough fabric beneath her skin she could shrink the years, reaching through that thin curtain of time to when she had been a child, transporting herself back to River View, the cottage she had shared with her parents. If she stared into the fire for long enough, concentrating on the familiarity of the sofa beneath her, she could almost smell the coconut and cardamom from her mother's breakfast paniyaram, or hear the tapping of her father's typewriter in the other room. She tried to get there now but her mind was in no mood for cheap tricks, rooting itself instead in the present moment with all its confusion and heavy surreality. Daniel was having an affair. *Daniel*. It was hardly comprehensible. She looked around herself – at the little oil painting of Rhossili beach they had bought from a gallery there during a rare, brief weekend away from work, at their silly collection of salt and pepper shakers that took up two whole shelves on the dresser, at the photo montage that told the story of *Millers,* their deli business – from a single family-owned green grocers to nationwide successful chain. She continued to drink, rejecting her rule of never more than three glasses.

When the bottle was empty, Uma stumbled upstairs and into her room, pulling a selection of warm, comfortable clothes from her bottom drawer, swaying as she negotiated them over her limbs. Back downstairs she pulled on her trainers and stepped out the back door, the moonlight bright, reflecting off the snow, lighting her way to the end of the garden and over the stone wall at the bottom. Snow found its way into her trainers, wetting her socks and her breath plumed ghost-like round her face in the darkness. She could hear the burbling of the stream as she picked her way through the undergrowth. She squeezed through a loose area in Ruth's hedge and looked up towards the house. *Please be home*.

**

Uma woke with a start, at the metallic clunk of her curtains being drawn. She lifted her head, struggling to open her eyes. The room swam and she let her head fall back onto the pillow.

'What on earth happened to you?'

It was Ruth's voice – soft, familiar, concerned.

Uma struggled to remember the details of last night, grappling with threads of memory in an attempt to tie them together. Her head was so full of thumping pain there was no space for remembering.

'I'm not sure,' Uma croaked, pushing herself up on her elbows. She tried to swallow – her mouth dry and sour – and forced her eyes open.

'You left me a message, saying you needed to talk to me about something important. You sounded upset Uma.'

Ruth perched on the end of the bed. The large linen scarf wrapped about her throat was the colour of a deep orange sunset. She wore one every day, and Uma had once asked to see where she kept them all, dipping her fingertips in the drawer-full of colours, taken aback at how it reminded her of her mother's wardrobe – her shalwar kameez hanging, tunics in every shade, heavily-patterned fabric that she sent for from India.

'You're still fully clothed,' said Ruth, as if trying to jog Uma's memory.

Uma was lying on top of the duvet, dressed in the thick joggers and layers of long-sleeved tops that she had pulled on so clumsily the evening before.

'Is my brother responsible for this?' Ruth asked, smiling.

Then Uma remembered. It was like stepping into a cave, the coldness hitting her. *Daniel*. She had drunk a bottle of wine and gone, in her drunken state, to tell Ruth everything. 'I went round to yours…' Uma mumbled. 'I was being silly. Drunk. I'd been out with Pippa,' she lied, keen to end the conversation.

'I was at a thing with James,' explained Ruth. 'Mum had the girls overnight. So where's Daniel?'

'Devon.'

'When's he home?'

'Around lunchtime I guess. What time is it now?'

Ruth glanced at her watch. 'Just gone ten. Shall I put the kettle on?'

'You don't have to stay. I know what Saturdays are like with the girls' dancing and swimming.' Uma imagined the awkwardness of Ruth being around when Daniel arrived home. 'You should get back.'

'It's fine. James is doing the running around today. I'll stay and make you breakfast, okay?'

Uma forced a bleak smile and made a show of rousing herself. But as the door closed behind her sister-in-law, Uma rolled onto her side, burying her face in the pillow, letting the sobs come in great heaves. She felt too wretched to fight it, and felt the shame of that rising up in her and elbowing everything else out of the way. *Life is tough*, her mother used to say. *If you're soft as a mango then expect to get eaten.*

Ruth lit the fire in the kitchen while Uma, watching, full of gratitude despite her anxiety, lay beneath a blanket on the little sofa. However hectic Uma and Daniel's schedule, Uma made time for the building of a fire in the kitchen on a cold morning, enjoying the rolling and twisting of newspaper into knots, the wigwam of kindling, the fizzle of the match as she grazed it against the box. It was why she chose to work in the kitchen most days, piling her papers and folders on the dresser each evening or leaving them strewn across the kitchen table if she was particularly busy. *You have a spacious office upstairs*, Daniel would say, glancing at the debris of Uma's day. *I like it down here*, she told him, countless times, in different ways. He'd never asked her why, grumbling, instead, *that chair of yours cost a fortune, you know*. He meant the one upstairs. The one she never used. *I never chose that chair*, she was tempted to say, every time he mentioned it. *I never wanted it in the first place.*

'Your back door was open, by the way,' said Ruth, carefully positioning some small logs on top of the flaming kindle. She closed the small glass door and turned to Uma.

'Was it? Unlocked, you mean? Or *open* open?'

'*Open* open. Just swinging in the wind.'

'This is why I don't drink,' said Uma.

'Well at least you remembered to bolt the front door.'

'Did I?'

'You did. I went to check when I first came in. I thought maybe you'd been burgled or something.'

Uma grimaced. 'I feel so silly. I can't remember the last time I got so drunk.'

Immediately she did remember – the night of her wedding. The first morning she woke as Daniel's wife the world had been spinning, her regret a bitter pill that she would struggle to swallow down for the rest of the day. She had created the *never more than three glasses* rule that evening as they made their way to Scotland for their honeymoon. *Sure*, Daniel had laughed, oblivious to the depth of her pain. *That's what we all say*. But Uma had stuck by her rule, realising several years later how like her father she was in that respect. *Once you've made a decision, you stick to it*, he'd told her once, his stiff-upper-lip Englishness as clear and bright as those harvest moons he loved so much.

Ruth disappeared from view and Uma closed her eyes, listening to the sound of the kettle coming to the boil, the cafetiere being located in the cupboard, the top removed, the bag of coffee being opened. Uma imagined the smell of it – rich, pungent, a comfort despite her delicate state.

'I'll have it black,' she called.

Ruth was pouring water from the kettle, Uma could hear it sloshing into the cafetiere.

'Sure.'

Uma stared into the flames, trying to get things straight in her head. What was she going to say to him? What was *he* going to say to her? Uma knew there was every chance this thing, whatever it was, was significant. Daniel's motto was *let's wait and see*. He preferred saving to investing. He'd never left the UK, not even for France, not even for a day. He went alone to his father's grave on the anniversary of his death, every year without fail. And he had a little notebook with scores of names and dates inside – the significant events for everyone that mattered. Daniel was as dutiful as he was cautious.

Ruth appeared in front of her, holding out a cup of steaming coffee.

'Thank you,' said Uma, sitting up a little, fighting the wave of nausea, reaching out for the cup.

'Are you sure you're okay? I mean, I know you're not feeling okay *right now*. But is everything okay? It's just...' Ruth trailed off, and Uma's heart tugged for her friend. She knew Ruth meant well.

'I think everything's okay.'

'You *think*?'

'Daniel and I had a falling out about something. It so rarely happens, that's all.'

'Ahhh.'

Ruth sipped her coffee, looking at Uma over the top of her mug, her spare hand stroking the folds of fabric wrapped around her throat. Uma felt a pressure to say more. But what? She couldn't concoct a whole alternative story.

'Well, we don't have to talk about it,' said Ruth, smiling her sympathetic, GP smile.

'I wouldn't want you to feel in the middle,' said Uma, wondering what Ruth would have said last night if Uma had stumbled into their home at midnight, cold from the biting wind and overflowing with her bitter news. She pulled at a tuft of wool in the blanket over her knees, picking at it and working it free.

'You'll sort it out when he's home,' said Ruth.

But would they? Uma realised as she sipped her coffee that Daniel being unfaithful wasn't a scenario she had ever given much thought to. She simply hadn't imagined it, not seriously. And the experience of finding out yesterday, that sensation of coming out of the darkness into the light, of suddenly knowing, had been so shocking. Like a balloon expanding inside of her, filling every tiny space until there was nothing but *it*. *There is another woman. Nothing is what I thought it was. The last fifteen years have been a waste.*

Ruth's voice found its way into her thoughts and Uma looked up.

'Sorry?'

'I said what have you got on this week?'

'Oh God,' said Uma. 'There's so much happening in the next couple of weeks. Our new deli's opening in Manchester a week today. We've got tons to do for that. Daniel's interviewing for a new manager down in Devon on Wednesday.'

'He's going back down?'

Uma nodded, flaring inwardly at the thought of what his trips to Devon involved. She had always been so grateful that he'd taken on the burden of the long, tedious journeys and all those nights away from home. It had seemed almost chivalrous the way he'd reassured her from the beginning that he *really didn't mind*.

'You two are amazing – working together's tough.'

It will be from now on. She thought about the weeks ahead and how they could possibly steer through all that needed to be done. Their lives were so intertwined it was impossible to imagine untangling them, even temporarily. Uma sipped her coffee, the starkness of it in her dry mouth a relief of sorts. She sighed, leaning back into the cushions.

Three short, sharp knocks shattered their quiet conversing. They looked at one another.

'The bolts are on,' Uma said, speaking the thought aloud, looking at her watch. 'He must have left before five a.m.'

'I'll get my things,' said Ruth.

'Thank you for looking after me.'

They hugged, Uma's face disappearing into the sunset folds of Ruth's scarf, wishing it was possible to stay right there. There were only two people who hugged her like it really mattered. And Ruth was one of them.

In the hallway the tiles were warm beneath Uma's bare feet. Daniel had promised that she would love the underfloor heating in the winter. *Some things are worth the extra effort,* he had said.

Uma unbolted the door, readying herself for the sight of him, arranging her face into something steely. She unlocked the deadlock, inserted the yale key and twisted, stepping back as the door swung open. She was already turning away, ready to leave him on the doorstep, the cold air raising goose bumps on her neck, when she realised it wasn't Daniel.

Two police officers, a man and a woman, introduced themselves, ascertaining that Uma was Uma. There may have been a moment when she realised – perhaps when they asked whether it was okay to come in, whether they could speak inside. The wind rushed down the hall ahead of them, and Uma felt swallowed up in blackness as she stepped back to make space for them. Their boots were heavy on the hallway tiles. Their radios crackled. And somewhere in the depths of her she knew what she had just invited into her home.

Chapter Two

2015

'Is it okay to sit down?' one of them asked, motioning for Uma to sit, shaking hands with Ruth, introducing themselves all over again.

'Is it Daniel?' Uma asked.

There was no one else it would be. There were no parents, no children, no siblings, even. No one for whom she would have to be the first to know. There was only Daniel.

'We're so sorry to give you this terrible news,' is how they started.

It didn't seem possible, but they said it was.

'I only spoke to him…'

When did she speak to him? She looked to Ruth, unable to remember.

The officers were sure there had been no mix up. They were certain that it was him, killed in a collision with another car on the M1. They checked his details, from the wallet in the pocket of his trousers.

'What happened?' Ruth asked. 'How did he…'

Uma's arms felt hollow. She let her head fall into her hands, her elbows digging into her knees as she leaned forward on the sofa.

'From initial reports it looks as if the car in front of him lost control. I'm afraid he was pronounced dead at the scene.'

'Was he alone in the car?' Uma asked, looking up, and the officers confirmed that he was.

Her thoughts struggled for air. She opened her mouth to say something, but there were no words. She tried to swallow but her mouth was sticking together.

'Would you like us to call anyone for you? Family members perhaps?'

The floor seemed to fall away as Uma thought of his mother, Mary. How would she survive the news? How would Uma survive the *telling* of the news? How did *they?* Uma wondered, looking in turn at the officers. They were talking to her still, she could see their mouths moving, hear the sound of their voices. Ruth had her arm around Uma's shoulder. She was squeezing her tightly, holding her upright.

'I can make those calls,' said Ruth, her voice thin and raspy. She was addressing the officers, answering for Uma, sparing her the need to form coherent sentences.

'I think you need a cup of something sweet,' said Ruth then, squeezing Uma firmly.

'We can do that,' said one of the officers.

Ruth nodded. 'The kitchen's just through there. Everything's obvious.'

'We'll give you a few moments,' they said, standing up.

Uma watched them go. She listened to them disappearing down the hallway, to the faint sounds of them moving round the kitchen, to the mumble of their quiet, imperceptible voices.

She looked to her sister-in-law. Tears were streaming down Ruth's cheeks.

'I thought it was him at the door,' Uma muttered.

Ruth nodded, her face crumpling.

Half an hour ago his arrival had been imminent, his presence almost tangible, the conversations they were about to have taking shape in Uma's mind, her anger a knot she was slowly tightening. Any moment he would step through the door and hang his coat on the right-hand peg in the hall.

Anything else was incomprehensible. He might not be back tonight. Or even for the weekend. He was away often enough that his absence wasn't unusual. But forever?

'He told me he loved me,' Uma muttered.

Ruth looked pained. 'He *did* love you.'

'It was the last thing he said.'

**

Later, when the house was empty of people, Uma peeled away her clothes and stepped into the shower, turning the water to its hottest setting. It pummelled her skin, the heat stinging. She reached for Daniel's soap, needing two hands to grapple with the large cube – a deep honey brown with flecks of black. He ordered it from somewhere on the internet. Uma brought it to her face, inhaling the fragrance. This is what he smelt of when he came to bed with no deodorant or aftershave. This was Daniel. Bergamot and black pepper.

Uma let the soap slip from her hands, watching it slide across the shower cubicle floor and lodge in the plug hole. A memory surfaced, bobbing up from sometime long ago, shortly after they had moved into the house, their belongings still in boxes. The bathroom had been new – the paint matched fastidiously to the iridescent green in the tiles. It had been a very grown-up bathroom, and they had christened it in an appropriately grown-up way in the walk-in shower. Water had flowed over Uma's breasts and down into the valley their bodies made. Daniel had lifted her, holding her, his mouth on hers and for a moment it felt like a scene from a film. It had fleetingly been the kind of sex Uma imagined other people had – the kind of sex she felt that they *ought* to be having. But then he had slipped, cracking her head against the tiles, his teeth cutting her lip as their mouths collided. There was blood when she touched her fingers to her face, and she had laughed, embarrassed. *I'm sorry,* he kept saying, *I'm so sorry.*

**

Uma wrapped a towel around herself, her gaze pausing on Daniel's toothbrush, his shaving cream, the little plastic sticks he used to clean between his teeth, his bottle of mouthwash. She had belligerently rejected his kisses after he had swilled his mouth, hating the strong chemical smell, the faint taste of it on his lips. She tried to remember the last time she and Daniel had kissed, *properly* kissed, but couldn't think of when it would have been, what occasion would have warranted it. Immediately she imagined him with Mystery Caller, offering up long, meaningful kisses to her, as if long, meaningful kisses were the easiest thing in the world instead of the most difficult. He had probably taken hold of the sides of her face. Or paused to look at her in wonder before kissing her all over again. Uma couldn't stop the thought of them running through her mind. She shook her head as if she could shake them off, grasped the bottle of mouthwash, snatched off the lid and poured its contents down the sink.

Turning away he was there again. His dressing gown and pyjama bottoms hanging on the back of the bathroom door. In their bedroom, his jumpers draped over the back of the little sofa, mingling with jumpers of hers, as if everything was just as it had always been. His favourite sweatshirt was hanging on the back of the bedroom door, ready for him to grab tomorrow morning before going downstairs to put the coffee on. His soft leather slippers poked out from beneath the bed like a faithful dog awaiting his return. *He's not coming back. He'll never need them again.* She kept looking, unable to keep her gaze from the sight of his things, deflated and empty. She reached out and leaned on the end of the bed, shivering despite the heat still rising from her skin. It was the early hours. She had promised Ruth that she would try to sleep, but the notion now was such a vague idea. Ungraspable. Instead, she pulled on her pyjamas, eased a loose jumper over the top of them and rummaged in her drawer for some thick woolly socks.

Lifting the lid of the laundry basket to deposit her towel she caught sight of one of Daniel's shirts. She snatched her eyes away, standing up straight, the woven wicker lid hanging in her hand. It was some minutes before she moved again, replacing the lid, heading back out onto the landing, reaching for the long metal pole that was hidden behind the radiator. She unlocked the hatch to the attic, letting it fall towards her, reaching for the wooden steps. She climbed into the darkness, reaching blindly for the light switch. Looking round she saw the plastic boxes she had come for and shuffled to them on her hands and knees, grabbing several and pulling them towards her.

Back in the bedroom she lined the boxes up on the bed, lids off. She picked up everything of his that she could see – the jumpers that he'd left slung over the back of the sofa, his tracksuit top, his wooden box of cufflinks, his aftershave, his dirty laundry from the laundry basket, the small pile of books from his bedside cabinet. She went through into the bathroom and plucked his things one by one from the shelves. She scrabbled for the slimy cube of soap that was lodged still in the plughole and threw it into the bin. She glanced around for anything else – any of his things that were now cast adrift, any of his things that might evoke pity. When she was satisfied that she had removed him enough, for now, she replaced the lids on the boxes, clicking them down into place. Then, one by one, she hauled them up into the open mouth of the attic.

**

Uma didn't have to light a new fire when she came down in the morning. Several tiny embers trembled in the white-grey ash and she coaxed them back to life with some match-thin kindling, opening the bottom vents, closing the burner door and watching the embryonic flames grow strong. Her eyes itched from lack of sleep and she squeezed them shut, covering her face with her hands. After a moment of waiting she added several small logs to the fire and turned away, filled the kettle, took a cup from the shelf, put her hands on the worktop and waited, listening for the gradual crescendo of water boiling. Staring at the walls sparked a memory of her and Daniel choosing the colour of the paint together, Daniel complaining that the pale, brown-pink was the colour of the bare, recently plastered walls. *Why bother painting them at all?*

She was pouring coffee when she heard the sound of a key in the door. *Mary.* Ruth kept a spare key for Uma and Daniel too, but she wouldn't dream of using it. Ruth always knocked at the front door or came straight round to the back. Mary, on the other hand, liked to assert her place in their lives by letting herself into their house. Uma waited where she was, listening to the rustling sound of Mary hanging her coat, the dull clunk of her keys on the hallway sideboard, a long pause into which Uma put the image of her mother-in-law bending to remove her shoes, reaching beneath the sideboard for her slippers – great furry things she had always felt the need for, no matter the season or the underfloor heating. Then the small sounds of her slippers on the hallway tiles, bringing them closer to the moment of seeing one another. Uma felt an urge to turn away at the last, but resisted.

They didn't speak but fell, instead, into one another's arms, breathing in unison. Mary smelt of rose geranium and when they parted her face was wet with tears, her powdery make-up coagulating in streaks down her cheeks. Still neither of them dared to say a word. Mary's hands clutched Uma's forearms and they looked into one another's eyes. Eventually Mary shook her head in disbelief and released her daughter-in-law.

'I made a cake yesterday morning,' she said, stooping for the carrier bag she had deposited on the floor when she first came into the room. She extracted a colourful tin and removed the lid, showing Uma inside. 'Chocolate,' she said, her voice barely audible, the tin shaking in her trembling hands. She put it on the table and Uma stared at her blankly. She didn't feel that she would ever eat again.

'It's good to have things to offer people,' said Mary, running a hand through her short, silver hair.

'Yes, of course,' said Uma, remembering that death, and all it entailed, was new to neither of them. They had both been here before – Mary, barely middle-aged when her husband, Clive, died suddenly. She reached out and cupped Uma's face in her hands.

'He's with us, you know,' said Mary.

Uma wasn't sure if she meant God, or Daniel, and realised it didn't matter anyway. *He's not with us*, she wanted to say. *He's just not.* Mary exhaled a long, wobbly sigh, turning away, making her way to the kettle, shaking it.

'It's not long boiled,' said Uma.

Mary ignored her, emptied and refilled it, returned it to the cooker top and turned on the ring beneath. 'My baby boy,' she whispered.

Uma turned and pulled a chair away from the table. She eased herself into it, remembering her conversation with Ruth earlier that morning, about identifying him, and whether she and Mary would be going to see him.

'Ruth said he looked… okay,' Uma said. She nearly added *considering*, but stopped herself at the last minute.

'He's at peace.'

It wasn't what Uma meant.

'I know I should have been the one to do it.'

'It's not an easy thing,' Mary said, coming towards her, fingering the gold cross around her neck, sitting down on the chair closest to Uma.

'I'm so grateful to her,' Uma said, imagining Ruth looking down at Daniel's lifeless body, confirming what the authorities already knew.

'We help each other through. That's what families do.'

Uma felt queasy with exhaustion. She had hardly slept

last night, at times escaping consciousness for a moment or two, slipping beneath the first silk-sheet of sleep, before jolting awake, lurching nauseously from tentative dreams. All night she had collected thoughts of him like pebbles on a beach, turning them over in her hands, inspecting them for flaws, inspecting them for beauty. Never before had she felt so completely full of him. She had tried to push him away and make space for sleep, but he had refused to go. And as the light began creeping in round the edges of the curtains she had pressed her face into her pillow, imploring him to leave her be.

'I'm going in to see him later today,' Mary said, getting up and going to the kettle, lifting it off the heat, rinsing the teapot at the sink. 'If you wanted, we could go together.'

Uma shook her head.

'To say goodbye…' Mary said.

'I don't want to see him like that.'

Uma shook her head with certainty. *You think it's the same for me as it was for you. But it's not.*

'Maybe another day then,' Mary said, after a pause.

Climbing the stairs, Uma's legs ached. She was breathless, her lungs refusing to fill properly. She sipped from a sports bottle, but still her mouth was dry. Closing the bedroom door behind her she sat down on the bed. Her hands were shaking as she punched in the mystery number. She listened to it ringing until it went to voicemail.

'It's Uma here. I need to tell you that Daniel died yesterday. I have no idea what this will mean to you. But I think we should talk.'

She surprised herself by sounding so matter of fact – as if she was changing the date of a meeting or cancelling a yoga class, and she wondered what Mystery Caller would make of that. What stories had Daniel told about his wife? How much *husband* had remained when he had been with his lover?

**

Uma put the plug in the bath and turned on the taps, watching the water for a while before removing her clothes one by one, laying them over the wicker chair in the corner of the room. She unhooked her dressing gown from the back of the door and slipped it around herself.

The room was fuggy and she heaved up the heavy sash window to let the steam tumble away into the city air, relishing the cold breeze that replaced it and how refreshing it felt after the stifling warmth of the house all day. She tugged at her dressing gown, exposing her chest, welcoming the icy touch of the winter night, her skin responding, flushing with goose bumps. The chill released her momentarily from the sense of unreality – the haunting sensation that she wasn't really there at all, that she was just an onlooker, a ghost version of herself walking through what remained of her life. As if it wasn't Daniel who had died, but Uma.

She went down the hallway to his office, stopping at the closed door, staring stolidly at the painted wood before reaching out for the door knob – grasping it, feeling its surprising warmth, but not turning it. She imagined him there on the other side, sitting at his desk. He would turn to her when she entered, his shirt would be tucked into his dark jeans, his father's cufflinks might not be obvious, but he would be wearing them. Everything about his person would be neat. But his desk would be strewn with piles of paperwork, chewing gum wrappers, paperclips that he had joined together into great long snakes. And she would ask him *what the fuck happened?*

She opened the door. Dark floorboards stretched across the room, shelving in matching wood covered the entire wall to the left, and the great hulking oak desk that had been passed down from somewhere in his family squatted centre stage. Pictures, photographs, certificates, all in dark, matching frames covered the wall to the right. They were all so familiar that, ordinarily, Uma was blind to them, but today they drew her eye, luring her into the room. She stepped across the threshold. There were several of Anna, Daniel's much younger sister, the baby of the family, away now at university. The largest photo, in more or less the centre of the wall, was a picture of her and Daniel on honeymoon – crystal waters in the background, white sand that could have been the Caribbean, but was actually the Isle of Mull. It was the only one they had of their honeymoon. Daniel had insisted on getting *one at least*, stopping a passer-by despite Uma's whispered protestations. He had loved that photograph, but Uma only ever saw her awkwardness when she looked into their faces. She imagined destroying it, there was no one to stop her now, she could just remove it from the wall, take it from the frame and fold it into the bin. She also imagined being caught in the act and being unable to explain herself – how utterly unacceptable such a thing would seem.

Next to the picture of them in Mull was a picture of Daniel and Aaron – skinny teenagers, sweaty after a rugby match, their arms around each other's shoulders. Uma reached out and traced her fingertips across the glass. Peering into a time before the three of them had met, a time when it had been just the boys.

Inseparable since their first day at school, *more like brothers* is how people described their friendship. As kids, they had supported Derby County, preferred *The Dandy* to *The Beano*, spent hours every evening outside – climbing trees or building dams in the brook that ran through the park – and, one winter, aged eleven, Daniel had rescued Aaron from a freezing lake after he'd fallen through the ice. *I'd told him not to go out there*, was how Daniel always started the story.

Uma turned away from the photographs and cast her gaze around the room. This was Daniel's space full of Daniel's things. She had never been a wife to pry. But right now she wanted to dismantle this room piece by piece.

She went towards the gloomy toad-desk and slipped her fingertips beneath the brass handle of the top drawer. It was locked. She yanked on it, rattling it back and forth. She imagined emptying the drawers one by one onto the floor and scrabbling through their contents. She wanted – *needed* – evidence of what he had all but admitted to her. Their last conversation was fading in her mind, she had strained throughout the day to recall it, desperate to hear it afresh, the silences between them and their unspoken meaning, his words of apology, the tone of his voice. Each time she brought it to mind it had faded a little more.

She eased herself slowly into his chair, pulled it up to his desk and reached for a piece of paper from the printer. She took a pen from the brown leather pen-holder, then upended the lot, plunging her fingers into the mess of pens, pencils, rubber bands and paperclips, scattering the items, looking for the key to the desk. It was a pointless exercise. She knew already where the key would be, and she presumed that at some point it would be returned to her by the police, along with everything else. She tried to imagine the moment of taking possession of his things, and felt a sliver of shame at her impatience and the beady focus of her mind on that tiny little key that she knew she would find somewhere on his cumbersome, clanking bunch of work keys.

Uma picked up the pen again and wrote down what she could remember of their phone conversation. She stared blankly at the paper, the words swimming in front of her eyes. She waited, hoping that she would remember more. Her head felt fuzzy, unresponsive, and in the end she placed the pen down on the paper and rested back in his chair. Her eyes were heavy and she closed them, her head lolling almost straight away, sleep snatching at her for brief moments. Resisting it she stood, glancing round his office once more. *All your things*. Where might he have left evidence of her? Of *them*?

She looked at his dumbbells pushed to the side of the room next to an exercise bench. She thought back to when he had first taken an interest in toning up, concerned about his gradually expanding waist. He had been disciplined, getting up on Saturday mornings in time for the local park run, and Uma tried to remember when all of that began – perhaps a year ago? Had all that been for his lover's benefit? She stared at the dumbbells, remembering when they had first appeared in the house and how uninterested she had been in what he was doing and his motives for doing it. It seemed obvious now. *Is this how it will be?* Will she not have to search at the back of drawers after all? Perhaps there will be plenty of evidence right in front of her, hidden in plain view if only she cared to open her eyes.

It was dark outside and Uma reached forward to let the blind drop. She opened his diary, looking through it, turning the pages, reading over the entries for the days he had been away this week, looking for any indication of his plans, any small, secret note to himself. She was aware only vaguely of the thumping sound of Mary coming up the stairs, of her exclamation somewhere out there in the house. The door swung open.

'Uma!'

Uma looked at her mother-in-law in confusion, feeling somehow caught out.

'You've let the bath overflow. It's running through the light fittings in the kitchen.'

'The bath?'

'What are you *doing*?' Mary said then, her voice quieter, taking in Daniel's room, glancing back at Uma. 'Oh *Uma*,' she said with such feeling.

Don't pity me, Uma thought. *Please don't pity me*.

Chapter Three

1997

From her parents' bedroom window Uma watched the estate agent hammering the *For Sale* sign into the ground at the point where the lane met the main road. The sign had been uprooted by the gales, lifted into the air by the angry gusts, sent tumbling, and splintering. She had been tempted to leave it in the ditch where it lay, as if that might mean that River View wasn't for sale after all.

Pippa and Daniel had taken a car filled with boxes and bags of Uma's parents' belongings to the charity shop in town. Uma was supposed to be sorting through her parents' clothes while they were gone. So far she had shoved an armful of clothes into the washing machine, made some masala chai, and taken her cup from one window to the next, staring out at the view, pushing away the thought that she was making a terrible mistake. *There is no other way*, she chastised herself. *The decision's been made*. She kept repeating to herself what it was that she needed to do. *Sell River View. Go to university. Get away from everything*.

But her heart was telling her otherwise, rebelling at every opportunity, cantering like a jittery foal.

Uma looked at her father's empty wardrobe, doors gaping, its fabric lining peeling away, hanging limply from the wood. She had taken his clothes and laid them on the bed. Good quality shirts, beautifully soft, pristinely clean, whites and creams, long-sleeved for the winter, short-sleeved for summer. Two suits, one navy and one grey. A handful of ties.

Her father had never been a casual dresser. If the situation warranted it then he opened the top button of his shirt and left off his tie. If he had something to do outside – mow the lawn or wash the car – then he rolled up his sleeves. If Uma closed her eyes she could see him fingering the soft cuffs of his shirt, rolling them neatly, carefully, until they reached his elbows. If he was washing the car he would unfasten the brown leather strap of his watch, slip it from his wrist and lay it on the little telephone table. Never profligate in his dealings with the world there was something mesmerising about these small, delicate actions – unrushed, considered. He had been the same in his giving of affection. Why take his daughter in his arms when a kindly word and a smile would suffice? She remembered the touch of his hand on her shoulder the day her mother died. Uma had been looking out of the window when he had appeared behind her. His hand was warm and she had wanted to cling on to it, to turn and bury her face in his clean white shirt. But she didn't. And after the shortest of moments he let his hand slip away.

Uma glanced now at her mother's wardrobe. They were a matching pair, like sentinels on either side of the bed. The doors were open, revealing a rainbow of colour as varied as her father's clothes were limited, and Uma plunged her hand amongst the fabrics, rifling through, grasping a grey tunic with yellow hummingbirds that she pulled out and held against herself. Uma was smaller than her mother had been, even at the end when the cancer had ravaged her. It would be too big for her but she undressed and slipped it on anyway, looking at herself in the mirror. It swamped her tiny frame. Would she ever wear her mother's shalwar kameez? Could she have them altered so that they fitted her properly? Her mother's clothes smelt of moth balls and sandalwood and Uma brought the fabric to her face, inhaling slowly, breathing her in. She had done the same as a child, sitting in the corner of the wardrobe with a book, reading in amongst her mother's clothes, touching them idly with the tips of her fingers, stroking a hem across the soft flesh of her cheek, tracing the contours of her lips, her nose, the arch of her eye socket.

Uma gathered the soft, grey tunic around her and stepped into the wardrobe, bending, making herself small like a child again, turning, sitting, pressing herself into the corner. Memories flooded her and she pulled the door shut. She closed her eyes, trying to conjure her parents downstairs – her father wandering out of his study with a book open in his hand, reading something aloud to Uma and her mother, some little bit of poetry or some snippet of ancient history.

Long after Uma's legs had stiffened, her buttocks numbing, she heard a faint sound that might have been the sound of a car. She pushed open the wardrobe, waiting, hearing then the sound of a door slamming, footsteps on gravel. She eased herself from the bottom of the wardrobe and went to the window, expecting Pippa, but seeing Aaron – suntanned, Depeche Mode t-shirt, his untidy, blond hair pulled back into a short ponytail. She pulled off her mother's clothes, hurriedly dressing, laying the tunic on the bed with her father's things, feeling a lurch of sadness at the sight of them together. She wondered how she would ever throw these things away. She didn't like the idea of other people wearing her parents' clothes. Other women, less witty than her mother. Other men, less careful than her father. Uma heard Aaron calling her and she turned away from her parents' things.

'Uma!'

She registered in his voice a sense of urgency. Opening the bedroom door and striding across the landing she heard him shouting her name, over and over. She took the stairs two at a time, calling out, running across the small living room, throwing open the door to the kitchen, taking in the sight of Aaron, broom in hand, sweeping water out through the back door and into the garden. Uma looked down at her feet, water sloshing around them, cold and incongruous.

'Where's it coming from…?' She looked around herself aghast.

'The washing machine! Where's the stopcock?'

Uma stared at him blankly, thinking desperately to what her father had told her, knowing that he had pointed out its whereabouts at some point.

'Big tap thing, turns the mains water off,' Aaron prompted.

'I know what *it is*.'

He looked up at her but didn't stop brushing, waves and currents swirling across the kitchen floor with every forceful *fffshtttt* of the broom.

'Under the sink! I think it's under the sink.'

Aaron threw Uma the brush and she began brushing water as quickly as she could out of the door, adding to the rivulet that was swirling down the garden path.

'Oh my God!'

Aaron knelt in the water, reaching into the dark space beneath the sink in search of the stopcock.

'Got it!'

After a few seconds the gushing from the open door of the washing machine began to slow, gradually stopping, but Uma continued brushing, frantically, desperate to get the water outside.

'Have you got another brush?'

Uma shook her head.

'Then let's take it in turns,' and he held out his hand for the brush. She passed it to him, and looked around for something useful to do. She lifted the chairs onto the top of the table like they had done in primary school at the end of the day to make the sweeping easier. Then she grabbed one of the rugs from the floor, heavy with water, sidling past Aaron in the doorway, out into the garden, hauling the rug over the washing line. It took all her strength, water flowing from the twisted cotton down her arms, soaking into her t-shirt.

She went back for another. A lump formed in her throat at the memory of her mother making these rag rugs – ripping the cloth, folding and pulling, listening to the radio as she worked, persisting patiently with each project until it was finished. That had been her mother's way. Focused. Diligent. Seeing things through to the end.

Her mother had sanded and painted the floorboards the year before she became ill. She had shown Uma the clutch of colours she had tested in the corner of the kitchen, asking her daughter which she preferred. They had all agreed in the end on white, even her father appreciating the bright colours of her handmade rag rugs against the starkness of the white boards.

Aaron showed no sign of tiring or of wanting to pass Uma the brush and so she ran to the airing cupboard upstairs, pulling down all the towels she could reach, then running back downstairs, thinking about the people booked in to view the cottage tomorrow. She could hardly bear to think about it anyway. *And now this*. Back in the kitchen she released her armful of towels, flinging them around the floor, dropping to her knees and spreading them out, mopping as best she could.

'It's nearly gone,' said Aaron, breathless, sweeping round the edges of the room, pushing the last of the water towards the door.

'It'll be in the cellar,' said Uma, her hands going to her hair, grasping clumps of dark curls, imagining the water that will have poured through the cracks in the floor, soaking the carefully labelled boxes below – the hard, painful work already accomplished. She looked back to her mopping, feeling dizzy, her breathing shallow, stars pinpricking her vision.

'It'll be okay,' said Aaron, joining her on the floor, so close Uma could feel the heat of him. He took the sodden towel from her hands and passed her a drier one, lifting the wet one away outside. Momentarily he was gone and Uma felt the lack of him, but then he was back, kneeling next to her. 'We'll go into the cellar after this,' he reassured her, his voice quiet and steady, as if everything was perfectly fine. 'If stuff is wet it'll only be the surface – we'll get it dry. I can bring things up. It's sunny today.'

Uma felt the nausea rising as she stood and headed for the door, trying to get away from the dreadful fear that was wrapping itself around her. She reached for the broom as she went, as if she could distract herself from what was happening. In the doorway she gulped the warm muggy air, desperate for something colder and fresher.

'Where are the others anyway?' she managed, trying to force a return to normal.

'They'll be here later,' said Aaron, coming up behind her.

She leaned against the stone of the house, readying herself for what was coming.

'*Hey*,' he said, his voice soft. 'Are you okay?'

She half turned towards him, vision swimming, hands shaking as she placed the tips of her fingers on her chest. How could she explain, this feeling that the world was about to end?

'I'm just a little…'

Her fingers fluttered over her chest as she tried to describe it in a way that made sense. She willed air into her lungs, silently pleading with herself, breathing and breathing, great deep breaths. It wasn't enough. She closed her eyes, forgetting Aaron, scrabbling for something, *anything*, she didn't know what. She felt his hands on her shoulders, he was moving her away from the wall, his arm coming around her.

'Let's sit down in the sunshine.'

'Not the sunshine' she said weakly.

'The shade then.'

She let herself be manoeuvred.

'Breathe *slowly*,' he said, pulling her gently to the ground in the dappled shade of the apple tree. It was her mother's favourite – sweet, early apples, tinged with red, softening quickly once they were ripe, falling in early September. There was always a rush to eat them, to make the most of the brief harvest, although Uma still liked them when they were well past their best – their skins wrinkled, thickened, sweetened up.

'I can't breathe,' she said, heart hammering.

She looked to him, suffused with panic.

'Sit up straight,' he said. 'Look at me, breathe *slowly*.'

'I'm trying,' she said, hardly able to enunciate.

'*More* slowly. In through your nose, out through your mouth. Breathe in… two, three, four.'

He breathed with her, taking her hand, holding it firmly, looking into her eyes. She closed them, listening to his voice as he counted, slowing her breathing as best she could, trying to keep pace with him, slowing every breath to his count of four. In and out. Everything fading away, nothing else existing, just the sensation of her breath. And the sound of his voice.

Eventually, the world coming back into focus, Uma lay down in the grass, the sun warm through the dappled shade, Aaron laying down beside her, propping his head on his hand. They were silent and still, and the breeze rustled the leaves, birds shifting from branch to branch.

'Thank you,' she whispered after a while.

She shivered, her skin damp with sweat. He looked down at her, holding her gaze, smiling his straightforward smile.

'My dad used to get panic attacks,' he said.

'Panic attacks?'

'You know that's what they are, right?'

Uma shook her head, thinking to herself that she had probably heard those words before. They sounded vaguely familiar.

'Sudden attacks of panic.'

'I suppose,' she said.

'He says they're like quicksand. The more you struggle the more they suck you under.'

Uma didn't know how to do anything *but* struggle. There seemed to be no choice in the matter when they came.

'There's something wrong with me,' Uma said, but Aaron shook his head.

'No. It's fear. And it's not surprising. He says as soon as he stopped being afraid of them they went away.'

She looked up at his pale eyelashes, his freckled, tanned skin. He was looking at her earnestly, biting the end of his thumb, which was a habit of his when he was concentrating hard on something.

'There's nothing wrong with you,' he said.

Uma rolled her body towards his, propping her head on her hand, mirroring him, reaching for his fingers and gently moving them away from his face. He smiled, shifting towards her an inch or two, encircling her with his free arm, pulling her close, resting his face in her hair. He smelt of incense and marijuana and she relaxed into the safety of him. She sensed his breathing quicken. She closed her eyes. There was only one person who held her like it mattered. And that person was Aaron.

Chapter Four

2015

Uma woke, fully aware, as if she had carried the knowledge with her as she slept. She felt like a slab of stone in the soft sheets. And she imagined Daniel in his coffin – his lifeless body, leaden and waiting. She closed her eyes again and turned onto her side, pulling the duvet over her face.

'You can't prevent the day from happening.'

Uma jumped at the sound of Mary's voice, there in the room with her. She twisted round, her eyes slowly focusing on her mother-in-law, her hair neatly blow-dried, her features defined with heavy makeup. One hand stroked the gold cross pendant that rested on the black silk of her blouse, whilst the other proffered a cup of steaming tea in Uma's direction.

'What time is it?' Uma asked.

'Nearly nine.'

The cars were due at 10.20am.

'I should have been up ages ago.'

'I know you've not been sleeping well…'

'Is everyone here?'

'Yes. Aaron too. Anna's meeting us at the church.'

Aaron had flown in from Nairobi yesterday. Uma had tracked his journey in her mind, imagining the plane making its way over the vast deserts of Sudan and Libya, crossing the Mediterranean and coming in to land at Heathrow. She imagined him heavy-hearted, collecting his bags, getting a taxi to the train station. Perhaps he had been mulling things over just as she had been, rolling thoughts of the funeral round in his head, trying to get the measure of it, wondering just how awful it would be. He had texted her several times throughout the late afternoon and evening, letting her know of his safe arrival and his whereabouts. Uma hadn't offered him a bed for the night, deliberate in her decision, and in the end he had said that he would be staying with his parents.

Uma peeled back the covers and stood.

'Thanks for the tea Mary. I'll have a shower and be down.'

**

In the kitchen, Ruth and her husband James were overseeing a game of *pick-up-sticks* on the large table, their girls in shades of dark pink and plum – velvety dresses that made Uma think of coffin linings. Ruth kissed Uma on both cheeks and James gave her a silent hug.

'Is this okay?' he asked, motioning to his daughters' game. The three girls erupted with shrieks and laughter and Uma gave his arm a quick squeeze. 'Of course.'

Aaron had his back to her at the sink, the sleeves of his collarless black shirt rolled up to his elbows. He was wearing the kind of trousers he always wore – utility trousers with large pockets down the outer edges. *At least they're black.* Uma wondered how he had managed to wrestle the task of washing up from Mary, who was fixing up her make-up by the window, holding a little mirror to the light. Aaron turned towards Uma and they gave one another the faintest of smiles. He kept his dark blond hair short these days – when they were younger it had been long and straggly, bleached almost white in the summer and always in need of a thorough combing.

Uma went towards him and he lifted his hands from the water, shaking them into the sink, looking round for a towel. She didn't give him a chance to find one, leaning against him instead, closing her eyes.

'My hands are wet,' he said.

She could tell he was holding them away from her.

'I don't care.'

He folded his arms around her and for just a moment there was only the rise and fall of his breathing. If the room had been empty she wouldn't have moved. As it was, before she was ready, she pulled herself away. They stepped back from one another, eyes meeting. He'd often remarked on the colour of her eyes – *so dark they're almost black*. His, the palest of blue, were full of tears. She tightened her jaw and swallowed.

'How you doing?' he whispered, looking at her with concern.

'Surviving.'

He nodded.

'I'd have asked you to do the eulogy…'

He shook his head as if to say *it doesn't matter*.

'You know there won't be one?'

'How come?'

'There's never a eulogy at a catholic funeral.'

'Oh. Okay.'

'Otherwise we'd have asked you.'

He rubbed the side of his face with his palm, his bottom lip tremoring with emotion. His face was usually covered with stubble – thick and blond. But today his skin was freshly shaved.

'And he'll be at the church already. He's been there overnight.'

'Okay.' Aaron nodded, looking into Uma's face.

'That's just how they do it,' Uma explained.

The previous afternoon Mary, Ruth and Uma had accompanied Daniel from the undertakers to the church. Father Michael had been there to meet them. The church had been ablaze with candles and the three women had followed the coffin to the front, sitting together afterwards in silence, holding hands. Mary had wanted to keep vigil next to his coffin until late into the night but Ruth had persuaded her it wasn't a good idea. *We all need our strength for tomorrow.*

Mary had said she didn't like the idea of Daniel being alone. Father Michael had said *but he won't be alone. He's in the house of God.* And Mary had seemed satisfied with that.

'I should go and get dressed,' Uma said to Aaron, meeting his gaze.

Pippa came through the back door, stamping snow from her feet, bringing with her a blast of freezing air. The weather had not improved during the last two weeks and Mary had repeatedly brought Uma her worries, voicing her concern that they would fail to get Daniel to where he needed to be, or the cars would fail to get them all to the church. Her recurring nightmare was everyone trapped for hours in the snow, her son's funeral dissolving into farce. Uma had tried her best to reassure Mary, settling in the end for some notion of God-given justice. *We've had our bad luck already. Don't you think?*

Pippa and Aaron hugged, exchanging the quiet pleasantries that were unavoidable on a day like this – even for childhood friends. Then Pippa turned to Uma.

'Where are we up to?'

'Where's Holly?'

'Mum's bringing her. They'll see us there.'

The smell of Pippa's perfume made Uma want to turn away. She ran a hand through her wet hair, remembering all of a sudden that she needed to get dressed. The smallest of tasks felt monumental.

'I'll come up with you,' said Pippa, her large hoop earrings swinging about her face.

She took Uma's hand and led her out of the room.

'We've plenty of time.'

'We haven't, not really,' said Uma.

The arrival of the cars felt imminent and Uma stopped at the bottom of the stairs, gripped the bannister and looked into Pippa's eyes. 'I don't feel very well.'

Pippa nodded. 'You'll be okay.'

Uma shook her head. 'You don't understand.'

'Understand what?' Pippa whispered.

'I can't…!'

'Let's get upstairs,' Pippa said, prising Uma's fingers off the banister, guiding her with both hands.

'I am *so angry* at him. Last night in the church… I was actually glad he was dead,' she whispered.

'Up we go,' Pippa said, manoeuvring Uma up the stairs.

Uma couldn't shake the idea of Mystery Caller being at the funeral, anonymous in a sea of faces, unremarkable in amongst all that grief.

'I am so angry at him,' she muttered, staring down at her feet, concentrating on one step at a time, her legs heavy and unresponsive.

'You're grieving,' said Pippa.

'You don't understand.'

Pippa looked her in the eye.

'Uma, what is it?'

She wanted to tell the truth. To *everyone*. It seemed that not an hour went by without somebody telling her how wonderful Daniel had been, how proud she must be, how devastated. Cards fell through the letterbox. Emails flooded into her inbox. And today it was all she was going to hear. She wasn't sure how to survive it – how to pretend and pretend and to keep on pretending.

'I'm just so tired,' she said, sidestepping all the words that threatened to seep from her. 'Mary wants me to stand at the church door to welcome people as they arrive.'

'You don't have to do that.'

Uma shook her head. 'I do though. I have to do my bit.'

Pippa opened the door to Uma's bedroom.

'It's freezing,' she muttered.

'The window's open,' said Uma.

Pippa closed the door, opened the curtains and shut the window.

'Nothing feels real,' said Uma. 'It's like déjà vu all the time.'

'You're still in shock. And you're exhausted.'

'Everyone'll be crying today, except me.'

'It doesn't matter.'

'I haven't cried since it happened.'

Uma looked to Pippa for her response, gauging her reaction. Pippa slipped a hip flask from her handbag, unscrewed the cap and passed it to Uma. It was heavy in Uma's hand, warm and solid, more real than herself. She lifted it to her lips and drank.

'What will people think if I'm not crying?'

'No one cares whether you're crying.'

They'll see straight through me. It was all she could think.

'It's the shock. No one's expecting anything of you.'

Maybe Pippa was right. Maybe people would only see what they expected to see. And perhaps it all dovetailed together – shock, anger, grief. They weren't so very different once you swallowed them down. Uma sat on the edge of the bed.

'Do you know what you want to wear?' Pippa asked, walking over to the wardrobe.

'Something black, I don't care.'

Pippa rummaged, pulling out a plain dress which she lay in Uma's lap.

'Where are your tights?'

Uma gestured to a drawer. There was a knock, and Ruth appeared, her head around the edge of the door, a string of pearls swinging from her neck.

'Just wondering if I can help?'

She came into the room, a mottled black and grey scarf clutched in her hand like a child's comforter.

'Have you eaten?' Ruth asked.

Uma grimaced at the thought.

'You need something,' said Ruth. 'Even if it's just a mouthful.'

Uma looked at her blankly.

'I'll make something, okay?'

Uma nodded, watching her sister-in-law retreat, wondering at the ease with which she had appeared, asked sensible questions, and taken herself away again, downstairs into the milieu of familial grief.

Pippa held out her hand for the flask and Uma passed it.

'You need to put those on,' she said.

Uma looked down at the clothes in her lap, nodding. Pippa went to the window and opened it, lit a cigarette, inhaling, staring out at the winter sky – a washed out, white-blue.

'I can't believe he's gone,' she said.

Uma said nothing, but stood, undressed and dressed again in new, clean clothes, all of them black. She was aware of Pippa talking, but the specifics of what she was saying didn't make it through. Uma had learned that the details didn't really matter. Everybody said more or less the same thing. She thought of her mother, suddenly in need of her, and scrabbled through her jewellery box for her mother's earrings. She pressed the cold metal through the soft flesh of her earlobes, one at a time, looking at them in the mirror, glad of the bright flashes of blue.

Pippa was grinding her cigarette butt on the outside window ledge and Uma stood in front of the mirror, staring at herself, unable to shake the feeling that she was missing or forgetting something. Eventually, turning away, she went to the wardrobe and chose a pair of shoes with little thought. She stepped into them and fastened them around her ankles. She picked out a coat – her favourite, long, black, woollen one – and placed it on the bed. She wrapped a scarf around her throat just as Ruth returned with a bowl of porridge. She smelt the spice straight away.

'I was just thinking of her,' said Uma, looking at Ruth in wonder, touched that her sister-in-law had remembered something Uma said years ago about her mum making porridge with raisins, nutmeg and honey.

'I wish I'd known her,' said Ruth.

'I know.'

'Daniel said how lovely she was.'

'She was ill by then, though.'

She had died when Uma was seventeen. But her illness had stolen her away more than a year before that – depleting who she was, washing away the nuances of her character. If she hadn't been sick from her rounds of treatment then she had been full of worry for Uma. Her squirrel-like energy and dry sense of humour had been spirited away and Uma, even now, could remember the elation she occasionally felt when she glimpsed those aspects of her mother's character towards the end. Splinters of light in the darkness of dying.

Pippa shut the window and zipped up her leather jacket. Ruth wrapped her mottled scarf around her neck. Uma looked at them both.

'I think it's nearly time,' said Ruth.

**

The black cars skulked up the road, slow as lions in the grass. Uma watched from the window, willing it now to *just begin*. Mary had been waiting at the front door for half an hour or more, peering into the sky, letting the freezing air into the house, anxious that the snow was going to come again.

'They're here,' she said, coming into the front room, her face already ravaged by a constant flow of tears. She looked to Uma across the room. 'Ready?' she asked.

Uma nodded, reaching for her coat. She pulled it about her, buttoning it up, remembering the clumsy fingers that had unbuttoned it once after a late night of dancing. She had been tipsy, shivering with anticipation, watching his face as he pulled the buttons from their holes, slipping the coat from her shoulders, his hands on her hair, her face, her waist.

**

Mourners had gathered, spilling around the sides of the church, dispersing beneath the scattered trees. From the safety of the car Uma hefted the weight of their collective grief, measured

49

out in black, and sombre handshakes and eyes that searched the ground as if the right things to say might be found in the sodden confetti flecked across the newly cleared paths. Uma searched the crowd for Anna, and saw her eventually – a thin wisp standing alone, the smoke from her cigarette curling up around her shaved head.

Uma stepped out of the car, averted her gaze from the throng of friends and family – up close a murder of crows, indistinguishable in their mourning wear – and looked instead only to Anna who ground her cigarette beneath her foot. *You look like death.* Dark grey smudges ringed Anna's eyes. Her cheeks were hollow. Her new short haircut – cut close to the scalp – exaggerated the skeletal look. Nothing could soften the wrench of seeing her looking so wretched. Uma opened her arms and pulled Anna towards her. She was stiff, unyielding, unresponsive. She *felt* like death.

'I love you Anna,' said Uma before she could think better of it.

'Thanks,' Anna muttered, glancing askance at Uma as they moved away from one another.

'How was your journey?'

Anna shrugged, looking away.

'You must have left so early.'

Anna pulled out her packet of cigarettes and put one in her mouth, lighting it with a long drag. They stood in silence as Anna smoked, both of them shifting their weight from one foot to the other. Anna's clumpy black shoes spun her ankles into matchsticks but her bright tartan socks were a burst of welcome colour.

'I ought to go really,' said Uma after a moment or two. 'I'm supposed to be greeting people with your mum.'

Anna snatched a look at her. '*Really?*'

'It's what she wants.'

Uma pulled a resigned face, noticing her attempt to align herself with Anna, as if she too knew what it was like to be on the receiving end of Mary's disapproval.

'It's a great idea,' said Anna, speaking through chattering teeth. 'Really relaxing for everyone. Especially you. I guess you're totally pumped for a little chit chat.'

Uma smiled without effort, wanting to grab Anna and hug her all over again.

'Come with me then,' she said, hopefully, taking a chance. 'Come with me and we'll go in together.'

Anna looked into Uma's eyes, weighing it up, then flicked her cigarette away.

'Okay Moo, let's go.'

Uma wasn't sure whether she reached for Anna's hand or whether Anna reached for hers, but their fingers clasped each other's as they made for the dark doors of the church.

Very little remained of anything that Uma recognised as faith, but she couldn't help but feel moved by the thought of Daniel lying in the church all night, the candles burning around him. It was, if nothing else, how he would have wanted it. He had never doubted his catholic faith, just as Uma's mother had never doubted hers, despite peppering it with the teachings of Shiva, Krishna and Lakshmi. Her mother had often fingered the beads of her rosary, sitting quietly in River View Cottage, staring out of the window or into the fire, her lips moving in prayer. Some weeks after Clive had died, Uma had witnessed Mary similarly, praying with her rosary, the beads tapping together. The gentle sound of it had provoked in Uma tears from nowhere – tears that had streamed down her face as she had stood in the doorway. Mary must have sensed the silent grief happening behind her. She had turned and sprung to her feet, clasping Uma to her. *We'll pray together*, she had said, and Uma didn't like to tell her that she didn't see the point anymore. Her father's atheism, as unbending as her mother's love of God, had insinuated its way into her heart. She hadn't welcomed it, not really. Her childhood faith had been a soothing balm, company as much as comfort.

The church began to fill behind her and Uma stared resolutely at the colourful stained glass, studying the detail of the figures, fathoming the stories as best she could from remembered snippets of her mother's catechisms. *Just keep breathing*. For long moments at a time it was all she focused on – the cold air coming into her lungs and leaving again, warmed by her living body. *Just keep breathing*.

Just when Uma sensed that the church was full, that mourners had crammed into the back of the church and were spilling out of the doors, Mary appeared at the end of the pew and met Uma's gaze. Mary's face probably mirrored her own, strangely vacant despite the surfeit of emotion.

'Someone kept vigil all night,' Mary said, leaning close to Uma's ear, whispering the words.

'What do you mean? *Who?*'

Mary shook her head, eyes wide in disbelief.

'But how do you know?'

'Lily who does the flowers told me.'

The music started and they stood. Uma hardly managed to mime the words of *Abide with Me*, but held the hymn book for Mary who was singing for her son as if it was the last thing she could do for him. Mary's fingers massaged the handkerchief she clutched in her hand. And she fidgeted with her pendant, stroking it against her blouse as if it needed soothing.

Uma tried hard to empty her mind and think of nothing, but the image of somebody sitting through the night with Daniel's coffin was hard to dismiss. She imagined the same woman that she imagined every time Mystery Caller came to mind: tall, blonde and fair skinned. Everything that Uma wasn't. She hadn't managed to create a face for this woman. She was just an impression, a ghost that Uma didn't want to believe in. The temptation to deny her existence was strong. *Where are you now? Nobody sees you back there in the throng of mourners. You are not important*. And yet, as Uma imagined this woman silhouetted by candlelight, sitting alone with Daniel's coffin throughout the night, she couldn't deny the significance of such an act. Those hours after midnight will not have passed quickly and there was an intimacy in it that made Uma feel hollow inside.

**

Aaron and Pippa came back to the house after the wake which gave Uma an excuse to send everyone else away. *I am so tired*, she said, shaking her head as Mary and Ruth tried to suggest she might need their company. *Aaron and Pippa will drop me back and then I just want an early night.* It was a lie and perhaps they knew it but Uma was beyond caring. She had offered Anna a bed for the night but her sister-in-law had said she was going home. *All the way to London?* Uma had asked, and Anna had frowned disparaging. *It's six o'clock,* she said. *And a three hour journey.* So Uma had let her go, but not before she had pulled Anna's stiff, unresponsive frame into an awkward hug. *Come stay,* Uma had said. *Anytime you want a break.*

Pippa disappeared upstairs to find something more comfortable to wear as Aaron lit a fire and Uma put the kettle on, dropping teabags into the pot, opening the fridge for the milk.

'You used to make it in a pan,' said Aaron, and Uma smiled, twisting to look at him. She hadn't made tea in that way for a long time. It was how her mother had made her masala chai and Uma had carried on making it that way for years after her mother died. But then, for no particular reason, she had let that tradition slip from her daily routine.

'Shall I put some music on?' he asked, closing the door to the wood burner, opening the bottom vents, watching as the smoke billowed and the air pulled at the flames.

Uma nodded.

'I'll find a playlist,' he murmured, scrolling through his phone.

'Easy tunes for after a wake,' Uma said, pouring tea into their mugs, stirring in the milk.

'We're not drinking tea,' said Pippa, arriving in the doorway with a bottle of whisky in one hand and three glasses crunching together in the other. She had changed into one of Uma's nightshirts, leaving several of the top buttons undone. 'Black Rock,' she said, holding out the bottle of amber liquid. '*Peat smoke, treacle toffee, burnt orange.*'

She held out the glasses towards Aaron and he took one in each hand. Uma watched as Pippa leaned over to pour the whisky, her pale breasts falling forwards, filling the space where the fabric of the nightshirt parted. Uma looked to Aaron for his reaction, studying his face, gratified when he kept his eyes on the flow of the whisky. Uma resisted the temptation to take the place next to him on the sofa and sat, instead, on the floor, in the firelight next to the wood burner, leaving Pippa to sit on the sofa, crossing her legs and tucking the nightshirt between them. She leaned back, staring up at the ceiling. Aaron had gone back to searching his phone for music, the silence between them as comfortable as ever.

'Oh Danny-boy…' Pippa began to sing, quietly, her voice clear and high, no effort needed to find the right notes. 'The pipes, the pipes are calling…'

'From glen to glen, and down the mountain side,' Aaron joined in. 'The summer's gone and all the flowers are dying. Tis you, tis you must go and I must bide.'

Uma listened to them gently singing. She alternated between staring down into her glass and taking sips from it. *Danny-boy*. Still it seemed incomprehensible, to think he had become someone's *Danny-boy*. To think of the excitement there must have been between them – the longing, the secret messaging, the daydreaming about each other when they weren't together. Uma had spent so much time over the past two weeks trying to piece things together – to create some certainty in her mind. But how could she, when so much was left to her imagination? She thought about Mary, how she had squeezed Uma's arm several times throughout the wake, leaning in, an urgency in her voice as she asked, *who do you think it was, sitting there all night with him?*

'It's a shame there wasn't any music,' said Pippa.

'There were hymns,' said Uma.

'You know what I mean. And no *eulogy*. As if he wasn't important at all.'

Uma was too tired to explain the reasoning behind a catholic funeral mass.

'It's what Daniel would have wanted,' was all she said, finishing the whisky in her glass.

And it made it so much easier, she wanted to add. No music to choose. No words to think about. *No fucking eulogising*.

'Was it strange, having different beliefs?' Pippa asked.

'Not *strange*,' said Uma, thinking about her parents, their opposing beliefs, their differing cultures, and growing up between them, segueing between their worlds, sensing somehow even from an early age the benefit of it, the richness of it, her tolerance of difference, and also the downside – that underlying, nagging sensation of never completely belonging.

'At least, it wasn't strange for me,' she clarified. 'Maybe it was for Daniel. He'd often ask if I fancied going to church with him. *It's never too late*, he used to say.'

She laughed to remember it, the implication of what he'd been saying. 'He was the same with Ruth. Always asking, as if one day one of us might turn round and say *do you know? I think I will.*'

'He never tried to persuade *me*,' said Aaron, smiling.

'That's because you're a lost soul,' said Pippa, leaning over and patting Aaron on the back.

That's all we get of him. It was a feeling she couldn't shake. The finality of his death. That everything he would ever be had already been. Every situation had played out. Every conversation had happened. Every opportunity. Every relationship.

'We've had it all,' she said, looking up at them, speaking the thought aloud. 'That's all we get of him.'

Aaron was nodding, sitting forward on the sofa, resting his elbows on his knees. He looked her in the eye, holding her gaze, and Uma wanted to go to him, to collapse against him, to ask him to hold her until she fell asleep.

'What can I do for you?' he asked, as if the thought had seeped out of her mind and into his. *Hold me*, she wanted to say. *Just hold me*. She mustered the strength to lift her glass in his direction and he fetched the bottle of whisky from the table, pouring her an inch. He turned and topped up Pippa's glass too.

'Come sit here,' he said, gesturing to his space on the sofa. 'I'll sit on the floor.'

But Uma shook her head.

'It's nice here,' she said, turning her gaze to the orange glow of the fire. She took a large swallow of the fiery spirit, enjoying the warmth in her throat, the sensation of her insides coming alive. They listened to the music for a while, not saying much, finishing their whisky.

'Oh, by the way,' Aaron said eventually, reaching into the large side-pocket of his trousers. He pulled something out and passed it to her. It was small, circular, white, with tiny knobbles stretching upwards like miniature mushrooms, but on the underside there was a whorl like a flattened shell.

'Coral?' she asked, looking at him.

'I'm presuming so, although I found it in the desert nowhere near any water, so that was a bit weird.'

She rubbed the skin of her thumb across the rough surface of the rock, inspecting it, turning it over in her hand.

'Thank you,' she said, closing her fist around it, looking at him briefly. She eased herself to standing, every part of her body aching, walked out of the kitchen, down the hallway and up the stairs. On the landing was a south-facing stained-glass window and crammed on its deep sill were rocks and shells and fossils. On sunny days they were bathed in a rainbow of colour. Uma placed the coral-rock-shell in amongst the other rocks, looking at it alongside everything else.

Since leaving university Aaron had worked abroad as a civil engineer, building dams and roads and bridges, exploring the country once his contract was up, moving on to the next job somewhere else on the globe. *Do you have to go?* she had asked him, all those years ago. She had just married Daniel, and *I do*, had been his reply. She hadn't said *but you're our best friend*. And she hadn't said *but we love you*. And she hadn't said *it won't be the same without you*. And they hadn't looked each other in the eye.

He brought her a rock or shell from every country he went to. *I know you like rocks* he had said that first time, passing her a stone the colour of bloody liver. It had been tiny in her palm, almost a perfect sphere, and she had carried it in her pocket for so many months that its surface had worn shiny and smooth, polished over time with no effort at all. It was on the windowsill now with all the others and Uma picked it up, feeling its familiar shape, remembering how it had felt to carry it around, to rub the pad of her thumb across it in her pocket, out of view, unbeknown to anyone else.

She was holding it still when she became aware of him behind her. She didn't have to turn to look to know that it was Aaron, not Pippa.

'It's quite a collection,' she said, continuing to stare at them.

'It is.'

He was right behind her, but not touching.

There were so many things she wanted to ask, so many things that she wanted to say. *He was cheating! Did he tell you?* She was simply too tired to begin that conversation now, but she realised that she did at least *want* to have that conversation with Aaron. With anyone else – Ruth, Pippa, Mary – there was still that squabble of voices warning her not to relinquish the information. *Once it's out there you can't take it back.*

So grateful to him, she reached for his hand, interlacing her fingers into his, looking down at his skin next to hers. He rubbed his thumb over hers, gently stroking her as if to say *everything will be okay*. There was a beat, a breath, a pause, where a swirl of thoughts and questions and moments from the past seemed to rush at her all at once, but then there she was, on tiptoes, with her lips on his. He hesitated, she was sure of it, before he pulled away.

'*Fuck,* Uma.'

It was all he said, running his hands through his hair, his face unreadable. She felt the adrenalin flooding through her, horribly conscious of the line she had crossed, her fuzzy exhaustion finally gone.

She took a step towards him, reaching out for his arm, an apology stuttering on her lips. He stepped back as if he didn't trust her to be any closer, looking up at the ceiling, turning away. He stopped at the top of the stairs and twisted round to look at her, Uma's desperate *I'm sorry* colliding with his barely audible *don't*. He turned back to the stairs but didn't move, Uma staring at the back of him, willing him to turn around, to forgive her, to let her explain. She opened her mouth to say as much just as he moved downwards, one step at a time, disappearing slowly from view. It was another whole minute before Uma headed in the direction of her bedroom, pushed open her door and collapsed face down on her bed.

**

It was as if the embarrassment woke her. *Time to remember*, it seemed to be saying, the light showing round the edge of the curtains, her insides churning with regret. She didn't remember drawing the curtains last night and wondered who had let themselves into her room and made the decision to close them. And to tuck a blanket around her by the looks of it.

Down in the kitchen Pippa was making pancakes, Holly on a chair beside her.

'Auntie Uma!'

Holly jumped to the ground and ran across the kitchen, embracing Uma's legs. Uma lifted her into her arms and kissed the warm softness of her cheek.

'Are you still very sad?' Holly asked, scrutinising Uma's face.

Uma smiled a small smile and stroked Holly's hair.

'I *am* still very sad, yes.'

Holly flung her arms around Uma's neck and she let herself be pulled her into one of Holly's forceful hugs.

'I'm sad too,' Holly said into Uma's hair.

'I'm sure you are. Uncle Danny loved you very much.'

'He made me broken biscuit chocolate cake.'

'He made a big fuss of you,' said Pippa.

It was true.

'And you wrapped him round your little finger, didn't you?' said Uma, tickling Holly until she wriggled out of Uma's arms. Unwittingly, unwillingly, Uma thought about children, her and Daniel's lack of them, their subtle tussle over the years, her *not the right time* utterances, the implication of *maybe one day*. She felt the familiar tug of guilt.

'Are you having some?' asked Pippa, tipping the pan in Uma's direction.

Uma shook her head, turning to Holly.

'When did *you* get here, little one?'

'Nannan bought me.'

'And where's Aaron?' Uma asked Pippa, arranging the syllables as nonchalantly as possible.

'Gone,' was Pippa's quick reply.

'Sorry about last night, I was suddenly so tired.'

'You must have been out like a light.'

'Did you close my curtains?'

'And found you a blanket. I wanted to make sure you would sleep as long as possible.'

The disappointment was like a stone in her chest. She wanted it to have been Aaron – to know that he came to look for her, to check on her, to tell her things were okay between them.

'Did he go this morning?' Uma asked.

'Last night. He said he had an early start. Did he tell you he's been seeing Jo-Jo?'

'*Seeing her*… seeing her?'

'I think so.'

'You're joking.'

'I know!'

She had been his wife. They had met in Brazil, not long after Daniel and Uma had married. One minute Daniel and Uma were hearing about this amazing woman, getting photos through the post – two tanned faces, smiling into the camera, looking strangely alike with their white-blond hair, blue eyes and freckles – the next thing they'd married. On the beach, not wanting any fuss. *I just can't believe he'd marry someone without any of us meeting her,* Uma had said to Daniel. It had sounded silly, exposing, as soon as she had said it. But Daniel had felt hurt too. She had seen the disappointment in his face, in the twitching of his mouth as he'd looked at the picture of Aaron and Jo-Jo draped in flowers, denuded on the white sand, the turquoise water in the background.

'But she… ' Uma searched for the words. *Did his head in. Betrayed him. Messed with his life.* 'He said that her leaving was the best thing she'd ever done for him.'

'I told him.'

'That he's crazy?'

'Yup.'

'What did he say?'

'That it was fifteen years ago.'

'So…?'

'He says she's changed. *He's* changed. They've grown up.'

Uma could feel the incredulity plastered across her face. She couldn't have hidden it if she'd tried.

'I'm just telling you what he said!' said Pippa.

'What does that even mean?' said Uma. 'Doesn't growing up mean not falling for people like Jo-Jo anymore? Isn't that one of the *great* things about getting older? Being able to spot a narcissist at a hundred yards and walk in the opposite direction?'

Jo-Jo had been intoxicating, whispering sweet nothings to anyone with an ear to listen. She coaxed those around her into a pool of intimacy, her laugh like a bell. *She smelt like strawberries* Aaron had said, after it all fell apart. And Uma had understood. *Good enough to eat.* Even Uma had hungered when Jo-Jo was around to work her magic.

Chapter Five

1997

On New Year's Eve they met at a friend's house – aglow with fairy lights and jumping to the sound of something that someone called *balearic beat*. Uma heard it from way down the street and, despite herself, was glad that she'd ventured out. She had been feeling something she might have described as brittle. And all heart – as if that beating, pounding, rushing thing was all that she was. She'd been tempted to stay at home, but there had been too many times already that she'd ducked out of invitations. Her parents wouldn't have approved of moping.

The house was heaving, from the front door right through to the kitchen. Uma squeezed through the packed bodies, feeling their muggy warmth, the pulsing of ravers who couldn't stop moving, the up-close smell of perfume, tobacco, sweat. Someone spilt something down her back but there was no room to turn, so she pushed on, smiling at people she knew, hugging the occasional friend, looking for Pippa and Aaron. In the kitchen Uma opened one of the cans of beer she had brought and glugged a few long swallows. The door to the garden was open and she stood in the path of the icy wind that gusted into the kitchen.

Just as she was opening her second can of beer, three girls from sixth form blundered in with the wind, embracing Uma one by one. They demanded to know how Manchester was, whether she was loving it, what the nightlife was like, whether she'd met anyone. Uma offered the details they wanted, shouting them above the music, accepting a baggy joint from one of them, asking them about Liverpool and Bristol, picking loose tobacco from between her lips.

When the can was nearly empty she caught sight of Aaron looking at her from the hallway. The girls in the small circle around her were talking and talking, one long tale after another, and Uma found it hard to break away. Aaron was similarly engaged. They held each other's gaze and Uma felt an urge to go to him, to drag him by the hand outside, to tell him how she felt, to pin him against the wall and kiss him. Her vision was blurring, she felt giddy, but suddenly happy, as if everything made sense and was about to change for the better. Someone close by laughed, grabbing Uma's arm. *You're fucking miles away.* And then Uma was back in that little circle of old school friends listening to a rambling story about inter-railing and lost luggage and a man with snakes for tattoos who had a tiny cock but was an amazing cook.

By the time Uma looked round the kitchen Aaron had gone. There was a blue cocktail after that, and something the colour of a swamp, which provoked hilarity but they all drank it anyway, and Uma tripped as she made her way outside, scraping her knees, aware of the pain but more concerned about finding her friends. She needed to find Aaron, but Pippa would do. She would tell Pippa how she felt – confess all.

There shouldn't be secrets between us, she was saying to herself. Then Daniel was there, putting his finger to his mouth, miming for Uma to be quiet, dragging her by the hand down the garden to the summer house. Uma tried to pull away, unsure of his intentions, unwilling even in her drunken state to have to hurt his feelings.

'There shouldn't be secrets,' she tried again, pulling on Daniel's hand, trying to get his attention. They were at the summer house now and he pulled her to the window, peering inside briefly, turning to Uma, grinning. She looked where he

63

was looking, her eyes and brain taking a moment to register what she was seeing – Aaron and Pippa fucking in the darkness, their exposed skin lit by the moon, parts of them obscured by shadow.

Uma was kissing Daniel furiously by the time they were halfway up the garden. She pulled him into the shadows of a huge willow, its branches reaching almost to the ground, making them a tent of sorts. She lay back on the freezing ground, taking her knickers off, pulling him down onto her. His hands were confident, but hers more so, stripping him of his clothes, reaching for his cock, guiding it towards her without hesitation, pulling at his buttocks so he was deep inside of her, making it an encounter that sealed their fate – a moment that he would mention throughout their marriage, laughter in his eyes, full of pleasure at the memory, and she would think *please don't please don't please don't*.

**

They drove most of New Year's Day afternoon looking for a chemist that was open.

'I can't believe we were so stupid,' Uma said, over and over. Daniel looked slightly hurt, as if he didn't think they had been stupid at all.

'I could get pregnant,' Uma said, spelling it out.

'But what are the chances, really?' he asked, driving carefully, looking across at her.

'Oh my God.'

'I just mean...' but he didn't finish the sentence. 'I'm not saying we shouldn't be trying to find you this pill thing.'

'The morning after pill,' she said.

'Do you need it *today*? Everywhere is shut.'

Daniel was driving and Uma was directing him from one village to another.

'There's always a chemist open somewhere. We'll find one in Derby.'

'And you can just walk in and get it?' Daniel asked. 'You don't need to, like, see a doctor?'

Uma shook her head, wondering how she knew this stuff and he didn't.

'What *did* they cover in your sex education?' she asked.

'How to put a johnnie on,' he said, after a pause, looking across at her, a smile playing at the corner of his mouth.

'I can't believe we were so stupid,' she said.

And Daniel looked hurt all over again.

Standing outside the chemist she swallowed the pill with a glug from a warm can of Tango that Daniel had fished from the glove compartment. She relaxed. It was like blotting out their mistake. Not quite as good as turning back time, but the next best thing. Daniel put his arm around her shoulders as they walked back to the car and she was glad when they got there so she could slip away from his grasp. They hardly spoke on the journey back, Uma resting her head against the cold window, closing her eyes. He dropped her home.

'Do you want me to come in?' he asked and she shook her head. She put her hand on his arm and smiled at him.

'But thank you for coming and helping to sort it.'

He shrugged as if to say that it was nothing.

**

The four of them didn't see each other over the next week or so. Uma was relieved that none of them seemed that keen to get together. She had spoken to Pippa briefly on the telephone. *You'll never guess what I did New Year's*, she had said. Uma feigned ignorance. What else could she say?

**

Two weeks later she began to feel unwell. Queasy. Tired. Her period was late, but she had assumed that was nothing to worry about – a disruption of her cycle due to the pill. She kept telling herself that everything would be okay. What were the chances of her being pregnant? It started as a rhetorical question, but soon became real. She searched for the pill packet in her dustbin – emptying out the black bin bag full of rubbish, sure that she had only thrown it away a few days ago after discovering it in her coat pocket. She found it eventually, and tore it apart, fumbling the leaflet until it was spread out in front of her. She scanned through the information, searching, she realised, for some reassurance that what she suspected was impossible. She scavenged the words off the page, swallowed them whole and screwed the leaflet into a tight ball afterwards, hurling it back to the rubbish that was spilling across the ground. Being pregnant *was* possible. Sitting on her kitchen step, her breath pluming white in the freezing air, Uma looked across the surrounding fields. By the time she started scooping the rubbish back into the bin liner her hands were numb with cold. Her fingers were stiff and unresponsive as she tried to knot the ties at the top of the bag.

When a pregnancy test confirmed her suspicions, Uma lay on her parents' bed, looking up at the ceiling, missing them both, but desperately glad that her mother in particular, wasn't here. She held the plastic stick and brought it up in front of her face every so often, just to check that what she remembered was right – two thin blue lines. Then she let her hand drop back down onto the eiderdown.

At least she didn't have to hide it from them. At least she could prowl around the house, weeping, heart pounding, imagining the procedure, not knowing what to expect – the extent of her sex education lessons now exhausted. She couldn't imagine asking anyone for advice, terminating a pregnancy wasn't something that women seemed to talk about. Uma certainly didn't want to talk about it.

She went to the doctors, feeling sick as she waited for her appointment, her hands shaking. Images of glinting surgical instruments flashed into her mind. So, too, the image of a life beginning. However tiny, just a few cells, barely visible, but there, multiplying, doing their thing. The guilt was like a boulder in the pit of her belly. But it didn't feel like a choice. It wasn't that she didn't *want* this baby. It simply couldn't be. There was no future for herself and this child. She felt it in every part of her.

The doctor – a sympathetic woman in a pink top, with glasses on a gold chain round her neck – explained the procedure to Uma, telling her what she could expect. Uma felt faint at the idea of being in hospital, waiting for the medication to work, waiting for the pregnancy to leave her body. There would be blood, *just like a natural miscarriage*, the doctor said. The room began to dissolve, Uma's eyes unable to focus on anything. She gripped the arms of the chair, trying to ground herself, to steal some of its solidity for herself. The doctor led her to the examination table, laid her back, encouraged her to take some *nice, slow breaths*.

'You're getting some colour back now,' the doctor said after a minute or so. 'You were very pale.' She was patting Uma's hand.

The week's wait for her hospital appointment was interminable, and reminded Uma of the time when her mother was ill. The prognosis was so terrible that there had been no treatment, only palliative care. There had been no false hope and no remission. There had just been the bad news, followed by the adjusting to it, swiftly, and the sense of doom that stretched them all so thin. There was no relief, only waiting. And waiting was what Uma had hated the most. Waiting for the end to come. *Impatient* for it even, knowing that this thing they dreaded, this thing that was ripping their life apart, would also be the thing that delivered them – it would end her mother's suffering and give Uma and her father some semblance of life again. Death had been their foe, but as they became slowly acquainted over the months, it also became their insidious friend.

However much she was dreading what she knew had to happen in order for the pregnancy to end, she was impatient for it. She wanted to be beyond it, the experience receding into the past so she could think of it dimly, from a distance. During the week between going to the doctors and her hospital admission, Uma woke one night convinced in the dark hours of that early winter morning that she should have the baby. In a moment of night-time clarity she realised that this new little life would embody parts of her parents, characteristics that had bypassed Uma and died with them. Little bits of her mother and father that would come alive again in this child she would create. And wouldn't that bring them back to life just a little? But by the time the sun came up Uma could hardly believe she had thought such a thing. *There is no way I can have this baby.*

**

She made excuses to Pippa and Aaron, staying at home as they made their way back to Manchester. *Chores to do before the house sells*, she told them vaguely.

**

Uma spent the day in a ward with other women, most of them young like herself. A nurse came round in the morning, seeing them each in turn, pulling the curtain round for privacy but speaking loud enough for everyone on the ward to hear. She gave Uma a hospital gown.

'Put this on,' she instructed. 'And put your clothes in here,' she said, patting the bedside cupboard. 'You didn't bring any valuables did you?'

Uma shook her head. She had been diligent, following the instructions, hoping to be rewarded with some kind of simplicity – a straightforwardness that, deep down, she didn't believe she deserved.

'You'll need these,' said the nurse, putting a handful of thick sanitary towels onto the bed.

'There are bedpans in the toilets. Use them every time you pass water or open your bowels throughout the day, okay? And then call one of us by pressing the button in the cubicle. It's important you don't use the toilets today.'

Uma nodded, reticent to think too deeply about what she was being told.

'How long will it take?' Uma asked, almost whispering.

'It's different from person to person. You should be able to go home by five or six.'

The nurse took a little paper pot from a tray and upended the pill into Uma's hand. She passed Uma a cup of water and Uma swallowed the pill, their eyes meeting briefly. The nurse smiled kindly and disappeared through the fabric curtain, leaving Uma to undress, put on her gown and get into bed. A little while later the nurse pulled back the curtains throughout the ward and Uma stared at the rain that was spattering against the grubby windows.

She had brought a book to read, but struggled to concentrate on it, distracted by the conversation that a couple of the women had struck up down the other end of the ward. At some point Uma turned onto her side and pretended to be asleep, listening still, wishing for the peace of unconsciousness.

The pains were like period pain and Uma cried without moving her face or making a sound. There was a small amount of blood throughout the day, but not much, and each time Uma called for a nurse and showed the contents of her bedpan the nurse shook her head. 'Nothing yet,' she said, recording the details on her clipboard.

The women on the ward grew smaller in number as the light outside began to fade. Uma waited, anxiety building as the city lights gradually flickered into life, oranges and reds blinking across the cityscape, blurred by the droplets of rain on the windows.

At seven o'clock someone arrived to examine her.

'It happens occasionally,' the doctor said, resting Uma's legs in stirrups. 'I'm looking for the pregnancy sac, it's really just like a large blood clot at this stage.'

Uma fixed her gaze on the ceiling. Practising not thinking. Practising not feeling.

'Ahh,' said the doctor. 'Just here, at the neck of the womb.'

She tweezered it away, putting it into a metal dish, covering it with screwed up blue paper, all in Uma's peripheral vision. Uma did everything she could not to feel any of it too clearly, closing her eyes tightly when she felt the tears coming.

She lied when they asked her if someone would be collecting her, and she lied when they asked her if she would be alone that evening. *Yes, someone is coming to take me home. No, I won't be on my own this evening.*

Chapter Six

2015

When Uma finally had his bag in her possession she opened it without hesitation, half expecting there to be a letter from him balancing on top of his things. A full explanation. A message from beyond the grave. She removed the items one by one. A jumper, a dirty shirt, a t-shirt, underwear, sweatpants that he sometimes slept in and a toiletry bag. There was also a copy of *The Wasp Factory* and a half eaten bag of salted crisps. And in the small, inside pocket, beneath a tightly rolled sports top, there was a cheap mobile phone that she had never seen before. Hands trembling, she brought it to life. It was empty, no messages stored, no record of calls. Uma shook her head, understanding all too well what this phone had been for. And she saw Daniel in all these things, as careful and meticulous as ever.

His bunch of keys lay heavy in the palm of her hand and she shuffled them, identifying the ones she recognised, searching through the rest for something small. She tried a couple that resisted the lock. But then there it was, sliding in easily, brass against brass.

She took a deep, steadying breath and opened the top drawer first, looking briefly through the clutter of stationery. Opening the second she pulled out the pile of folders and envelopes. Sitting on the floor, cross-legged, she opened everything, one item at a time, making sure nothing was overlooked. It was all to do with Millers – accounts, stretching back several years, and tax returns. She looked through it all at least twice, but didn't find what she was looking for.

Uma opened the next drawer and repeated the process, bringing everything out onto the carpet, searching through, piece by piece. In amongst hundreds of bank statements from an old, closed account, Uma found what she was looking for. Statements from the same bank, but for a live, current account in Daniel's name – an account that had been opened ten months earlier. The statements showed several deposits of cash and scores of transactions over the previous year. Heart pounding, Uma traced her fingertip down the pages, one at a time, scribbling some of the details, names and mystery words, onto a scrap of paper. Then she searched online, finally sketching an outline of Daniel's affair, his predilection for rooms with a view, flowers in the bedroom, chocolates on pillows and amuse bouche at dinner. She scrolled page after page, website after website, examining the accommodation on offer, checking the corresponding hotel bills, punishing herself with thoughts of which rooms they might have stayed in, studying the sample menus, imagining their evenings together, their conversations over drinks in the bar.

She investigated the surrounding countryside, the picturesque villages, the market towns. She imagined them there, dreaming them up, watching them like a voyeur from a window.

She carried on looking through the files and folders and envelopes until she was sure there was nothing more. She opened the last drawer and pulled everything out in one go. The first file she opened held all of their original plans for Millers. Scraps of paper more than fifteen years old. Drawings that documented their vision. Uma remembered sitting in River View cottage with Daniel, working on the kitchen table, dreaming up the finer details of what Millers should be. What they *didn't* want. How it would be different to anything else. How Uma would create a range of South

Indian food to sell in the delis – her specialities would become their trademark. There were scrappy pictures of Uma on a plane to India, a little stick figure holding up a cookbook, a big smile on her face and exclamation marks all around her head like stars.

**

Uma bent to pull on her boots and her mobile fell from her coat pocket. She regarded it there on the hallway tiles as she took her time threading her laces. Reaching for it she straightened up, tapping the screen to bring it to life. She composed a new message to Mystery Caller: *Sometimes I think I imagined you.* Pressing send, she slipped the phone into her bag, knowing that the message, like all the others, would go unacknowledged.

As Uma was pulling on her coat she heard the metallic clank of the gate latch outside. She slung her bag over her shoulder and opened the door, greeting Mary with as genuine a smile as she could muster.

'I'm just on my way out,' she said, pointedly pulling the door closed behind her.

'I'm only here to drop this off,' said Mary, proffering a baking dish covered in tin foil.

Uma looked down at it, hesitating before reaching out for it.

'Thanks.'

But Mary didn't let go. 'I'll just pop it inside,' she said, easing it back out of Uma's grasp. Uma turned towards the door to open it again.

'You get on Uma, don't mind me,' Mary said, slipping past Uma into the house. 'I'll lock up when I go.'

Uma sighed, standing on the doorstep, watching Mary disappear down the long hallway into the kitchen. Left to her own devices Mary would spend the rest of the day in Uma's house, making herself busy with preparing food and cleaning out cupboards or doing laundry. Uma thought about Daniel's office, his unpacked drawers, and papers strewn around the place.

'Mary?!'

'Yes?' Mary called from the kitchen.

'I'm going through a load of stuff from Daniel's desk, for work. There are things in piles and I'd appreciate it if you didn't move anything. I'm halfway through sorting.'

Mary flapped a hand in Uma's direction as if to say *don't be daft, as if I would!* Uma rolled her eyes, subtly, too far away for Mary to notice. She knew her mother-in-law would still venture into that room, its carpet blanketed with documents. She would stand in their midst, looking for some remnant of her son, any morsel of him that she hadn't previously devoured.

'See you when I'm home then,' Uma muttered beneath her breath, closing the door.

**

She hadn't been sure that the church would be open, but it was. The still familiar smell hit her before she entered, the vague aftermath of incense and the dankness of wet stone.

Inside, her footfall echoed and she lightened her step. The font was there on the left, at the back of the church, and she reached out to touch it, running her fingers over its curves and down into the shallow puddle of water. It meant nothing, but all the same she touched her wet fingers to her forehead, and between her breastbones, faltering there, the gesture unfinished, letting her hand drop to her side.

She looked up at the intricate colours of the stained glass windows, remembering their detail from her scrutiny of them on the day of Daniel's funeral. She had concentrated on them for great stretches of time, counting the colours in every pane, losing track, going back.

She walked down the aisle, looking at the Stations of

the Cross, transfixed by their morbidity. At the front of the church she felt an obligation to sit, but instead she stepped from the cold stone onto the carpet and walked towards the altar, pressing her palm against the cold marble as she passed, continuing towards the chancel lamp that hung in a little alcove to the left. The flame of the candle, glowing red through its glass holder, flickered as she moved towards it. She reached up and touched the ornate glass, the colour of blood, sensing her trespass, snatching her hand away when the door to the vestry opened. Father Michael appeared. Seemingly unperturbed, he smiled at her.

'*Uma*,' he said, closing the vestry door, stepping towards her.

Neither of them spoke.

'Sometimes I let it go out by accident,' he said, after a moment.

'That's terrible.'

He smiled.

He was younger than Uma, perhaps by as much as ten years. She scrutinised his calm, pallid face for nervousness, but found only a sense of ease. In the silence that stretched out between them Uma searched for some way to explain her presence.

'Would you like a cup of tea?' he asked. 'We could go through to the rectory. It's a little warmer.'

Uma followed him through the vestry into the sparsely furnished rectory. He led her into the kitchen and she sat down at the small table, watching him fill the kettle and position three small cups into a neat line.

'Just the one cup or would you like two?'

'One is fine.'

'They're very small,' he explained, but Uma shook her head.

'A teacake?'

He opened the cupboard above his head. It was empty apart from two packets of teacakes. He took a packet down and opened it, reaching for a bread knife from a drawer, slicing one teacake before turning to Uma with eyebrows raised.

'Okay,' she said, thinking that it would be good to have something to do during this conversation. She watched him make the tea and toast the teacakes, neither of them speaking.

'I wondered if I could talk to you about something,' she said, eventually.

'Of course,' he said.

'Confidentially.'

'Of course.'

Uma wondered what made her think she could trust him.

'Do you remember the person who sat with Daniel's coffin throughout the night?'

'Yes,' he said, slowly buttering the teacakes.

'I want to know who she was.'

'She isn't one of my parishioners,' he said, turning to look at Uma.

'But did you recognise her? Is she from round here?'

Father Michael shook his head in a slow, non-committal way.

'Did you speak to her?'

'Yes.'

'Did she tell you her name?'

'No.'

'Who was she? I mean, did she say that she was a friend or…?'

Father Michael hesitated before answering.

'She didn't say.'

'What did she look like?'

This time the silence stretched out between them until Uma was tempted to speak herself. She resisted. Father Michael leaned over the table and put her cup of tea down, followed by her toasted teacake on a flowery plate with a crack that ran from one side right across to the other.

'You put me in a difficult position,' he said.

'Why?'

'She wanted anonymity. Discussing her feels like a betrayal.'

Uma stared at him, dumfounded.

'A *betrayal*?'

Father Michael sat opposite and took a sip of tea.

'But Daniel was my husband.'

He looked uncomfortable.

She shook her head, looking down at the teacake with its pool of butter on top. Her throat tightened at the thought of eating it. Father Michael had taken a bite of his and she could hear him chewing, his jaw clicking slowly, rhythmically. After swallowing he said, 'I'm so sorry Uma.'

'I don't need you to feel sorry for me,' she said, fiddling with the delicate handle of the tea cup. 'I just need to know who she was.'

'I don't have the answers you're looking for.'

'It's not as if I'll *do* anything with the information.'

But she would. She would find Mystery Caller. She would track her down to see her in the flesh. To hear the sound of her voice. And then to question her until she had all the answers she was looking for. Was that really so terrible?

'Even if you were to find out who this woman is, what would that tell you?'

Uma sipped her tea.

'You'll only hear what she wants to tell you. Even with the best of intentions it's hard for people to be honest in situations like this. Emotions are running high.'

I'll be the judge of that, Uma thought. *If I look her in the eye I'll know if she's telling me the truth.*

'All of us are tempted at some point in our lives, and all of us make mistakes. If Daniel were here I'm sure he'd be the first to acknowledge that.'

'I don't need a sermon on forgiveness.'

Father Michael shook his head. 'That's not my intention.'

'I found out the day before he died! The *day before*.'

Father Michael took a deep breath as if he was about to speak, but didn't, and they finished their tea in silence. Afterwards, he collected their tea things from the table and put them in the sink.

'I've actually got a favour to ask,' said Uma.

He looked at her without replying.

'You might not want to help,' she said, preparing herself as much as him.

'I'd *like* to help,' he said, sitting down opposite her again. 'If I can.'

'I wouldn't have even known about anybody sitting with Daniel's coffin if the lady who does the flowers hadn't told Mary. I suppose it was good gossip.'

Father Michael's right eyebrow twitched.

'Well, it was unusual,' he said, clasping his hands on the table between them, steepling his fingers. 'Although not unheard of.'

'Could you think of something to tell Mary? Everything is bad enough without her obsessing about who this person might have been. *She* wanted to sit with his coffin, remember?'

Father Michael nodded.

'I can't tell her the truth,' said Uma. 'And I just don't know if I can keep pretending.'

'Can you *not* tell her the truth? Do you *have* to keep pretending?'

'For Mary's sake, I do. I *really* do.'

Uma imagined Mary's added grief if she knew. The *disappointment* she wouldn't know what to do with. She would come to Uma with it. *Over and over and over.*

'Maybe it's for my sake,' said Uma, looking away from Father Michael, around the sparse, tidy kitchen.

'There are people who attend stranger's funerals,' he said. 'That's a thing, you know.'

He looked at her, and they regarded each other silently for a moment.

'And there are people who stay in church to pray for days at a time.'

Uma kept her eyes on his face.

'It really could have been anyone.'

**

On her way out, choosing to go back through the church, Father Michael tried to say something about the chancel lamp and how like a marriage it is, but Uma concentrated on the solidity of her footsteps on the stone floor, forcing his gentle, well-intentioned words as far into the background as she could get them.

**

Uma practised a straightforward, giving-nothing-away smile as she walked down the street towards her house. She knew that Mary would be there to welcome her, ready to warm her something to eat, a cup of tea conjured within seconds of Uma stepping through the front door. Mary meant well and Uma was doing her best to remember it. The house smelt nice when she opened the door – like one of Mary's shepherd's pies. If Uma had any appetite at all it would be a happy situation, with much to be grateful for.

Mary appeared in the hallway.

'Hello,' she said, wet washing draped across both arms. 'I'm just...'

She held up the washing as if it wasn't obvious enough.

'Thanks for that,' said Uma, taking off her coat and hanging it.

'There's a postcard from Aaron. He's going trekking with a friend. It's on the table in the kitchen.'

Uma headed straight there, snatched up the card and turned it over, gobbling his brief message, reading it three times. *Hope you're doing okay. It's been such a terrible time for all of us. It would be good to meet soon. I'm booked to walk the Sultan Trail with a friend I've been working with. But after that???* Uma took a deep breath, thinking about it all over again, cursing her stupidity and wondering whether she had ruined things between them.

'Where is the Sultan Trail, exactly?' Mary asked, appearing at Uma's elbow, pulling her glasses on and peering at the postcard.

'I don't know,' Uma said, turning away, holding the postcard to her chest without thinking what that might look like. *Get away*, she wanted to say. *You shouldn't even have seen this.*

'I've made a Lancashire hotpot for tea,' said Mary, bending to open the oven door, grabbing a tea towel and pulling out the baking dish to inspect its progress. 'Half an hour?'

'Shall we see if Ruth and the girls want to come over too?'

'I'm not sure they'll eat hotpot,' said Mary, running a hand through her short, silver hair. 'You know how fussy they are.'

'They could have fish fingers. I have fish fingers in the freezer.'

It would be so much easier to have other people round the dinner table. Uma wasn't sure how many more meals she could eat with Mary staring balefully at Uma's barely touched food. *You must eat*, had become Mary's mantra, her mission. And all Uma could do was protest that she *was* eating. Just not very much. Her insides felt full of something alien, something she didn't quite recognise, and there wasn't space for anything else. *You're wasting away*, Mary kept telling her. And Uma couldn't argue with that.

'I'll give Ruth a ring,' said Uma, glancing at her watch and calculating where Ruth would be in her daily routine. *Just about to collect the girls from after school club*. Uma scrolled through her phone for Ruth's details, dialled, and stared, unseeing, out of the kitchen window as she listened to Ruth's mobile ringing. It went through to voicemail and Uma left a message explaining the offer of tea, stressing *it would be really nice to see you*, before returning her phone to her back pocket.

'So what about the Manchester opening?'

'What about it?'

'Have you decided to go?'

Uma continued staring out of the window at the waterlogged garden. The slushy mounds of snow left here and there made the place look messy, and she imagined taking a kettle outside, melting all those last little bits, thinking how satisfying it would be.

'I'm not sure. I thought I might feel okay to go by now, but...'

'You've postponed it once.'

'I'm not talking about postponing it again. I just think maybe someone should go in my place.'

'But who else is there?'

'Emma, the new manager?'

Mary frowned, shaking her head.

'Not Emma. She's just a girl.'

'The evening just needs to happen. I'm not sure it matters who's there. Anyone can say a few words.'

'Of course it matters! Listen. Ruth and I can help you. We'll book a nice hotel nearby. You can keep your speech short, leave early – everyone will understand. It just feels as if it would be tempting fate to not be there at all. As if... oh, I don't know! I just think you need to tell yourself you can do this.'

Uma put the base of her hands into her eye sockets and pushed, disappearing herself from the moment. Most of the time she could hardly imagine navigating the next few hours, let alone a celebratory work event in another city.

'It will be the start that you need,' Mary continued. She came over to Uma and put her hand on her back. 'It's going to be okay. I know it feels as if it will never be okay again, but I promise you that it will be.'

**

On the day itself, before it was even light, Uma found herself at the bathroom mirror, staring stolidly into her gritty, bloodshot eyes. *You can do this. This time tomorrow it will all be over.* She reached for the bottle of eye drops that Ruth had given her, squeezing the calming fluid into one eye, and then the other. She blinked, rolling her eyes in their sockets, coating her eyeballs with liquid, soothing the grittiness. She relished the comfort of her eyes feeling almost normal. These moments each morning were the most pleasant of her whole day. And she wished there was something similar she could administer to her fractious, splintered mind.

**

They arrived as the caterers were arranging canapes onto wooden boards and lining champagne flutes onto trays. Transparent, buoyant balloons swayed in clusters around the shop. Quiet music was playing and Emma, blond curls shifting round her face, greeted the three of them with a wide smile. She kept her hand on Uma's arm as she talked, explaining the plans for the evening, that Uma should just enjoy herself, that everything was taken care of.

Uma helped herself to a glass of champagne, downing it quickly, impatient for that first rush of relaxation. She poured herself another and sipped it slowly, running through her short speech in her mind, repeating the words to herself, smoothing them down, layering them with familiarity. She had practised it hundreds of times at home, knowing it was important to strike the right tone, and deliver it with ease. It was the kind of thing, ordinarily, she would have enjoyed.

'You look really nice Uma,' said Ruth, coming to stand next to her.

Uma smiled. 'You too.'

They were both in black. Ruth was wearing a black dress with the same black and grey scarf that she had worn to Daniel's funeral.

'I love this,' said Ruth, reaching out and running the back of her hand across the shiny silk of Uma's shirt.

They sipped their drinks in silence, the room filling around them, the hubbub building.

'I suppose I better go and do my bit,' she said, flashing Ruth a woeful smile. '*Circulate*, and all that.'

'Two hours and we'll be tucked up in bed.'

'Can't wait.'

Uma swapped her empty glass for a full one and moved from small group to small group, forcing conversation from somewhere deep inside of her, placating the anxieties of others, reassuring them that she was surviving. *Yes, it's hard but I'm doing okay.* And *it's lovely of you to be here.* She squared up to images of Mystery Caller, dismissing them as best she could. *I will not think about you tonight. I will not think about you tonight.* But she couldn't help herself. Her thoughts circled round like a boomerang. Each time she shook hands with a woman, or accepted a kiss on the cheek she couldn't help but wonder. *Is it you?*

'It's probably time, don't you think?' said Emma, appearing at Uma's elbow. 'Everyone's here.'

'Okay,' said Uma, following Emma round to the front of the room, noticing the blurring of her vision, the focus required to walk in a straight line. Emma was speaking, and then she wasn't. The room turned to Uma, silent with anticipation. She could *feel* their thoughts, crashing over her like a wave. She was awash in their pity and had no choice but to step towards their curious faces and be seen. It was like sacrificing herself. They hungered for her words, greedy for her grief. *What choice do I have?*

She turned to thank Emma for the introduction and collided with her, the champagne flute flying from her grasp and smashing across the floor.

'*So sorry,*' they both said together, Emma turning to the room and making a joke which Uma didn't hear as she crouched, ungainly in her too-tight skirt, to collect the pieces of glass from the floor.

'We can leave it for now,' said Emma, crouching with her. 'Do it after.'

Someone had fetched some kitchen roll though and was mopping the floor.

'I'll just get these big bits,' Uma said, reaching for the last couple of pieces of glass, toppling forward slightly, putting her hand down instinctively and cutting it against a barely visible shard. She balled her fingers against the sharp, quick pain.

'Damn,' she whispered beneath her breath, hiding the cut from Emma, holding out the pieces of glass to the person with the kitchen roll. Uma stood, hitching down her skirt, smoothing it self-consciously, ignoring the pulsing pain in her finger as she clenched her hand into a fist. She turned to the room that seemed alive now with shuffling, and nervous clearing of throats. She tried to make light of the incident, but the humorous words she was searching for stuck somewhere in her dry mouth.

'Thank you all for being here,' she managed.

She struggled for the sentences she had prepared – the simplicity of several paragraphs, strung together on the page. They had been easy. Straightforward. One following the other, quite naturally. But her mind had emptied itself.

'We're all here…' she tried again, thinking immediately of Daniel. *We're not all here at all.*

Uma felt her face flushing, her heart pounding. There were no words to rescue her. She couldn't remember a thing, and turned to Emma, who strode towards her, passing her some tissues before turning to the room. Uma unclenched her fist and blood dribbled to the floor, spattering the tops of her shoes. She scrunched the tissues over her wound, listening to Emma talk about what a difficult couple of months it had been, how sad it was that Daniel wasn't here, but how proud he had been to be opening another deli. A continuation of his father's business.

As soon as the applause rippled through the room, Uma turned and headed for the door, desperate for the cold winter air and the dark anonymity of the night.

Chapter Seven

1998

The pain had a rhythm, pulsing through her with the rocking of the train, oscillating knives in the pit of her belly. She told herself it was only after-pains – the hospital had said to expect them. *Everything is as it should be.* Breathing into them, willing them to pass, gripping the edge of the table she turned her head towards the window, watching momentarily the scenery hurtling past. It made her feel queasy, a damp perspiration breaking on her face, so she closed her eyes, shutting everything out.

As the train drew into Manchester she tried to imagine reaching for her bags, having the strength to alight the train, to make it out of the station, to manage the long bus journey across the city to her almost-derelict student house. Shivering with cold, the carriage heaving in and out of focus, she knew she couldn't do it. She needed help, but something was suddenly clear – she would rather allow something terrible to happen than ask a stranger for assistance.

When the train pulled into the station, Uma waited for the other passengers to gather their things and leave. *The train terminates here. Please take all your belongings with you.* Keeping her eyes closed for as long as possible, Uma only moved when she felt unable to delay it any longer. She heaved her bags from the overhead racks and dragged them off the train. She made it out of the station and looked towards the taxi rank, thinking that perhaps she could just about manage that. The queue snaked all around the side of the building. The pain was coming again, a rise of panic with it. She dragged her bags towards a phone box, opened the door with both hands, slumped inside, retching at the smell, wiping her palm across her sweaty face. She fished her purse out of her coat pocket and scrabbled through it for change, lifting the receiver. *Please be there, please be there.*

A stranger's voice answered.

'It's Uma here, is Aaron about?'

There was the clatter of the phone being thrown down, the sound of footsteps receding, a door banging and muffled voices. Then the sound of footsteps again, and Uma's own heart hammering in her chest. *Please let it be you.*

'Hey,' Aaron said.

'I'm at the station. I'm not well... I...'

'I'll come for you.'

'Thank you,' she whispered, weak with relief, fatigue, gratitude.

'Wait for me near the taxi rank. I'll be as quick as I can.'

She slumped down onto her bags, vaguely aware of wetness on the floor, the smell of ammonia. Pain pulsed through her again in deep, long waves, taking her consciousness with it, returning her briefly, vaguely, momentarily. She whimpered, fighting against it, doing her best to hold on to some semblance of clarity. She woke to the sound of her name, to Aaron's voice, to the welcome relief of cold air on her face, maybe rain. *Is it raining?*

'Uma!' Aaron was saying, over and over. He was calling out to somebody to help, for somebody to bring Uma's bags. His body was close to hers, lifting her onto her feet, his arm firmly around her, guiding her towards his waiting car she realised, seeing it ahead of them, the doors open. Uma took those last steps as best she could, focusing only on the interior of the car – of how much she wanted to be there, to enter and lie down and drift away again. Hazily, Uma was aware of just that happening – the familiar smell of his car, the doors slamming, the safety of it.

She could hear the sound of the engine, the familiar rhythm of her name, the urgency in his voice, drifting in and out. He said something about the hospital and *fuck fuck fuck*. She knew she should answer him, but the words wouldn't come. She knew, too, that it would reassure him if she were to sit up, to communicate with him a little. But she was unable. She could lie still. She could make the occasional sound. Or attempt a word, but not necessarily anything that made sense.

Aaron must have been driving fast because she was moving and shifting on the back seat, tipping forward at times as if she might roll into the foot wells. She put her hand out vaguely to steady herself.

I'm freezing. Everything was freezing.

And then the doors were opening.

'You need to help me,' said Aaron.

He was pulling at her arm.

'I'm not a fucking ambulance, I can't get right to the entrance. *Uma*.'

She did her best to sit up, his words sinking in.

'I'm coming,' she muttered, looking up, opening her eyes, trying to get them to focus on something. She gave up, concentrating instead on moving her legs, pressing her feet into the ground, standing, leaning into Aaron. They walked together into the hospital and then Aaron was talking and someone brought Uma a trolley. People swarmed, their hands on her skin, lifting her, rolling her, cold metal against her wrist, *sharp scratch*. Her limbs tremored. Her teeth chattered.

'Where is the pain?'

Questions were coming from nowhere.

'How long have you been feeling like this?'

Uma moved her hand to her abdomen.

'Are you taking any medication?'

'A termination…' she managed, barely a whisper.

The lights of the bright corridors flashed by overhead. Aaron's hand took hold of hers. And Uma let go.

**

He brought her home from hospital, as soon as she was well enough to leave. She had been threatening to discharge herself and eventually the staff relented, agreeing that if she had someone with her for a day or two then they would let her go.

'You're a terrible patient,' Aaron had said when they were in the car.

'I don't like to be ill. And the food was horrible.'

'You're also *way* too fussy. I would make the most of lying in bed having my meals brought to me three times a day.'

Uma had been in intensive care for five days with a septic blood infection. She'd spent another five days on a ward and Aaron had visited every day. Even during her less conscious moments Uma had been aware of him there. He had punctuated the long, sleepy days that had no night-time. It was his hand she could sometimes feel wrapped around her own. It was his voice that cut through the heartbeat of bleating machinery. Once she was conscious and sitting up he had offered to take her home with him – his mother had suggested it. *Just till you're back on your feet*, he had said. But Uma had declined, insisting that she should go back to River View – it was on the market still but hadn't sold.

'Then I'll come look after you there,' Aaron had said, fighting against Uma's bravado, adamant that the hospital staff were right – for a couple of days at least Uma ought to have someone around.

'Because you can't be trusted to look after yourself,' Aaron had said, as Uma had been packing up her things in hospital, removing her clothes from the bedside cupboard. She sighed, looking at him with exasperation, although secretly relieved that she wouldn't be alone at home. Empty of the vast majority of her parents' belongings the cottage seemed to ache for them. Uma had been efficient in clearing things away, knowing it was a job that needed to be done, remembering her parents' encouragement to face the jobs that needed facing. Their advice applied more to practical tasks than to matters of emotion. They would have approved of Uma sorting through their clothes, their letters and photos, their books and jewellery. They would have been proud of her ruthless decision making, her choice to keep only those things that she would actually use or that she truly loved.

'What about lectures? You're gonna miss stuff,' she objected weakly.

'It's fine. I'll sort notes from someone. I'll catch up no problem.'

He drove fast, hurtling round the country bends, the Rolling Stones blaring from the stereo. She wasn't afraid. She couldn't shift the feeling that fate would strike when it chose. If she was meant to die in this car on the way back from hospital – *today* – then it would happen whether she fought against it or not. He looked across at her, and she saw a sadness in his face.

'What?' she asked.

'Will you really not tell Daniel?'

Uma looked away and out of the window again. She shook her head.

'I should have told him before. It's too late now.'

'What if he finds out somehow?'

'How would he ever find out?'

Aaron shrugged, tapping his fingers on the steering wheel. She could tell he was anxious about it and she felt a pang of guilt.

'I'm sorry that you got involved. I didn't mean for that to happen. Obviously I hadn't meant to tell anyone.'

'I know that Moo. It's just…'

'Just what?'

'Wouldn't it be better if he knew?'

'He'd hate me.'

'Would he?'

'Catholics don't agree with termination.'

'And they don't agree with sex before marriage either, but he was okay with that.'

She was too tired to talk about it. Her brain was mushy, unable to concentrate on anything for too long.

'Let's talk about it another time,' she said, turning away from him. Closing her eyes, she tried to imagine the next few weeks and months stretching away ahead of her. River View might sell. In just a few days she would need to think about getting back to Manchester to resume her studies. She dredged up the idea of herself in lecture theatres, taking notes and making sense of the lessons, completing assignments and contributing to discussions during tutorials. She tried to remember that version of herself that had managed all those tasks. *That* Uma, who had been capable. The Uma that had wanted.

**

She lit a fire in the grate as Aaron made them tea. When the kindling was burning well she added some larger pieces, sawn tree branches, well-seasoned wood that her father must have gathered years ago. They had been dead for eighteen months and the wood stores still seemed full. He had been good at keeping the stocks up – going on long walks, collecting sticks in a rucksack for kindling, thicker branches clenched in his hands, or balanced on his shoulder, like a window cleaner carrying his ladders.

Uma waited for it to catch, carefully positioning coal around the pieces of wood. She balanced them, and watched for several minutes until she was sure the fire could take care of itself. Then she went to Aaron. He was at the kitchen table, the tea brewing in a pot beside him, and he was just finishing rolling a joint, pushing a little piece of rolled up card into the end.

'How do you get anything done?' said Uma, taking the joint from his hands, putting it in her mouth and lighting it.

He didn't suggest that she shouldn't be smoking.

'You scared the fuck out of me by the way,' he said, watching her.

Uma pulled an apologetic face.

'Thank you for being a super-star,' she said.

He held his fingers out for the joint and Uma passed it to him. She regarded him casually as he smoked, unable to release herself from the pull she felt towards him. It had always been the same. Maybe not right from the beginning, but pretty early on – as soon as they got to know each other during lower sixth. He had been one of those rare friends – one of those people that made Uma feel like a good person, as if she was worth something. He had made her feel interesting, seeking her out during free periods. And she had always been better for seeing him. He had often, back then, asked about her parents, and never offered platitudes. He remarked how shit it was and let the silence stretch out away from them. No one else had been as brave as Aaron. Daniel and Pippa had been afraid of what was going on in Uma's life and it soaked into everything they ever said. It made Uma feel afraid too. They wanted her to feel better, to forget, and she understood that – she wanted those things herself. But Aaron knew as well as Uma did that those things weren't possible. And if they weren't possible then she needed someone to stand in the swamp of grief alongside her.

When Uma's mother died, Aaron had appeared at River View, sitting in the garden, keeping himself out of the way, like some kind of promise beneath the apple trees. Daniel and Pippa had been thinking of her too. But they put their sorrow into words in a card and dropped it through the letterbox.

They played cards in front of the fire, and Aaron heated them some tomato soup, grating cheese into it, buttering them crusty French bread. They watched Cinema Paradiso and afterwards they went to bed. Aaron in her parents' bedroom and Uma in her own.

In the early hours she woke, as she often did. Bright moonlight cast shadows across her bedspread and she felt the weight of Aaron's presence in the house. She was glad of it. Since her father died and Uma had been living there alone the cottage had almost swallowed her with its emptiness. And she felt it most when she woke in the night and couldn't find her way back to sleep.

Eventually she folded back the heavy covers, reaching for her dressing gown at the end of the bed. She pulled on a pair of thick woollen socks and crept silently down the landing, stopping outside her parents' bedroom, waiting, listening for the sound of him sleeping. But only silence rang in her ears as she strained to hear him, and she wondered briefly if he was really there at all. Perhaps she had imagined him. Conjured him up because that's what she wanted.

The flames devoured the knots of paper that she folded and fed to them, and soon the kindling she piled on top was burning fiercely. She balanced a handful of thicker sticks around the paper and left them to be consumed as she heated butter in a pan and fried cinnamon toast which she dipped in sugar. Her stomach growled at the promise of food and she ate the first piece straight from the pan as she fried the second, heating her masala chai at the same time. With a plateful of cinnamon toast and a mug of masala chai she went back to the fire, turning all the lights off so the flickering orange warmth filled the room. Her skin was bathed in a fiery glow. She ate the last piece of sugary bread slowly, savouring it, washing it down with hot tea.

'I don't want to sell you,' she said, aloud.

The words hung in the silence. The thought, like her hunger, had reared up unexpectedly in the shadows. But she *needed* to sell River View – it still had a mortgage on it, albeit small. Uma had inherited her parents' debts as well as their small savings account. The mortgage was paid, at the moment, from the savings which would last until the end of the year. *I have to sell you*. She had said this sadly, remorsefully, months ago, speaking aloud, over and over, as she had moved around the house sorting through her parents' things. The rising tide of change had threatened to engulf her. She had tried to think through the alternatives – grasping at them hopefully. She could get a job, but that would mean no university, which in turn would mean being away from her friends, missing out too on the possibility of meeting the kinds of friends she might keep forever. That's what university promised – people had told her so. *It's a special time*, they said. *You'll never make the same kind of friends again*.

She could rent out River View, but it didn't comply with any legislation and would eat up more than every penny she had getting it ready for tenants – and even then she would have to advertise and manage the process of being a landlord, which seemed unfeasible from another city.

If there had been a wider family to go to then perhaps other possibilities would have presented themselves. But there *was* no family now. She tried to remind herself that she wasn't really alone in the world. She had her friends. Her kind neighbours. *I'm not alone. I'm not alone. I am not alone*.

Sat now in the firelight, *I don't want to sell* running through her mind, Uma knew that she'd made the wrong choice. River View cottage was the only remaining part of life with her parents. It was her only connection. She didn't *have* to sell it. She didn't *have* to go back to university. She wasn't even enjoying it that much – unable to ignore the feeling that she existed in a parallel universe to many of her friends. Being away from the watchful parental eye was a novelty for them. Their excitement was palpable, their greed for freedom. Drink. Drugs. Sex. Parties. The drama of fucks gone wrong. The dreadful hangovers. Uma was there, but she wasn't there. If her parents had been alive then Uma would have been just like everyone else – desperate to get away from home. As it was, she dreamt of the house, of sleeping in their bed, sitting in the wardrobe in amongst their clothes, inching closer to the memory of them.

By the time she heard Aaron moving around upstairs, Uma was brimming with certitude. The pieces of her decision had closed together in her mind, welded and fused as if it had always been the way it was going to be. As if she hadn't ever really packed up and moved to Manchester. As if she had only ever been right here.

**

She made him tea and cinnamon toast before he appeared downstairs, feeling the gratitude in her chest when she heard his footfall on the stairs, the old wooden rises creaking indignantly. His hair, the colour of straw, was wild around his head. She laughed and he ran his fingers through it, smoothing it half-heartedly.

'*I* should be cooking breakfast. That's what I'm here for.'

'Come sit down,' she said, ignoring him, moving out of the kitchen, drawing him towards the fire. His shirt was tatty, fraying round the edges, tiny holes scattered down the front of it. She passed him his food and sat with him on the sofa, turning towards him and crossing her legs. She clasped her hands together in front of her chest as if in prayer.

'I've made a decision.'

He stopped, motionless, food halfway to his mouth, his eyes locked with hers. His pale blue irises were ringed with navy. Freckles speckled his nose and cheeks.

'I'm going to stay here and get a job.'

'Give up uni?'

She nodded, searching his face, realising how much she wanted to hear from him that this was a good idea. He put the piece of cinnamon toast back on his plate.

'What will you do?'

Uma shrugged. 'I need to think of something. But it

94

doesn't really matter for now. I just want to keep the place, and I want to *be in it*. I don't want to rent it out and have other people living here.'

He nodded. 'It makes sense,' he said.

'Does it?'

'Of course. It's a big decision to sell your family home.'

'I grew up here…'

Aaron took a bite of toast and his face broke into a wide smile.

'How do you *do* this?' he gestured the piece of toast in Uma's direction. 'It's amazing.'

She grinned.

'Well that's something I was thinking I could do,' she said, excitement bubbling up, deciding to share the details of her longer-term plans.

'I want to do something food related. Maybe something around South Indian food. Run classes or write a book. I could visit my mother's village, take pictures, gather recipes and write it all up. No one eats South Indian food in this country. It's so different to the kinds of curries that people are used to eating.'

'Sounds cool, Moo!'

'Obviously I just need to find a job to start with. But in time it's what I'd love to do. The whole cookery and travel thing really excites me.'

'You could open a restaurant on the back of the book,' he grinned.

'Or the other way round! Do the restaurant, make it madly successful and *then* write a book.'

'*Do it!*'

'Do you think?'

'Absofuckinglutely!'

And Uma laughed with the sudden joy of it.

**

Pippa barely met Uma's eye when she walked into the messy kitchen of their shared house in Manchester. Uma certainly wouldn't miss this. She glanced briefly at the piles of washing up, the over-flowing bin, lid missing, food stains covering the paintwork behind. Envelopes and junk mail covered the back door mat – a door that never opened.

Pippa was at the table, eating a bowl of cereal, reading a magazine. Uma began making a cup of tea.

'Do you want one?' she asked, and Pippa shook her head.

'You never say no to a cup of tea,' said Uma.

'What?' demanded Pippa, scowling.

'What's wrong?'

'Where the fuck have you been for two weeks?'

'I had stuff to do.'

'What stuff?'

'River View stuff.'

'What stuff, specifically?'

'Stuff to do with selling it.'

Uma felt the lies flowing out of her.

'And Aaron needed to help you with that did he?'

'Uh... I...'

'His mum told me, Uma.'

Heat flooded Uma's face, her scalp prickling. *What* had Aaron's mum told her? She stared, wrong-footed but unwilling to say anything that might make things worse.

'It's not what you think,' she said after a moment or two.

'One sign that maybe he was interested in me and bang! You're on him like a ton of bricks.'

Uma shook her head.

'Nothing happened between me and Aaron.'

'You're welcome to him.'

'It doesn't sound that way.'

'Don't let me stand in your way.'

'What?'

'Don't let me stand. *In. Your. Way.*'

Pippa stared Uma straight in the eye. Her face was stony cold. She obviously didn't know about the termination or she wouldn't be behaving like this. This was jealousy, pure and simple. But, how to explain herself? *Don't tell her*. Pippa wasn't good with secrets. If Uma told her, then there was every chance the information would slip through her fingers and seep out into the world. She trusted Aaron never to breathe a word. But if Pippa knew then Uma would forever wonder where in the world her secret had ended up. Out there, unleashed, it might find its way to Daniel and she couldn't let that happen. She opened her mouth to speak, but it was too late. Pippa had gone, slamming the door behind her.

Tears in her eyes, Uma went to her room and began taking down her posters, rolling them and putting elastic bands round their middle. She probably wouldn't use them again. Posters seemed necessary at university, but they wouldn't at home.

She brought in the cardboard boxes that she and Aaron had picked up from a supermarket on the outskirts of town. She had left them out the front of the house, intending to break the news to Pippa first before bringing boxes inside.

I need to leave on good terms. I can't leave like this. The thought of their friendship crumbling made Uma's stomach clench with anxiety. The scattering of people who were important to Uma was so few. She pulled the photos off her mirror, scraping away the blue tack, lifting the mirror down and wrapping it in newspaper. Her hands were trembling.

She packed away her books and folders, her clothes and trinkets, cassette tapes and her handful of CDs – boxing up her brief interlude of university life in just an hour or so. When the job was done she sat on her bed, flooded with a mixture of fear and exhaustion. She was still at a low ebb after her infection and even small exertions left her feeling weary. She took a deep breath, running through what she was going to say in her mind. After a moment or two she went to Pippa's room and knocked on the door.

'Pippa?' she said, knocking again.

When there was no answer she opened the door. The room was empty, as was the rest of the house. Pippa hadn't returned by the morning and so Uma wrote her a letter at the kitchen table, explaining what was happening and apologising – suggesting that they talk very soon. She blamed her staying away at home on her ambivalence about returning, her dread at leaving her family home and also on her panic attacks. She explained that she felt embarrassed about the attacks – that she felt weak and stupid and Aaron had been helping her with all of that. It was a lie. But it was a lie washed through with shades of truth.

Pippa would be okay. She gathered new friends everywhere she went. Uma wasn't essential to Pippa's happiness. Pippa was at the centre of things, whilst Uma was on the outer edges looking in. *You need to find your own place in the world.* Uma needed to find that place where she would feel at home in the centre of things. A place where she was really living, not just observing her life unfolding, as if it had been foretold already. She couldn't imagine where that place would be. But it wasn't here.

She walked round to Aaron's and picked up his car. He had offered to help her load up her things but she had told him that she could manage on her own. He hadn't pressed her. Perhaps he felt some of what she felt, a sadness bubbling so close to the surface that it might overflow at any time, threatening to get in the way of all the things that needed to be done.

As she was finishing loading the car, fighting the tears, her hands shaking at the idea of Pippa arriving home knowing nothing, not yet having seen Uma's letter, she felt the familiar anxiety begin to take hold. It gripped her chest and throat, doing its best to suffocate her. She opened the car door, sat behind the wheel and breathed. Slowly and evenly, focusing just on her breath. *Don't fight it, let it come.* She tried to let the feeling wash over her. *Don't struggle. It makes things worse.* She breathed in, and out, closing her eyes, remembering his words.

**

She withdrew from university, took River View off the market and returned Aaron's car, all on the same day. He dropped her at the train station afterwards, parking the car so he could come and wait with her on the platform. They sat on a bench together sharing an egg mayonnaise sandwich. After they finished he reached out and took her hand and Uma rested her head on his shoulder.

'I feel like we're parting company,' he said.

'Don't be dramatic.'

'I was taking it for granted we'd spend another two years in the same place. Round the corner from each other.'

'What difference does it make?' She knew she was testing him.

He sighed a deep sigh.

'What's happening with you and Pippa?' Uma asked.

'Nothing.'

'What about New Year?'

'It wasn't anything. I figure I was just next on her list.'

'I'm not sure it was nothing to her.'

Silence.

'Would *that* make a difference?' Uma said. 'If it meant something to her?'

Uma lifted her head from his shoulder to look up at him. He looked away from her, down the platform. Uma waited, needing to hear him say it.

'No, it doesn't make a difference,' he said eventually. 'It wasn't the start of anything. Pippa knows that.'

Uma started to tell Aaron how things had been with Pippa, but the train pulled in and there was nothing for them to do but stand up and hug, Uma trying not to disappear too deeply into it. She could feel her eyes watering as she turned away and boarded the train, so she didn't look back, not even to wave, busying herself instead with finding space for her bag in the overhead racks. The train had almost left the station before she dared to look out of the window, knowing she wouldn't be able to see him, tears streaming down her face by then. He was right. It did feel like they were parting company. It felt as if the chances of them ever being together were growing smaller. Floating away like Chinese boat-lanterns on a lake.

**

Daniel was sitting in the garden when Uma arrived home. She was shocked to see him, and walked towards him, concern bubbling up inside of her, sensing that something must be wrong.

'Daniel?'

His face was blank, kind of hollowed out. He didn't answer immediately and Uma realised he was trying hard not to cry.

'Dad's had a heart attack.'

'Oh *Daniel*.'

She took him inside and it was only as she was asking him further questions that she realised Clive was dead. He hadn't just had a heart attack. Clive had had a heart attack *and died*.

'It's awful at home,' he said. 'Really awful.'

Uma imagined Daniel's mother, aunts, sisters. She imagined that flood of female emotion, the tears flowing freely and Daniel surrounded by it – not wanting to add to it, holding it in as if he could set some kind of example. As if by not crying he might lessen their collective grief.

They talked for a while, and much later, after they had watched some TV, she made them cheese on toast because it was Daniel's favourite snack.

'It's all I've got in the house,' she said though, because that was also the case, passing him a plate.

They ate in silence, their fingers and lips greasy in the firelight.

**

Daniel's family were grieving carnival style. Uma thought about what Daniel had said – *it's awful at home*. Was this awful? There were certainly tears, and they were hard to escape. Uma could imagine Daniel feeling trapped – *hemmed in* is how he described it. But there was also laughter and the most delicious homemade cake with thickly whipped cream and chocolate ganache and stories dredged up from the past that made all of them howl so much that eventually their laughter dissolved into tears all over again. And there was gin and tonic, in large quantities that required a constant restocking of the ice cube trays in the freezer. Uma thought back to the whispered silence at home in the aftermath of her father's death and couldn't correlate the two.

Mary's three sisters had decamped at Mary's house, leaving their various children with friends and neighbours. They kept the teapot full. And they intercepted calls, taking messages, reminding Mary what needed doing next – what tasks she must attend to before Clive could be buried.

They included Uma in their ranks from the beginning, giving her jobs to do as if she was part of the team, getting her to pass out the tea and cake when people came visiting. They entrusted her with their thoughts about what Clive would have wanted, and how they all needed to help Mary out with Anna. *I don't mind having Anna some of the time,* Uma had said, explaining that she had just left university. *Until I find myself a job I have plenty of time on my hands*. They had called her *a good soul*, putting their fleshy arms around her shoulders. Uma was a good soul and Daniel was a good son. *Thank goodness he stayed behind*, they said. *Thank goodness he became involved in Millers, because now he knows what he's doing*.

**

'I like to keep busy,' he said, when Uma asked him if taking on the family business was all a bit much.

'But can you cope on your own?'

'For now,' he said. 'We're in the middle of a big refurbishment. I wanted to strip out the shops and bring things up to date a bit. Keep the fruit and veg, but expand into other things, a bit like a deli. Kind of rebrand things a bit.'

'And your dad was up for that?'

'He took a bit of persuading in the beginning – the fruit and veg has ticked along well enough for decades. But people are going to these big supermarkets now, business is dropping off and we need to do something to compete. He didn't like the fact but he knew what was happening. Specialising is the way to go. Offering something the supermarkets *don't* offer.'

Uma thought it sounded like a good idea and they talked about it whenever they were together, Uma throwing ideas into the mix, suggestions for what he could stock, speciality ingredients for aspiring cooks. Good quality oils. Local cheeses and meats. Uma found details of food festivals that were happening around the country and they visited several, staying overnight in a local B&B, eating and drinking their way through the events.

There were moments when Uma was tempted to confide in Daniel about the pregnancy and her decision to end it. But the words never quite came. It always seemed that there would be another more suitable time in the future for those particular words; a time when they wouldn't have to fight their way out of her. They talked about all sorts of other things, and Uma told him about her idea for a cookbook, for starting a South Indian cookery revolution. 'I'm going to bring it to the masses.'

'Come and work for me,' he said eventually. 'It'll be so great. You could be our product manager. Fancy title and all. Would you like to?'

She had laughed at his enthusiasm, recognising her own then too, thinking what a convenient arrangement it would be, to solve his problem and hers all at once. But more than that. Being with Daniel and being part of his embryonic business, looking after Anna, being around Mary and the aunts. Suddenly, unexpectedly, Uma felt part of something.

Chapter Eight

2015

She had run away to breathe the cold air off the Irish Sea.

Just a month, she had promised Mary, who had run her hands through her hair continually as Uma broke the news that she was going. *You shouldn't be alone*, Mary had warned. *And what about Millers?* Uma hadn't dared to speak the words that sprang to her mouth: *Fuck Millers*.

The road that approached the cottage was gritty with sand. It trickled in from the soft curbs, whispering promises of undulating dunes and vast windswept beaches. The place belonged to Pippa's mother. *Nobody uses it,* Pippa had said. *Just go.*

Uma had known to expect something basic, a phone line but no internet, patchy mobile coverage, a lumpy bed and saggy sofa. But the ramshackle timber cottage was even shabbier than Pippa had described. Paint flaked from its window frames. The garden was wild. And the draughts that blew in beneath the doors tugged at the long curtains as if someone walked unseen behind them.

Uma hadn't just run to the sea, she had run away from Daniel. He might be dead but back at home he jumped out at her all through the day. The photos of him around the house. The letters addressed to him. His mug in the kitchen. The foods he liked in the cupboards. His clear, precise voice on the answer machine. His mother who had insinuated herself as Uma's shadow. The never-ending demands of Millers. He was gone, but her life was still *their* life, and none of it felt right anymore.

Four weeks had passed, peppered with calls from Mary *just checking in*. Uma had been spooning her reassurance, some of it nowhere near the truth.

She had been sending Aaron text messages, once a week or so, guessing at his whereabouts on the Sultans trail. Austria perhaps? Slovakia? She convinced herself his lack of response was inevitable. *He's in the middle of nowhere.* But doubt niggled her. Surely he would have passed through some areas with a signal by now. *Perhaps he can't charge his phone. Of course he can charge his phone!* Every so often she would slip his postcard from her diary, looking at the familiar handwriting, reading the words for the hundredth time, searching for the anger she feared he was hiding.

Almost as compulsively, she reached for her mobile phone and scrolled through her messages to Mystery Caller. *Who do you think you are? Don't you think we should talk? I spoke to Father Michael about you.*

But Mystery caller was ignoring her too.

**

Most of the time Uma ate in the kitchen, standing, tearing chunks from a loaf and smearing them across a block of butter, slicing cheese and scooping olives or tomatoes straight from a jar into her mouth. She was rarely hungry, but ate in an attempt to steady her persistent light headedness. Afterwards she threw the cheese and butter into the fridge and hid the remains of the loaf inside a saucepan with a heavy, tight-fitting lid to keep the mice away.

**

During the first few days at the cottage, Uma had distracted herself with useful tasks. She had hoovered away the layer of cat fur deposited on the collapsing chair in the corner of the veranda. She had emptied some dead plants from terracotta pots onto the remnants of a compost heap at the bottom of the garden, scrubbed the green slime from the pots and stacked them neatly. She had swept the inside the house and the veranda, and the steps leading down to the garden whilst a bony white cat had eyed her from beneath the plum tree. She had called to it, but it refused to come.

Moving inside, she had turned her attention to the dusty furniture, the skirting boards, the door frames, the top of the bookcases. She had pulled the novels down and hoovered the dust from them, wiping their covers with a hot, wet cloth, leaving them spread around the room to dry. She had scooped up the rocks and shells from the window ledges and taken them to the kitchen sink, submerging and refreshing them, marvelling at the colours coming alive in the water as she rubbed them to remove the layers of grime.

Pausing, hands submerged, she had traced her fingers over the grooves and spirals of the shells. *You must go to the beach*. And without even draining the sink she had found herself outside, hands still wet. Pippa had said the beach was a *short walk through the woods*. But in which direction? Driving through the gorse-covered moorland she had seen the coastline in the distance several times, but had lost sight of it long before the turning for the cottage.

Daniel and she had shared a terrible sense of direction. Neither one of them knew north or south without the help of a compass. Aaron on the other hand, like her father, had some innate sense about where he was, and if he didn't know it straight away it didn't take him long to work it out. If he had been there he would have known where the sea was in relation to the cottage. It would have been obvious to him. He would have said something about the gorse stretching towards the east because of the prevailing wind, which would be coming off the sea, which was of course to the west. *And if you look now at the sun…* Uma had smiled to remember those kinds of conversations, and how it was always Aaron that helped them find their way.

That first time out exploring, Uma had followed a narrow walkway round the side of the cottage, heading blindly into the gloom of the trees. Brittle branches and dry leaves scrunched and cracked beneath her boots. There was no clear path and she had been forced to push branches away from her face, stooping here and there, ducking under low boughs, startling creatures in the undergrowth. Every so often she had checked behind, reminding herself of the way she had come, the white of the cottage obvious behind the grey of the naked trees. She kept pausing to listen for the sound of the sea and eventually, just as the sight of the cottage diminished to nothing more than wishful thinking, she had realised that she could hear the roar of waves at last, and, even better, a path had appeared in front of her.

As she got close to the beach the undergrowth became sandier, softer under foot, the trees sparse, reeds appearing in clumps. She emerged onto vast sand dunes, the sea in the distance, the wind strong. She realised how protected the cottage was behind its screening of trees, how quiet and still it had been whilst here the wind was slapping at her face.

The tide was out and Uma strode towards it, walking straight at the wind, her eyes drinking in the vastness of the sea and the wonder of the sun coming down over the water. She knew that the crepuscular light would make her walk back to the cottage difficult, but she could hardly bear to turn away. She broke into a run, determined to meet the water where it lapped the shore before she had to turn back. Her boots sunk into the soft sand, tiny flies jumping away from her. It wasn't long before she reached wet sand and it was easier to run, her boots leaving deep indentations behind her. When she turned to look she laughed at the sight of them, something leaping inside her when she realised they were the only footprints for as far as she could see. She slowed to a walk, spinning round and taking in the expansiveness of the long beach. She couldn't see another soul and had called out at the joy of it, the wind lifting her hair and throwing it wildly.

**

Most evenings, Uma lay in the bath, topping it up at intervals with water too hot to touch, watching the steam rise and her breath condense. And during the night she did what she always did – attempted to read and attempted to sleep, and failed at both. Wrapped in several layers and thick woollen socks she wandered from room to room in the darkness, lying on the sofa to see if sleep might visit her there.

**

During the daytime she walked. Anywhere. It was the only thing that made sense. She explored the woods, watching jays and woodpeckers, listening for the rustle of shrews and field mice. She walked along the coast, welcoming, as the weeks passed, how familiar it became – the undulating, windswept dunes, the random clumps of reeds sharp enough to cut a careless hand or soft sole, the large piece of driftwood half a mile up the beach, its spider silhouette an eerie ghost on misty mornings. She loved the unfamiliar too, the surprise each day of what the tide had gifted the beach – thick, translucent jelly-fish, or hundreds of oyster shells, or heaps of tangled seaweed.

**

Uma woke from a broken half-night of sleep, filled with the sense of her mother – sandalwood soap, long hair twisted in a bun on the top of her head, small wisps framing her face. She turned to the window, taking in the blue sky unfettered by cloud, then closed her eyes, allowing her tired, fractious mind to sift through the memories – the poetry her mother wrote, and read over dinner to Uma and her father. The afternoons spent cooking together, peeling and chopping onions, rinsing rice, cleaning lentils. Picking produce from the garden in the summer, spinach, chard and beans, tomatoes and cucumbers, chillies, herbs and salad. The songs her mother sang beneath her breath, old songs from her childhood in India, the songs her aunts sang as they worked.

Sometimes Uma had asked about her mother's childhood, about her family and what India had been like, whether she missed it and whether they would ever go. If Uma was lucky and her mother was in the right kind of mood, she would offer a glimpse of her previous life. But her reluctance to talk was obvious, and there had always been something about the weight of her mother's silence when it came, like a landslide between them.

Uma had learned, over time, not to ask for too much at once, to be grateful for the snippets that came when they were cooking. And to be grateful for the cooking itself. Understanding even then that it was a sliver of India right there in their kitchen. As was her mother's Catholicism, shaded through with the teachings of Ganesha, Shiva, Hanuman and Durga. She taught Uma how to sit in silence, how to close her eyes and see the world through her third eye, how to observe without judging. *Sometimes it helps to quieten our minds*, her mother had said. *There'll be times when you'll be glad to know these things*.

Uma hadn't thought about it for years, and she threw back the bed covers and wrapped her tiny frame in several layers – jumper over shirt, over thermal top, over vest. She grasped hold of the memory, shining it, doing her best to get back to that time, sitting with her mother on the floor in front of the fire, contemplating Ajna, *that place between your eyebrows where wisdom meets your intuition*.

Uma scrabbled in the kitchen cupboards for the cassia bark she had brought for her porridge. She found a small pan and filled it with a little water. With no pestle and mortar she made do with the end of a rolling pin, grinding the cinnamon stick as best she could, sprinkling it into the water and waiting for it to come to a boil. She added the dry tea leaves from a tea bag, telling herself not to be so precious. After a few minutes she added milk and sugar and boiled the whole lot together. It was more than a decade since she had made masala chai and she took her cup to the sofa, inhaling the fragrance, tasting the sweetness and lack of pungency, promising herself that she would head out that afternoon to the nearest town and stock up on cardamom, cloves, ginger, pepper. And tomorrow she would make it properly.

For now, she closed her eyes, cupping the warm drink, bringing her mother's instructions to mind. Once upon a time she would have laughed at herself. *What's the point? Learning to breathe!* She wasn't sure that even now she had an answer to why she was bothering. But she closed her eyes anyway, desperate for anything that would help her find a way back into herself.

**

For the next week, Uma filled the cottage with the smell of mustard seeds, fenugreek and turmeric. The tiny black seeds popped in the oil, spitting at her, hot and fierce. She sliced chillies into slivers and grated ginger into small piles, juice running off the board onto the table. Handfuls of curry leaves fizzed and shrivelled in the pan, filling the kitchen with the aromas of Kerala, and her mother's cooking. It was like coming home. And it was like going somewhere new. She thought of Daniel. *You steered me away from this.* Somehow, Millers was never quite ready for the flavours of South India. *It's not the right time*, he'd say, all those years ago. And later on, more recently, when she mentioned India, when she mentioned Kerala, he'd say things like *let sleeping dogs lie*, and *you're chasing ghosts*. He told her that her mother left her family for a reason. *You don't know what you'd be walking into.*

Uma stepped outside into the warmth of the sunshine, the paving slabs hot beneath her feet, the cat making its way towards her across the grass, stopping a short distance away, as was its habit. It sat, looking directly at her, unblinking, as if trying to tell her something.

The sun was fierce for May. There had been no sign of rain all week, just a wisp or two of cloud in the sky and hardly any breeze, just the sound of the birds, trills and warbles and the squabbling of finches high in the trees.

The garden bench was silver-grey with age, the grain of wood open and cracked, rough to the touch. But sturdy, and comfortable too now that Uma had softened it with some cushions she had found at the back of the rotting shed. She had wiped away the cobwebs and dead insects and ignored the stains.

The bench was like the one they used to have at River View Cottage, and she wondered whether it was there still. That bench had been privy to every secret, every struggle. Beneath the apple trees, in the shade, it had been the place Uma had retreated to, whispering her thoughts to herself when there was no one else.

Why didn't we take it with us? She had never thought about it before. When she and Daniel sold it, in favour of a *proper house* in the city, they could have loaded the bench into the removal lorry along with everything else. But they hadn't. Perhaps Uma had realised that the bench belonged at River View – a cottage with, laughably, no view of the river at all.

She sipped her tea, savouring the sweetness of it and the warmth of the sun. She drank slowly, nothing to hurry to. Over the past few weeks she had stumbled into a lower gear and sometimes she wasn't sure she would ever get going again.

Anna was arriving later that afternoon. She had texted a

few days ago to say that she was coming and Uma's heart had leapt at the thought. She knew that Anna had a tendency to change her plans at the last minute and so had tried to pretend her sister-in-law wasn't really coming at all. It made her wonder if that had become a habit of hers over the years – keeping her expectations low, her hopes in check.

**

The phone was ringing in the other room before Uma was even out of bed. She rolled over and reached for her mobile, checking the time – 7.50am. *Who on earth?* She sat up and pulled a jumper over her vest top. She heard the ping of the phone being answered in the other room and saw, when she opened the bedroom door, Anna, dressed only in pants, with the phone against the side of her face. She turned towards Uma and rolled her eyes, letting the phone flop away from her ear.

'Mary?' Uma whispered.

Anna gave a nod and Uma held out her hand.

'I'll speak to you later Mum. Here's Moo.'

Uma took the phone, hesitated, then put it to her ear.

'Hi Mary.'

'She cut me off mid-sentence!'

'You're calling very early.'

'I wanted to be sure to catch you, that's all.'

'Has anything happened?'

Uma knew that nothing had happened.

'I'm surprised Anna's there,' said Mary.

'It's lovely to see her.'

'How's Warwick? Have you asked?'

'No, but I'm sure it's going fine,' said Uma, lowering her voice, watching Anna pulling on a pair of jeans. 'How are you?'

'Ruth said I should talk to you. You know I'm worried, it's not as if I've hidden the fact, and I know I shouldn't interfere, Millers isn't anything to do with me anymore but it's the family business and anyway, it's not really just about Millers. It's you I'm most concerned about.'

'O*kaay*.'

'When are you coming home? It's been five weeks, do you even have a plan? Ruth said she spoke to you a few days ago and you sounded as if you had no idea when you were going to be back. I probably wouldn't mind so much if you *did* have a plan but sometimes it just feels as if you've run away from everything. Do you think you might be depressed? Is that it? Because Ruth could help with that couldn't she?'

'It's just a bit of peace and quiet I need. A little time to think.'

'Millers can't run without you. It's difficult enough with Daniel gone.'

'It's temporary.'

'How temporary's temporary?'

'I'm calling every Monday morning, checking in, making decisions. They're recruiting a finance manager to replace Daniel.'

'They need you here. In person.'

'I'm not entirely sure they do.'

'And you need it too. You'll never want to come back home if you leave it too long. You're hiding from all the things that matter. You'll regret it if you're not careful.'

There was a sharp edge to Mary's voice, the kind of tone she used with Anna. Uma hadn't been on the receiving end of that before.

'I'll be back in the next few weeks.'

'*The next few weeks?*'

'I just need a little more time.'

'You'll feel so much better once you establish a proper routine for yourself. Get back to things.'

Uma thought about her routine here at the cottage. Her morning walk on the beach, the fragrant porridge she made afterwards, the lighting of the fire, replenishing the wood store with sticks and branches from the woods, the weeding in the garden if the weather permitted. *I have a routine*, she wanted to say.

'Your staff need you around. It's a terrible shock for everyone. It's not just about you.'

Uma bristled.

'People will be anxious about the future and you should be here to reassure them.'

Part of her knew that Mary was right. If her own parents were alive they would be telling her the same thing. Duty. Responsibility. She had prided herself on these things for so long.

'People understand,' Uma said, desperate to convince herself as much as Mary. 'For goodness sake. How long is long enough? How quickly should I get over it?'

Silence.

She felt like a fraud, knowing that if things had been just a little more straightforward she would have been back at work by now. She would have made the effort. Extra effort, in fact. She'd have stepped up to all the new challenges. And her shirts would have been just as crisp as before. Her colleagues, as well as Mary and Ruth, would have marvelled at her resilience.

'Somebody was here for you.'

'Where's here?'

'At the house.'

'My house? Why are you at my house?'

'You know how it is when a house stands empty. I don't want you coming back to that.'

Uma imagined Mary rattling around the empty rooms, searching through drawers and cupboards.

'She was here yesterday morning,' said Mary. 'Peering through the windows.'

Uma's heart picked up.

'I suppose she'd been knocking,' said Mary.

'What did she say?'

'Just that she was looking for you.'

'Did you get her name?'

'She said she'd call you and that was it.'

'What did she look like?'

'Like she was in a bad mood. As if something was wrong.'

Uma's mouth was suddenly dry.

'*Is* something wrong? With Millers, I mean,' said Mary. 'Money troubles or anything like that?'

'Absolutely not. You know what Daniel was like with the accounts, and how cautious he was.'

'So who was it, do you think? It seemed so strange that she was just there, peering in at the windows.'

'What did she look like?'

'Oh goodness, I just remember her hair, bright red ringlets, and so much of it!'

'Was she young? Did she… did she say anything else?'

'She was your age I suppose. Tallish.'

Uma took a slow, deliberate breath. Was this the image she'd been grasping for? She had an instinct that it was. Who else could it be? She didn't know anyone fitting that description.

'Oh, yes,' said Mary. 'And a Devon accent. Made me think she might have been something to do with the shop down there. I only thought about it afterwards, but she didn't say anything about being involved with Millers. You'd think she would have done.'

Uma was only vaguely listening to Mary's gabbling. She twisted the telephone cord round and round her fingers. And watched a spider crawling the skirting board, her mind scrabbling.

**

Uma slipped out of the cottage whilst Anna was in the bath. She didn't leave a note to say where she was going or when she'd be back. The urge to be alone on the vast beach with nothing but space had her striding towards the woods, pushing branches out of her way, her arms prickling with goose bumps in the heavy shade of the trees. She broke into a run when she could, slowing to negotiate fallen trees, ducking beneath low branches, walking every so often to catch her breath before running again.

At the beach she sat high on the sand dunes between several clumps of reedy-grass. The sand felt warm, but when she pushed her hands beneath the surface it was cold just a few inches down. She took off her boots, peeled off her socks and found the cold sand with her toes. She watched a couple in the distance, holding hands, walking a dog that was running ahead and veering in and out of the shallow water, yelping at the waves.

She took her mobile out of her pocket and typed a message, as brief and to the point as all the others. *You were at my house?? I know what you look like and I will find you if you don't contact me*. She stuffed the mobile back into her pocket, looking up again at the sea and the couple and the dog.

She could feel the engine of her indignation turning over, doing its best to get going. *How dare he? A whole year of lies! And who does she think she is – coming to my house!* But the thoughts changed quickly to something else, something murky and mutable. Her anger, so stark in the beginning, had become less reliable these last few weeks, rearing only briefly before fading, leaving an empty space that Uma filled with self-wrangling and doubt.

Mainly, she thought about all the things she and Daniel hadn't talked about, all the conversations they had skirted around. He'd never said *I really want to have children. Don't you*? She'd never told him how angry she'd been on their wedding day, by the time Aaron had finished his best man's speech. He never asked whether she really loved him. And she'd never said *there are things you need to know*.

His tendency had always been to keep his feelings to

himself, but Uma had never chosen to coax them out of him either. She hadn't wanted to know what was going on inside his head when she caught him watching her, or when she noticed him deep in thought, staring off into the distance, picking at the skin around his fingernails. She never offered him a penny for his thoughts. She left him alone with them. And in return, as if it was a bargain they had struck, he left her alone with hers. They circled the silence that came to live between them, making room for it as it expanded over the years.

Sitting on the sand, staring out to sea, Uma tried to work out whether he had been unhappy. Or lonely. She wanted to tell herself that he hadn't. That she hadn't. That they had been okay. Not perfect, but okay. The memories roiled, the good and the less good, the easy and the less than easy.

She plunged her hands even deeper into the sand.

I didn't love him enough. I didn't love him in the right way. I should never have married him. The lightening-strikes of thought were a shock, but hardly a surprise at all. It was like uncovering a memory she had buried long ago, something she had forgotten knowing. She lay back in the sand, digging for the truth, ferreting through the various versions of their story.

By the time she sat up again the sun was high in the sky. Her body was aching from lying still in one position for so long, and her head was heavy with everything she knew, and all the things she didn't. She had been trying all these weeks to filter her thoughts, dismissing those that didn't fit with how she wanted to feel. She wanted to be angry and indignant, hungry for their opacity. What she didn't want, was to think that what he'd done was understandable. She didn't want to think about loneliness. She didn't want to feel sad.

But the thoughts kept returning. There was no way around it. She could tell herself all the things she wanted to hear, fooling herself for short moments. Or she could hold what she thought was the truth, like a hot coal in her hand, barely able to stand it. *He must have been lonely. I was lonely. Both of us were lonely.*

The beach was deserted, the couple with the dog long gone. Uma looked to the calm sea, the tide retreating. She stood, took her jumper off and unbuttoned her jeans, pulling them down, stepping out of them. She peeled her top from her body and unhooked her bra. She ran towards the water, feet slapping the wet sand as she got close, obscenities bleeding from her as she met with the first low waves. As soon as it was deep enough she dived, eyes squeezed shut. She surfaced seconds later, gasping from the cold. Forcing herself, she swam away from the shore, refusing to think, one stroke after another, arms slicing the water, her face beneath the surface, twisting for mouthfuls of air. Swimming and swimming. Determined to feel invincible, for a moment at least.

**

Anna stood on the veranda to smoke and Uma stood with her, the two of them watching the rain crashing onto the ground and bouncing off the greenhouse roof.

'I love a storm,' said Anna.

It had been threatening since yesterday, the humidity building, the air thick with static. It was such a relief now it was here. Uma put an arm out, the rain collecting on her palm within seconds, running through her fingers.

'I was going to clean the greenhouse,' said Uma. 'Perhaps the rain will do the job for me.'

'I thought you were here for a rest.'

'I've time on my hands. And plants that need a home.'

She had grown tomatoes from seed on the kitchen windowsill. Yesterday morning she had pricked them out, lifting the baby plants into bigger pots, tucking them up in damp, crumbly compost.

'Sounds like Mum wants you back.'

Uma shrugged, looking off towards the woods.

'She's worried there are things I need to sort out. And there are.'

'Things?'

'I dropped out of my life overnight.'

'Don't you want to go back?' Anna asked.

Uma shook her head.

'Then don't go.'

'It's not as easy as that.'

'And it's not as hard as you're making out either.'

They stood in silence for a few moments, watching the rain, Anna finishing her cigarette. The white cat was sitting in the corner, next to its favourite chair, taking refuge. Like Uma and Anna, it stared out at the rain.

'Why don't you want to?' asked Anna.

'I'll get sucked back in.'

'To...?'

'Everything.'

It all seemed so connected. Daniel. Millers. The busyness. Wasted opportunities. Neglected dreams. How could she begin to explain? Anna was watching her.

'It's your chance to escape,' she said, scrutinising Uma as she said it.

'Maybe.' And then, after a moment: 'I feel bad.'

'Don't.'

'What, just like that?'

Anna shrugged. 'At least tell yourself not to. Wouldn't that be a start?'

'I'm not sure where to start. I haven't straightened any of it out yet.'

'Is there anything you're sure about?'

'The business.'

'Wanting it? Or not wanting it?'

'Not wanting it.'

'Then do it. Leave.'

The rain was getting heavier.

'I'd have to sell it. A clean break.'

'So sell it.'

Uma shook her head. 'Your mum would never forgive me.'

'So what?'

Uma took a deep breath and looked towards Anna.

'You're her daughter and can piss her off as much as you like. You know deep down she'll always love you. You'll always have a place in her heart.' Uma pressed a finger onto Anna's chest bone.

'You're her golden girl! What you talking about?'

'Mary loves that I supported Daniel in taking on Millers. She loves that we were all doing it together and that me and Daniel were like her and your dad used to be. Married and working together. Without any of that I'm not so sure how she'd feel.'

'Does it matter? Don't tell me all this is about Mum's approval.'

'I have no siblings, no parents, no kids. Mary always made sure I felt like one of the family.'

'You *are* one of the family.'

A lump tightened in Uma's throat.

'I suppose I am to you,' laughed Uma, thinking about it and realising that yes, of course, to Anna she *was* family. Uma had been around for as long as Anna could remember.

Anna turned her cigarette packet over and over in her hands, looking down at it. 'She'll get over it,' she said. 'And if she doesn't, you'll have to find a way to live with it.'

She made it all sound so simple. Uma looked out at the pools of water forming on the grass.

'Maybe I can help you out by telling her I've dropped out of uni, set up a band and shacked up with a woman twice my age.'

Uma laughed.

'What *is* going on for you?' she asked.

'I've dropped out of uni, set up a band and shacked up with a woman twice my age.'

'Really?'

'Yes, really. So she's going to flip one way or the other. We should just confess together. Test your theory she'll welcome me with open arms whatever choices I make in life.'

Uma tried to imagine Mary taking in this news. She had been so proud of Anna studying maths at Warwick. *Second only to Cambridge*, she had said, repeatedly, during Anna's application process, working it into every conversation.

'I hated my course from the start,' said Anna. 'I should never have gone along with it. I know I always found maths easy. You know, *I get it*. But I get music in the same way. The patterns. The logic of it. It makes sense to me and I love it. I never loved maths.'

'Daniel loved anything to do with maths. He never needed encouragement to sit down with the books and make sense of the business with figures. All those little black squiggles in their neat little lines.'

Uma remembered how he would shut himself away in his office for several days at a time, when the year-end accounts needing doing, or when the tax returns were due. He'd emerge, buoyed, almost refreshed from the experience. As if it wasn't just arithmetic he'd been putting to rights, but himself too.

'He was such a nerd,' said Anna, looking away. She waited a moment before saying 'but it all worked for him. Sure, he made Mum and Dad happy taking Millers on, but the whole thing made him happy too. It's the same for Ruth. All she ever wanted was to be a doctor. We've both heard those stories, right? How she used to play doctors and nurses and insisted on being the doctor, making Daniel be the nurse. It was easy for them, everyone cheering them on all the time.'

They watched the rain.

'So were you unhappy?' said Anna, after a while. 'Before he even died I mean.'

Uma paused, wondering what an honest answer might sound like.

'Maybe without realising. We were so busy we hardly noticed what we were feeling.'

Kept busy precisely so we wouldn't notice.

'Our lives were paperwork and planning. When I think about what I actually spent my life doing, it was so far away from where we started. It was a million miles away from what I'd loved in the beginning.'

Uma thought about the scraps of paper she'd uncovered in Daniel's desk, the scribbled plans, the child-like drawings of Uma on a plane to India. She thought about Daniel's reticence to help make that part of their plan happen, the subtle digging in of his heels. And she also thought about the fact that he'd kept those silly pictures all these years. As if, despite what it seemed like, they had mattered to him too.

'One thing leads to another,' said Anna.

'Exactly that.'

Small decisions that all add up. Little compromises here and there and all of a sudden you're somewhere you never intended to be. There had been no great leap to where they ended up. Just lots of little stepping stones.

'It looked great from the outside,' said Anna.

'It *was* great. As a business. I just mean, that it wasn't really what I'd hoped it would be in the beginning. I had all these dreams of travelling and writing a cookbook, maybe opening a café or restaurant.'

'So why didn't you?'

'Like you said, one thing leads to another. It just didn't happen.'

'Daniel never seemed keen to travel.'

'He didn't have to. It was my thing. I should have done it.'

'Didn't he want you to?'

What had he wanted?

'He was afraid of flying,' said Uma, almost to herself.

'Yes, but that wouldn't stop you, not if you really wanted to travel.'

'No, I suppose not.'

'He was a home bird,' said Anna. 'One of those contented types.'

'He was having an affair.'

She'd said the words almost before realising.

'Fuck,' said Anna. '*Fuck*.'

'I found out just before he died, but we never got the chance to talk about it.'

It wasn't the beginning of the story at all. She had just offered Anna the punchline. She had turned straight to the back of the book and read her the last few lines. And Uma had never understood it when people did that.

'I can't believe he did that to you.'

'It's complicated.'

'Who was she?'

'I think she lives in Devon. I've got her mobile number. She has lots of curly red hair.'

'How do you know?'

Uma described picking up the message from Mystery Caller, realising what it was, what it meant. She told Anna about the person who kept vigil, the unanswered text messages and Mary's description of a strange woman waiting at the house last week. Anna listened, face pinched, lighting another cigarette, blowing the smoke into the damp air, shaking her head again and again. The water was pouring off the veranda roof, splattering onto the ground.

'Really I'm just piecing it together,' said Uma. 'But I'm sure it's her.'

'How long was it going on?'

'About a year.'

'Unbelievable.'

'It was my fault too. We let things slip. I let things slip.'

It was a surprise to say the words aloud and to realise that they didn't, after all, feel so terrible. They were heavy with sadness, and light with relief; neither one thing more than the other.

'All that deceit though. Then trotting off to church every Sunday.'

Uma shrugged. 'We all find ways to justify the things we do,' she said.

Anna looked at her. '*Fuck*, though.'

'I don't want you to think badly of him. It's way more complicated than you know.'

'But what about you? Aren't you thinking badly of him?' asked Anna.

Uma reached her hand out into the rain again, letting the water pour through her fingers.

'I don't know what I'm feeling. I just wish we could have talked about it.'

'Of course.'

'It sounds weird to say it, but when they told me he'd died I was just so angry. It was like he'd got himself killed on purpose so he didn't have to explain himself.'

'Oh Moo. What did he say when you talked on the phone? I bet he was sorry. Did he say he was sorry?'

Uma didn't know whether he had or not. She could hardly recall their brief, last conversation.

'He told me he loved me.'

His last words had become moths in her mind, hiding in the dark corners, then taking flight, fluttering fitfully through the mess of her thoughts.

'He spent a lot of years really loving me,' Uma said, determined to be fair for Anna's benefit. It was the truth after all. Daniel spent more than half his life loving Uma as if she was the only woman on the planet worth loving. Her throat closed around the sadness of it, tears spilling suddenly, easily, from her eyes. Anna reached for her, but Uma turned away, towards the deluge, covering her face with her hands. She sobbed, shoulders heaving.

They were the first tears since his death and she hardly knew what to do with them.

'Oh *Daniel*.'

She repeated his name, those familiar, painful syllables again and again.

After a while Uma looked towards Anna and saw that she too was crying, her face smeared with tears, blotchy with emotion. They smiled small smiles simultaneously, then broader ones, then laughter. They reached for one another, grabbing each other's hands as they laughed. Uma pulled Anna, shrieking, out into the force of the rain. They gasped at the strength of the downpour, eyes wide in disbelief. They span, arms out-stretched, soaked to the bone in seconds. A flash of light in the distance silenced them. They waited, crying out when the deep rumble of thunder came.

After towelling themselves dry and pulling on clean clothes, Anna lit a fire while Uma made them eggy bread. They ate in front of the warm flames, shovelling the food into their mouths, Uma ravenous for the first time in months. They played backgammon, game after game, talking a little here and there about Daniel. They meandered over the years, recalling events and incidents, moments that Anna had cherished, and other moments that she was too young to remember – Uma filling her in, and Anna doing the same, recalling times when Uma hadn't been around, moments that had been just her and Daniel. Insignificant moments that were suddenly precious. And Uma ate them up like a delicious meal.

Perhaps it was the swimming in the cold Irish Sea, or the crying in the rain, or confiding in Anna, but for the first time since Daniel's death, Uma fell asleep before midnight and didn't wake until well after dawn. She could hardly believe it when her eyes fluttered open and she realised she had slept all night and sunshine was streaming in through the gap in the curtains.

Chapter Nine

2015

He'd said she would see his house as soon as she passed the derelict farm buildings. *You'll see my place on the left, just the top of the roof through the trees.* Uma slowed, looking out for the hidden driveway he'd described.

The bony white cat was mewing in a cardboard box on the passenger seat. Her name was Lily and she'd been missing for nine months.

Uma turned into the driveway, the overgrown privet hedge closing in on both sides, the dry leaves rasping against the sides of the car. She came to a stop in front of the 1930's brick-built house. A Harley Davidson was leaning in the open mouth of the garage – the reason he gave for asking Uma to drive over with Lily. *Not sure she'd appreciate a ride on the back of the bike.*

Uma tried the bell several times, waiting for a moment or two before rapping her knuckles on the wooden door. Lily cried and Uma jiggled the cardboard box in her arms, clicking her tongue to quieten her. Eventually, calling out, Uma made her way round the back of the house to the garden. It was large, open, slightly overgrown, but with signs of attention. The grass had been recently mown. Wind chimes chimed in a nearby tree. Daffodils had been bunched and tied together and were dying in their tethers. Tulips were in bloom, trees in blossom.

'Hello?' Uma called again, heading for the back door, preparing to knock.

'Down here!'

A man leaned out of a window in the large wooden building at the bottom of the garden. His name was Richard. Seconds later double-doors swung open and he stooped to come through them, approaching her across the lawn, brushing himself down with a cloth, dust flying away on the breeze. She clutched the box in front of her chest, like a shield that she might have cause to use. He reached out a hand, thought better of it and raised a palm instead.

'Hi,' he said.

'Well, here she is.'

Uma had found Lily a few days earlier, pitiful beneath the garden bench. She had taken her to the vet in town.

'I can't tell you how grateful I am,' he said.

'The wonder of microchips.'

He reached for the box and Uma let him take it, watching him hold it up and peer in through one of the holes, smiling at whatever it was he saw. His olive skin was dull with dust, his dark hair speckled with wood shavings.

'I'll let her out in the workshop,' he said. 'She used to like it in there.'

He turned and walked a few strides then stopped, looking back. 'You coming?'

Uma hesitated. 'Okay.'

She followed him inside, and Richard reached behind her to close the doors, balancing the box in his other hand. The smell of wood was warm, almost spicy, and she glanced around the light, spacious, workshop. Several guitars at different stages of construction leaned against the wall closest to her.

'She used to sit there while I was working.'

He gestured to a chair with a blanket on it, placing the box onto a work bench.

'So what happened?' Uma asked.

Richard lifted the flaps of cardboard and Lily peered up

at them both, mewing still but showing no sign of wanting to come out now the box was finally open.

'Did she just disappear one day?'

'Out of the blue,' he said, lifting Lily out of the box and putting her down on the work bench. 'It was a mystery, and after a few months I started to think she wasn't coming back. I suppose I thought she was dead.'

Uma looked down at Lily and stroked her.

'I'll miss seeing her out in the garden,' said Uma.

Immediately Lily nuzzled her hand, encouraging Uma to stroke her.

'Well, you seem to have bonded.'

'She's not been too friendly,' said Uma. 'This is the first time I've stroked her properly.'

'She always liked her own space.'

Richard turned and walked across the workshop to a little kitchen area. He raised a kettle in Uma's direction, a questioning look on his face, and she nodded.

She looked around the workshop again. Two dimensional guitar-shaped cut-outs hung from the ceiling. A guitar with no fret board or strings lay on the work bench in front of them.

'Do you do this for a living?' Uma asked, motioning to the instruments in progress.

'If you can call it a living.'

She ran her hand across the guitar that lay close by. It was black, shiny as water.

'What kind of wood are they?'

'Different kinds. The wood changes the tone of the finished instrument. This is Ash.'

Richard held up a wooden board and tapped it, holding Uma's gaze. 'Hear that?' he asked. He picked up another. 'Now this is Walnut,' he said, asking with his expression whether Uma could hear the difference. She imagined plucking the wood shavings from his hair. He turned, walking back to his tea-making things.

'So, the vet mentioned you're staying in a holiday cottage nearby,' he said, throwing the words over his shoulder.

'It belongs to a friend's family, it's not really a holiday cottage.'

'And you found Lily nearby?'

'She was hanging around outside the cottage. There's this little veranda and I think she quite liked it, kept her out of the wind and rain I suppose.'

'I hate to think of her living rough,' said Richard, coming towards Uma with two mugs of tea. 'Do you have sugar?'

Uma shook her head, lifting Lily and bending to put her on the ground, brushing cat hair from her jumper, taking the tea from Richard, conscious of their fingers touching.

'I can't thank you enough for getting her to the vets. I imagine I might never have seen her again if you hadn't.'

'It was no bother.'

'So how long have you been here?'

'A couple of months. Longer than I ought to have been!'

'Fallen in love with the place?'

'Something like that.'

Lily was snaking round their legs, rubbing herself against both of them, and Richard leaned down to her, murmuring, massaging the malleable scruff of her neck.

'It must be so satisfying,' she said, running her hand across the instrument closest to her. 'To make something so beautiful.'

He straightened, nodding, looking her full in the face.

'Let me cook you dinner,' he said. 'As a thank you.'

'You don't have to do that.'

'I'd like to. I'm a good cook you know.'

Uma smiled at his confidence – not brash, but candid.

'What food do you like?' he asked.

'All sorts,' she said, laughing as he rubbed his hands together.

As they were saying goodbye, Richard tried to give Uma a cheque for the vet's bill, but she refused.

'Take it,' he said, trying to force it into Uma's hand. 'Not everyone would have been so kind.'

'It's really fine.'

'I'd feel better if you took it.'

His green eyes searched for hers, still trying to find a way to sneak the cheque into her possession, but Uma resisted him.

'I did one trip to the vets. You're cooking me dinner. We'll be quits.'

She spoke with such certitude that he acquiesced, watching as she got into her car, raising his hand as she drove away.

Chapter Ten

1998

Uma woke on Christmas morning and looked out of the window before doing anything else. It was white with frost and she felt a rush of pleasure. No snow, but the next best thing. She went downstairs and lit the fire, only then going outside to give the hens some corn and feel in the nest boxes for eggs. She found two – a treat, for this time of year – and decided to scramble them.

The couple from the farm up the road had brought her a side of smoked salmon down yesterday. *A little something for Christmas* they had said, *from a friend's smokery in Scotland.* Overwhelmed by their kindness it had brought tears to Uma's eyes, but they had waved her gratitude away, insisting it was nothing. She took it out of the fridge and lifted the thick uncut slab to her nose, salivating at the smoky aroma. She sharpened a knife on the back doorstep so the slices she cut would be wafer thin. She put a pan on to boil, spooning in tea leaves and spices.

Pippa, Daniel and Aaron arrived late morning. They rustled in with bags and presents, like a wave of festive spirit.

'I love this place,' said Aaron, taking a bottle of fizzy wine into his hands, ripping away the foil. 'I'm so glad you've kept it.'

'Paying the mortgage myself!' said Uma.

'I can't imagine it,' said Pippa. 'Like, *really*, I can't imagine it.'

'I bring gifts,' said Daniel, unwrapping envelopes of greaseproof paper, looking round the kitchen. 'What shall I put them on?'

He rested his hand on Uma's back as he spoke. She found wooden boards and they arranged the meats and cheeses. They put the olives and sweet, stuffed red peppers and grilled artichokes into little bowls.

'I'm relieved it's you two in charge of feeding us,' said Pippa, peering over the offerings that were being arranged around the table. 'And that Aaron's in charge of intoxicating substances.'

'But what are *you* in charge of?' said Daniel, taking the glass that Aaron passed to him.

'I'm in charge of entertainment needs. And documenting them.' She lifted the camera and snapped a picture blindly.

'Then we're sorted!' said Uma, taking her glass, lifting it in a silent toast.

The kitchen was fuggy with steam and Uma went to the window, opening it a little.

'I couldn't bear Christmas without a proper pudding,' she said.

They had decided against cooking. Uma had not been sure her rickety old oven was up to the task of roasting a turkey. The flame, if she could get it lit in the first place, extinguished itself randomly and frequently.

'Tasty,' said Pippa, helping herself to a chunk of cheese and an oat cake, slathering it with a spiced rhubarb and chilli chutney.

'You can thank our product manager here for that,' said Daniel.

'You must be living in each other's pockets,' said Aaron, refilling his glass, having thrown the first down his throat with a couple of swallows.

'We kind of are…' said Uma, looking at Daniel. 'Although we work in different shops, so we're not with each other every day.'

'We speak at least ten times a day,' said Daniel.

'And have a planning day on Sundays.'

'Over Sunday lunch at mine,' said Daniel. 'Which isn't always the best work environment.'

'Think excitable two-year-old, incorrigible mother, a murder of aunts, a gaggle of lanky cousins,' Uma said.

'Is it awful?' asked Daniel.

'It's lovely,' said Uma.

She smiled at the thought of the hustle and bustle of Daniel's house – Anna negotiating time on Uma's lap, sucking her thumb and drawing pictures on their paperwork, the ubiquitous aunts always *not stopping for long*, smoking at the back door, their laughter reverberating through the house, their children hurtling up and down the stairs *like a herd of elephants*. Uma could tell that Daniel tired of the constant intrusions and Mary's flow of input, but he was ever patient.

'I miss your mum's Sunday roasts,' said Aaron.

'God, me too,' said Pippa.

'We were invited today.'

Mary had mentioned it to Uma a few weeks ago, grasping her upper arm.

We both know what it's like, she had said, her face close to Uma's. *And you are welcome here. Anytime. It would be lovely if you were here on Christmas Day. And I know Daniel would love you to be.* As soon as Uma mentioned that they were thinking of spending it with Pippa and Aaron then Mary widened her invitation. *Why don't you all come over? The turkey's big enough.*

'I feel a little guilty,' said Uma.

Daniel shook his head.

'She's got a houseful. It'll be mayhem.'

It was Mary's first Christmas without Clive. Uma knew what these milestones were like, fences to scale, one at a time.

'This cheese is amazing,' said Pippa, piling more onto another oat cake.

'It's the one I tried in Harrogate that time,' Uma said to

Daniel, slicing a corner and holding it up for him to try. 'It's great with honey.'

'So is that really your job? All those food fayres? Travelling round the country just eating stuff,' said Pippa.

'Basically,' said Uma, laughing.

'The shops are bursting at the seams so she might have to reign it in.'

'What do you do when you're not searching for gorgeous grub?' said Pippa.

'I manage one of the shops. Daniel manages the other one.'

'And most importantly she keeps crazy Eva under control,' said Daniel.

'She's amazing. She bakes, but like you've never seen. We've even had a kitchen put in for her.'

Eva's cakes were garnering a reputation throughout the whole of Derbyshire – chocolate offerings layered high with cream, ganache, cherries, threatening to topple from their stands, coconut cakes fit for a snow queen's secret feast, over-sized meringues, cherry bakewells that filled the deli with the fragrance of warm almonds.

Eva wore dresses from the 1950's, wrapped silk scarves through her hair and painted her lips a glace-cherry red.

'She just came from nowhere,' said Daniel, putting a piece of salami into his mouth.

'Walked in to the shop one day when it was being refurbished and said she was looking for a job. She brought us this beautiful box of pastries, all wrapped up with ribbons and said that the dark green and gold paintwork we were having put on the frontage looked too much like a funeral parlour. *You should go for something more like this*, she had said, pointing at two different shades of blue on the box she'd just given us.'

Uma laughed, remembering the encounter.

'She was bold as brass but she was right. We'd been dithering over the colour scheme for weeks, hadn't we?'

Uma looked to Daniel.

'And everyone had a different opinion,' he said. 'In the end we were just trying to go for something that suggested quality. But Eva was adamant we needed something lighter, more fun. That the quality of food would speak for itself.'

Don't try too hard to convince anyone, she had said. And Uma had liked that.

'She sounds like a keeper,' said Aaron, meeting Uma's eye, looking away too quickly and creating a moment of awkwardness that Uma later wondered whether she had imagined.

'We've sucked her into our food-obsessed craziness,' said Daniel.

'I *am* obsessed. I go to sleep thinking about food,' Uma said, helping herself to a slice of smoked salmon. 'And sometimes it's all the two of us talk about – so just tell us to shut up okay?'

'It's a different world,' said Pippa, unlacing her Doc Martin boots and easing them off. She reached for Aaron's bum bag off the table and took it through into the other room. Uma watched her sit cross legged in front of the fire and extract the smoking paraphernalia, preparing to roll a joint, bangles jangling her wrists.

Uma felt a pang of something, a fear of missing out, perhaps. She had almost forgotten her university life. It had been brief and seemed so long ago.

'I'm pleased for you guys,' said Aaron, leaning back in one of the kitchen chairs, offering up the bottle to Daniel and Uma before filling his own glass.

Are you? Uma wondered. Did she want him to be pleased? What would it mean if he was delighted everything was going well, that Daniel and Uma's lives had become so entwined? She turned away to the stove, checking the level of the water in the pudding pan, topping it up from the kettle. She sighed inwardly. There had been times over the last few months where Uma had forgotten all this – the push-pull, the longing. The business had given her a sense of purpose. She had imagined how proud her parents would have been. She was keeping the house. She had a proper job and plans for the future.

'Do you need a hand with anything?' Daniel asked, coming up behind her.

Uma shook her head, twisting to look at him briefly. 'There's nothing to do. Let's go play something.'

'I'll find the games.'

He went through to the other room and Aaron filled Uma's glass.

'Drink with me,' he said, and Uma slipped into a chair beside him, meeting his gaze. The world swam a little and Uma leant back in her chair, lifting her glass to her lips.

'I'll be asleep by the afternoon at this rate.'

'You're a lightweight.'

'A cheap date.'

Aaron smiled, but didn't take his eyes from the table top.

'How are you doing?' he asked quietly.

'I'm good. It's *good*.'

Uma was conscious of trying too hard to convince him, which was odd because things really did feel good. At least, they *had*. Yesterday. Last week. Last month. Now Aaron was here Uma felt that tug of sadness again, that old, familiar, sense of longing. Of missing something, even though it's there. Feeling homesick, even at home.

'If your mum and dad were here, what would you be doing?'

Uma smiled, looking away, remembering, memories popping open like the doors on an advent calendar.

'Mum would still be at church. The turkey would have been in the oven since dawn, the smallest one they could find. I'd be playing cribbage with my dad.'

'Was it always just the three of you?'

'It was *always* just the three of us…' Uma trailed off. 'And then there was one,' she added, saying what she imagined he was thinking, laughing hard, making light of it.

'What about your Indian family?'

136

Uma took a deep breath. It was a mountain she was yet to scale.

'Well they're out there somewhere. Mum cut herself off. I think she felt she had to. Marrying a white Englishman was a scandal. She ran away with him and didn't dare look back.'

'Do you know much about them?'

'Little snippets. I know they live in Kerala.'

'I'd go with you if you wanted to visit.'

Uma looked at him, resting her gaze on his face, watching him drink his wine. She tried to imagine the two of them setting off in search of her only remaining family. Her father had been an only child, with a few distant cousins he'd all but lost touch with by the time he became ill. His parents had died when Uma was young. She had a vague memory of being at a fairground with them, her teeth sticking together from too much candyfloss. There were photos of them on the wall of the room that had been her father's study. It was the only way she could imagine them, black and white on their wedding day and later, with her father as a boy stood beside them, serious and fully-clothed at the seaside. Now all of them were gone and Uma was cast adrift, although before her parents had even died there had been a similar sense. Other people's families were like ripples on the surface of the water – ever increasing.

'I'll go one day.'

'I'll go with you,' he promised, even though she wasn't asking for that.

'Thank you for what you did for me this year,' she said, speaking softly so Daniel and Pippa wouldn't hear from the other room.

'That's what families do,' he said. 'They look after each other.'

She reached out for his hand, just briefly, covering it with her own, wondering why it felt awkward, and where their ease with one another had disappeared to. After her stint in hospital he had touched her so easily. She had leaned into

137

him when she felt tired, curling on the sofa and resting her head on his lap, enjoying the feel of his hand as he stroked her hair. She had even slipped into bed with him one time, when she woke in the middle of the night and couldn't get back to sleep. She had wrapped her dressing gown over the top of her pyjamas, and crept into his room, lifting the covers in the dark, disturbing him. He had encircled her with his arms as if it was the most natural thing for the two of them to entwine themselves and sleep.

She thought about slipping into bed beside Aaron tonight, when Christmas day had disappeared into the early hours, all of them full and lethargic from eating and drinking all day. She thought about his body next to hers, naked this time, imagining him hardening against her, the soft escape of his mouth. Uma slipped her hand from his, pushing the thought away, looking up into his face.

'And things are okay with Daniel?'

'Things are… great.'

'And it's okay? Working together?'

'Why wouldn't it be?' She lowered her voice, glancing through to the other room, to Pippa and Daniel getting out the scrabble board, the unlit joint dangling between Pippa's lips.

Aaron shrugged, draining his glass.

'I just thought… after what happened.'

'It's water under the bridge,' she said.

He looked at her, his eyes searching her face for something, and Uma wondered whether he would find what he was looking for.

'So you're not trying to make it up to him?'

'What the fuck, Aaron?'

'I'm just saying…'

Uma glanced into the other room again, leaning forward so she was close to him.

'I don't owe him anything.'

Aaron leaned forward too.

'I know that,' he said, his voice quiet.

'So… what then?'

Anger was flaring inside her, like paper being lit.

'Come on you two!' Pippa shouted from the other room and Uma turned to see her leaning out the window, smoking.

Uma snatched up her drink and took it into the other room. She knelt on the floor at the little table, the warmth of the fire on her back, and began setting up her pieces for scrabble.

'We're playing the rude version,' said Pippa, passing the joint to Aaron when he joined her at the window. He was glowering but Pippa didn't seem to notice. *How dare he?* Uma felt the irritation bubbling inside of her, mentally navigating their unfinished conversation, shoring up her righteous indignation, preparing her response in case they revisited the subject.

It was later in the afternoon when that opportunity came. It was dark and Aaron put on his donkey jacket and red woollen scarf and slipped away into the garden. Uma watched him from the kitchen window for a moment or two as he slouched on the garden bench, pulling on a cigarette, staring at the ground. She wished she could read his mind. Did he know she was watching him? His legs were stretched out, one boot kicking at the other. His lips were moving as if he was talking to himself, and Uma softened, realising how defensive she'd been. She took two bowls of Christmas pudding outside with her. Cream for her, brandy butter for him. He threw his cigarette away and took the bowl from her.

'You took it the wrong way,' he said.

'I know.'

'*I* don't think you need to make it up to Daniel. I was just checking that *you* weren't feeling that. I know you and your catholic guilt.'

Uma thought of her mother. She would have done anything to prevent Uma entering that hospital and ending her pregnancy. Uma didn't like to think about it in too much detail. She had tried to reason with herself that her mother was dead. *She will never know*. But even so she still tried to keep the memory of her mother and the fact of the termination separate in her mind, as if thinking about the two simultaneously might cause the information to leak through the fabric of time, changing the order of events, bringing her mother back to life in possession of all the facts. It was horrifying. And the thought of Daniel finding out was nearly as bad. She didn't know why. If she really believed what she said to Aaron – that she didn't owe Daniel anything – then why did she fear him finding out. *It's my body. My choice.*

'Perhaps you're right about Catholic guilt,' she said.

'It's a bastard.'

'Not that you'd know anything about it.'

Aaron's parents were atheists.

'Actually there's nothing wrong with a bit of guilt now and then,' said Aaron. 'It's shame that's the killer. It should be called Catholic shame.'

'Not sure I know the difference.'

'Guilt is to do with something we've done, it can be helpful. Shame is to do with who *we are*. Shame is what makes you want to crawl into a hole and hide.'

Uma looked at him, taking in what he was saying.

'Maybe I feel both.'

'And maybe you shouldn't.'

'I can't help how I feel.'

'You should tell him.'

'What good would it do?'

'It would stop it being a secret, take the power out of it.

'I just wish it had never, *ever* happened.'

'And you'll feel terrible forever if you keep it from him.'

'It'd ruin everything. He'd hate me. His family would hate me.'

'You're thinking the worst. I think he'd understand. It's not as if he's ready to be a dad.'

'He's a practising Catholic, Aaron. He will *not* understand.'

'Okay. So he's angry, thinks badly of you for a while. Is that such a terrible thing?'

'I don't want to talk about it. I'm so fed up with moping around about stuff every time I'm with you.'

'I think you can justify a bit of moping.'

'It makes me boring.'

Aaron laughed.

'So, do some mushrooms with me. I'm going to boil them up into some tea.'

Uma shook her head. 'I don't want any.'

'It'll be fun.'

Uma thought about her anxiety attacks, how difficult it had been to get them under control. There was no way she could drink his mushroom tea.

'Oh *Aaron*. Please don't do them today.'

She put her hand onto his arm, looking into his eyes. He gave her a quizzical look, laughing.

'Just a few Christmas mushrooms?' he said, like a small child pleading for a chocolate biscuit.

Uma noticed Daniel looking out at them from the kitchen window and she pulled her hand from Aaron's arm.

'*Why*?' challenged Aaron, looking towards the kitchen window, watching Daniel disappear back into the house. 'Why did you do that?'

'I –'

'So don't tell him about the termination, but at least put him out of his misery.'

'I don't know what you mean.'

'Of course you fucking do. The guy's in love with you and you're…'

Aaron gesticulated, searching for the right words, then gave up and took a mouthful of Christmas pudding instead.

'I'm what?'

'You're… not being honest with him.'

'What does honest look like exactly?'

'Just tell him you're not interested.'

'When he's asked nothing of me,' said Uma, defending Daniel. '*Nothing*.'

'That means shit.'

'It would be arrogant to presume he has feelings for me.'

Aaron laughed, shovelling more pudding into his mouth, shaking his head. '*Tell* him, Uma.'

'Can you hear yourself?'

'It's not fair.'

'On who?'

'On Daniel. He's just hanging on in there. Waiting. It's fucking tragic.'

'Oh my God. And then what? I take Daniel aside and tell him, *oh by the way, you do realise that I'm not interested in you.* And then our work life becomes impossible and I have to go find another job and Daniel's left completely in the lurch and… then what?'

'And then we all get to move on.'

Aaron stood up, grabbing Uma's empty bowl, taking it away to the kitchen with him.

Cold, shivering, Uma eventually followed Aaron back into the house and found him boiling up his magic mushrooms in the little saucepan she used for her masala chai. The fragrant aroma was mixing with the pungent, earthy mushroom smell and she felt a flash of irritation. The saucepan had been the one her mother used every day for making her chai. She would never have permitted its use for anything else. Uma felt like snatching it away from his attentive hands and throwing the whole lot in the sink.

She joined Pippa and Daniel watching television in the other room, picking up the tin of chocolates on the way, positioning it on her lap, unwrapping the first of many and throwing it into her mouth.

'Who wants mushroom tea?' called Aaron from the kitchen. Only Pippa replied, getting up from the sofa, joining Aaron in the kitchen, leaning against him, peering down at the concoction they were about to consume.

Uma stared at the television screen, aware of the two of them in her peripheral vision, pouring out their little cups of revolting, hallucinogenic tea, laughing at something Pippa said, drinking it down at the same time as one another, clinking their empty cups afterwards.

Chapter Eleven

2015

The clouds were bulbous, and bearing down in shades of grey, like great plumes of darkening smoke. *The Gods are gathering* her mother used to say.

Uma filled the kitchen with the aromas of a Keralan feast. Curry leaves, coconut milk, mustard seeds and fenugreek. The bright curry, yellow from turmeric, was ready, resting on the stove, flecked chilli red and coriander green. Uma peppered her cooking with taking photographs, excited by the colours, already composing the words to accompany the pictures for her blog. It would have to wait until she was somewhere less remote. In the meantime she was creating posts in her mind and scribbling thoughts and notes on scraps of paper.

She prepared a coconut chutney – pale, creamy and thin – and a sweet carrot chutney the colour of amber, sticky as jam. The batter for the dosa pancake had been fermenting all night, frothing over the bowl, begging to be whipped back and poured onto a fire-hot pan. Her mouth watered in anticipation.

It had been years since she had cooked in this way, everything from scratch, sacrificing hours and days, enjoying the alchemy of recipes she had learned long ago by heart – food prepared by mothers and sisters and aunts over years and continents. The best nourishment.

She was taking her time, finishing the potato masala that

would fill the dosa, adding the cooked potato to the browning onion, silky and sweet. Her fingers smelt of ginger and garlic. They tasted of chilli when she put them to her mouth, leaving a familiar heat on her tongue.

Richard was coming to eat. It had become a thing, sharing meals. He had cooked for Uma that first time – chateaubriand steak with entrecote sauce. He'd left it rare, slicing the pieces onto Uma's plate where they oozed their juices into the creamiest mashed potato she'd ever eaten. They picked strawberries from the garden afterwards, eating them where they stood, the berries still warm from the setting sun.

She had risen to the challenge, feeding him a mutton curry that had simmered for five hours on her cooker top, filling the cottage with its piquant aroma. His response, a few days later, had been a Middle Eastern feast. Cinnamon, cardamom, cloves and pepper. Rich and warm. They had eaten stuffed aubergines and poached apricots with clotted cream and walnuts. Uma had reached out for his hand across the table and he had offered it, palm upturned, eyes meeting hers.

They kissed on the doorstep, his hand in the curve of her lower back and Uma drove home, heart full, remembering what it felt like to smile. She felt a stab of guilt at the thought of Mary knowing how she had spent the last few hours. But it had been so long since her heart had been full of anything as easy as this that she knew it couldn't be a shameful thing.

A text message arrived as she was driving and as soon as she stopped the car on the gravel outside the cottage she pulled the phone out of her pocket, eager to see what he had to say for himself, sure it was him.

Mystery Caller. Her heart hammered as she opened the message.

I don't understand what you expect from me.

After several minutes staring into the distance she answered.

One conversation. Face to face.

Uma got out the car and went into the cottage, heading straight for the kitchen where her mobile signal was strongest.

145

She waited, sitting at the table, the phone in front of her. More than twenty minutes later her phone blinked into life.

I'm sorry, but no.

But you came to my house.

Only because I knew you weren't there.

Uma pushed the phone across the table top, looking away from it. How dare she? Uma waited several minutes before reaching for the phone again. She took her time, thinking of all the things she wanted to say, composing sentences in her mind, punching them into the phone, deleting them, trying again. Eventually, she settled on the simplest version of everything she wanted to say.

Just one conversation. You owe me that, surely?

It seemed as if the message had hardly sent before the reply arrived.

I owe you nothing Uma. ABSOLUTELY nothing.

Uma stared down at the message for several long minutes, deciding what to do. She went into the other room and reached for her address book, then the telephone, cradling both of them in her lap as she curled her legs beneath her on the floor. She imagined the conversation that lay ahead, trying out the different ways the words might sound, how to tell the story without drama. It was a risk because Eva liked a little drama, but Eva was the only person who could help with this.

'*Uma,*' Eva said, in that way that people now said her name, weighed down with pity. 'How are things in the sticks?'

'Surprisingly restful.'

'Good. Just you take your time, okay? Everything else can wait, don't be told otherwise.'

Tears prickled Uma's eyes and she clenched her jaw, swallowing the emotion. She asked about Jessica, Eva's wife, and their twin daughters. She asked what Eva was baking that day. The Devon deli oozed Eva's passion – still a deli, but really a Parisian patisserie in disguise. Strawberry mille-feuille, cherry clafoutis, madeleines, macarons, profiteroles, meringues, roasted peach fanciers, all on twisted-glass stands in the window. *Food porn*, Eva called it. And people came from all the counties around to eat her offerings.

'I need your help with something,' Uma said.

'Of course. Anything.'

'I'm going to tell you something, and I want you not to be shocked.'

A thought occurred to Uma as she was saying the words, something she hadn't thought of in all these months. Something that now seemed obvious. Perhaps news of Daniel's affair wouldn't be a shock to some people at all. Perhaps there were people *in the know*. Old friends that he had confided in. Or old friends that simply knew. People who looked, and saw things for how they were. Daniel and Uma had known Eva for fifteen years. She had built Millers alongside them. There was very little she didn't know about their lives. And she saw Daniel plenty, down in Devon, without Uma, away from home.

Uma's mouth was suddenly dry and she had an urge to quietly put the phone back down, to head out into the woods, to go to the sea, to forget about it all. *Do you really need to see this woman face to face? Do you really need that?*

But somehow Uma ploughed on, explaining to Eva what it was she knew and what it was she wanted. And Eva, quietly, gently, told her how genuinely surprised she was to hear of it all. Uma believed her, relieved, wondering why it mattered so much to her that other people hadn't guessed. Perhaps it helped her feel a little less foolish. Perhaps it meant that he hadn't been too cavalier.

Eva explained about a woman called Alex Foley, a woman with tight red curls and plenty of them. A graphic designer who worked for a local firm. A graphic designer that Daniel had employed sometime last year.

**

She heard the throaty roar of his bike and went out, barefoot, to meet him. His lips felt soft against hers, his hand briefly on her waist. Inside, he put his motorcycle helmet on the phone table, unstrapped a guitar from his back and peeled off his leather jacket.

'Too warm for this get-up,' he complained.

'You should get a bicycle,' said Uma, knowing that Richard wouldn't be seen dead on a bicycle. She was folding a pile of clothes she had just brought in from the washing line as he opened the soft guitar bag, pulling out the instrument. She thought of Aaron, impossible not to. He was the only person who had ever played the guitar for her and a sharp sadness rippled through her. He had called a few days earlier from a town in Bulgaria. The reception had been terrible, their words snatched away before the other could hear them properly. They had persevered for many minutes, Uma grasping every word she could, none of it amounting to much. And then, without any indication he had been saying goodbye, the line went dead.

'Bottle opener?' said Richard, holding up some red wine.

Uma pointed to a drawer and watched him rummage through it. When they touched their glasses together, eyes meeting, he gave a short, happy laugh, reaching an arm around her shoulders, pulling her against him briefly.

'It's always so good to see you,' he said.

'You too.'

It was the truth. There was something about his nonchalance that made him easy to be around. Perhaps at another time, in another place, she might have found him too sure of himself.

'When do you want to eat?' she asked.

'Are you hungry?'

'Not especially.'

If she was as blasé as he, she might have told him she was too edgy to eat. Too expectant. Too full of thoughts of his hands on her body, of his fingers twisting through her hair. *Fuck me first*, she might have said.

He reached for the guitar and sat on the sofa, the afternoon

148

sun falling through the window behind him. He launched into something impressive. It was a world away from Aaron's strumming of chords and singing of songs they both knew. Richard could really play the guitar, and although Uma knew it deserved admiration, she wasn't sure if she liked it or not. She clapped though, when he stopped, and he fetched the wine bottle and topped up their glasses, sitting at the other end of the sofa, leaning back.

'So… not packed up yet?' he asked.

'Nope.'

'I thought you were supposed to leave last week. Or was it the week before?'

She kicked him gently, digging her toes into his ribs.

'I'll be gone one day soon.'

He grabbed hold of her foot, pulling her down the sofa towards him, leaning forwards, over her, planting a kiss on her mouth. He lowered his body onto hers and Uma groaned at the weight of him, the heat she could feel from his chest, the hunger she could taste on his lips.

**

A fortnight passed and she hardly noticed. They feasted like Gods as the summer sun burned down on them. They compared bronzed limbs, his forearms thick, hers slender, but both a pecan-brown.

'You're fattening me,' she said, noticing that her stick-like arms had softened over all the edges. He lay back in the sun, pulling her down to rest in the curve of his arm. He smelt like clean skin. His limbs were lithe, muscular, his movements like water, his body firm against the softness of her.

She photographed him. Greying stubble and sun-bronzed skin. Muscular fingers. The curve of his calf. The defined contours of his *gluteus maximus*. It became their joke, Uma unsure why she enjoyed so much his naming of body parts in Latin, running his fingers across her clavicle, pressing his thumb across her latissimus dorsi, saying the name in her ear, taking his time locating her gracilis, running his tongue along it, Uma reaching for his hair, pulling handfuls of it in her fists.

And each day she grew more ravenous. Sometimes she woke in the night and went to the kitchen to eat, standing in the moonlight, folding chicken into cold chapattis and pushing them into her mouth.

When they were together, nothing else existed. There was no grief, no Daniel, no guilt. No Millers or Mary. No Alex or Aaron. There was just the smell of his skin. The tautness of him. Their mutual hunger.

But at other times, when he wasn't there, he seemed like a dream – bursting with feeling, but evanescent, forgettable. There was nothing to weigh them down, and so much they didn't talk about. He knew almost nothing about her, beyond the physical, and she couldn't imagine giving all those parts of herself to him. It made her wonder whether there would always be part of herself that she was holding back. Different parts with different people. And the thought of it filled her with sadness.

**

Uma picked up the phone and unravelled the cord that she had wound round and round after unplugging it from the wall the day before. Mary had taken to calling incessantly. Uma couldn't bear the sound of the ringing, picturing Mary as a town-crier, standing over her with a large bell.

A few days ago she had written Mary a letter telling her that she would be coming back to the house in the next couple of weeks. Also letting her know that she had decided to sell Millers and had spoken to their accountant and the board of executives. She had received a reply that morning and Mary's words were eating their way through her like fire ants. *Daniel deserves better*, she had said. *He gave you so much and you're betraying him. You owe him more than this.*

Uma plugged the phone into the wall and pulled it into her lap where she let it rest for a few moments in the folds of her skirt. She hadn't quite worked out what she wanted to say, what she wanted to reveal. She was just about to lift the old-fashioned earpiece from its cradle when it rang, its strident trilling cutting into her reserve.

'Hello?'

'At last.'

Uma took a deep breath, wrong-footed, unprepared.

'Please don't sell,' Mary began. 'Give it a year. You'll feel differently by then I promise.'

'Oh Mary.'

'You're making the most terrible mistake. It's easy to do at times like this. I've seen it time and again. Rash decisions should never be made during times of turmoil. Millers has been your whole life and you've worked so hard to make it into what it is. You know what it's like when other people take over, people who don't know a company's history, don't have the ties we all have. It's never the same. No one will care about it in the same way.'

'Perhaps someone in the family would like to take it on.'

'I've been wracking my brains and I'm just not sure there's anyone. And there's the cost of it, who could afford to buy it from you?'

'I don't care about the money. If someone in the family is interested then we can come to some arrangement. But someone has to want to take it on. I'm so sorry Mary. This hasn't been a rash decision for me. I've had so much time to think it through. That's why I've been here. To think.'

'Being alone isn't the best way to think through something complicated. You need to be able to discuss it. I always need to talk a problem through.'

'We're different. I need space and peace and quiet and time.'

'But it's not just your decision.'

'Well, who else's is it?'

Mary was silent.

'I don't want to fall out about it,' said Uma. 'But I am going to sell.'

'You just don't seem like yourself at all.'

Uma let out a loud sigh, wondering where to even start challenging that statement.

'Is there something else going on?' said Mary.

'There's nothing going on.'

'I just keep thinking… that woman turning up out of the blue…'

'That was nothing.'

'Did she contact you again?'

'Mary, listen to me. I know it seems as if this is all wrong, as if I should be keener now than ever to cling on to Millers. But it's more complicated than that. I've been needing a change for a long time. It's just all come at once. Daniel dying has forced my hand, that's all.'

'Are you depressed do you think? Is that it?'

'I'm not depressed, Mary.'

'Sometimes it's easier for others to see.'

'I'm *telling you*, I'm not depressed.'

'What would Daniel say? It would break his heart. Think about that.'

'Don't you think I have? All these suggestions, I've considered them, I promise you. This is a big decision and I've thought it through. I'm going to sell Millers. I will sell it to anyone in the family if they want it. Goodness, I might even give it away. It's not about the money. It's about new beginnings and me working out what I want to do with the rest of my life.'

'He'll be turning in his grave, Uma. How can you do this? *Turning in his grave.*'

Uma put the phone down and snatched the cord from the wall. Her hands were trembling, her throat tightening. She didn't want to fall out with Mary, but didn't know how to stop it happening. Mary was stubborn as a stain when she wanted

152

to be. Uma had seen it over the years, the way she could cut people out of her life, justifying it quite easily to herself. Uma didn't want to become one of those people. Mary was nothing like Uma's mother, but she was a mother of sorts. Who else would stake a claim to a piece of Uma like Mary had, loving and defending her and calling her out all at once.

**

Holly was running, the navy-blue skirt of her dress billowing outwards, her ringlets bouncing round her face. Smiling widely, her eyes fixed on Uma's, she opened her arms, fully expecting that Uma would do the same, just as she always did when Holly came running across the playground towards her on a Friday afternoon. Automatically, without pause for thought, Uma crouched and scooped up the soft, light weight of her. Holly's little legs wrapped around Uma's waist, her arms around her neck, her warm pudgy cheek pressed to the side of Uma's face.

'Is this your house now Auntie Uma?' said Holly, pulling back to look into Uma's face. Her dark eyes were wide, her face earnestly open in the way that only a child's can be.

'I'm just on holiday here, and I have missed you so much,' said Uma, disappearing into their cuddle. Holly held on tight behind Uma's neck, and didn't let go until Uma laughed, pointing out she couldn't fetch the cake and milk with Holly swinging from her like a monkey.

Pippa's hug was equally fierce, her large hoop earring pressing into the side of Uma's face. She smelt the same as ever – warm vanilla perfume, just-washed hair. Her face was hot, her cheeks flushed.

'I've been thinking about you constantly,' said Pippa.

Her friend's energy was a gentle wave breaking against her – the urgent sincerity in her voice, the heat from her skin, the bounce and sway of her hair, her fidgety hands that stroked and squeezed and pressed.

'*Thank you*,' said Uma. 'It's so good you're here.'

Pippa pulled Uma into a hug all over again.

They went inside to make coffee and Uma cut pistachio cake into squares as they waited for the kettle to boil. She poured Holly a cup of milk, putting things onto a tray.

'Take this outside, would you,' said Uma, handing it to Pippa.

She fetched a couple of blankets from the top of the wardrobe and followed Pippa and Holly outside, shaking the blankets out, laying them on the ground. Holly ambled away, crouching to pick a few green stems, starting a posy of weeds.

'So, tell me how you are,' said Pippa. 'And I want the truth, okay? No putting on a brave face.'

'Good days and bad.'

'Tricky times with Mary can't be helping.'

'It's a nightmare.'

'She'll get over it,' said Pippa, with the air of someone content with conflict.

Uma nodded, as if she believed it, disinclined to pick over the bones of Millers all over again.

'You've been here a long time. I imagined a week or two.'

'Is it okay?' asked Uma. 'I mean, do other people want to use the place?'

'No, hardly ever. It's a little down at heel I guess.'

Pippa looked around the garden, and then towards the cottage, as if seeing it for the first time. Looking back at Uma she scrutinised her for just a second, then lowered her face to the plate of cake.

'Smells great.'

'It's spiced. Try some.'

Pippa picked up a small square and pushed the whole piece between her lips.

'*Oh...*' she said, through an over-stuffed mouth. 'That's incredible.'

'It's made with olive oil, not butter. And no flour, just

ground almonds and crushed pistachios and desiccated coconut. You'd think it'd be heavy, but it's not.'

Uma lay on her side, stretching out, propping her head on
her hand, watching Pippa eat.

'I've made us hot and sour fish stew for later, and fish
croquettes for Holly.'

She didn't say so but she'd also made vegetable fritters,
date and orange pastries and sweet kummayam with jaggery.

'You've put on weight,' said Pippa, mirroring her friend,
lying down to face her. 'Got some flesh on those bones now.'

'Yup. Slowly fattening.'

'This whole food, blog, travel, cookbook thing sounds
great. A new project.'

'New beginnings.'

'Good for you.'

'I've been taking pictures and writing a journal. I'm
incorporating some of my mum's stories from India, some
of my thoughts about travelling there, the cooking...' Uma
trailed off, thinking about the other aspects of her journal
writing, the parts about Daniel, and their marriage, and how
it felt to wake up into her own life and not recognise it.

'You always wanted to do this.'

'It just never happened.'

'So will you go, kind of *soon*?'

'Not sure.'

Her route through India had been taking shape in her mind.
Flying to Chennai, starting in the east, exploring the temples
at Kanchipuram, the beautifully carved shrines, the caves and
sculptures. The wildlife hidden in the Cardamom hills, the
mountains and shola forests of the Western Ghats. The train
she thought she might take to Mysore, city of palaces, then
down through the tranquil backwaters of Kerala, the lush
green hills of Munnar, the rocky landscape of Hampi. She
described it to Pippa and they meandered the journey as if
they were about to travel it together.

Pippa never once cautioned her to be careful, or questioned

155

whether she really wanted to go so far on her own, or to be away for so long by herself. She bolstered Uma's reserve with tales from her own travels. The goat curry on a Kenyan beach as the sun was coming down, the Bedouin twins in Dahab, the giant crabs swarming the beaches on Ilha Grande in Brazil. Uma listened to Pippa's stories, her attention only drawn away in the end by Holly hurtling round the corner of the house, her dark ringlets bouncing, a wide grin stretched across her face.

'Can I have another cup of milk, Auntie Uma?'

'Of course you can. Do you want to get it yourself?'

Holly nodded, swivelling away from them, skipping into the darkness of the cottage.

'Who does the guitar belong to, by the way?' Pippa asked.

Uma smiled, memories of Richard rushing blood to her skin, heating her face, betraying her instantly. She looked Pippa in the eye, biting her lip, supressing the giddiness that bubbled up.

'What the *fuck*?' Pippa whispered, leaning in.

Uma laughed.

'Here?' Pippa asked, incredulous, sweeping her arm in a wide semi-circle. 'You found a man *here*?'

Uma nodded. 'It's just a fling. Sex. Just really great sex.'

Pippa gasped, not taking her eyes off Uma for a second. Holly appeared in the doorway to the cottage, clutching her cup in both hands, dipping her tongue in the milk.

'How?'

'Well… there was this cat hanging around, obviously a stray, and it looked really ill one day so I took it to the vets. Anyway, turns out it had a microchip, and an owner who is so grateful to get his missing cat back he rewards me with a month of truly amazing, no strings attached sex. True story.'

Pippa grinned, shaking her head. 'That's unbelievable.'

'And bad of me?'

'Of course not. Tell me more about him.'

'He makes guitars.'

'So, good with his hands, an eye for detail.'

Uma suppressed a grin.

'Sexy?'

Uma shrugged. '*I* think so.'

Pippa nodded, casting her gaze across Uma's face.

'This is a *good* thing,' she concluded. 'I hope you know that. *Do* you know that?'

Don't feel bad, she was saying, comforting Uma with certitude.

'Nothing's going to bring him back,' Pippa said, her tone deferential momentarily. Uma ran her palm across the blanket, back and forth, staring down at it.

'I've been seeing someone too,' said Pippa, brightening again.

'Who?'

'Todd's dad.'

'Todd?'

'The crazy little kid with the ginger hair and freckles.'

'The one who buried your phone in the garden?'

'The very same, the little shit. His dad's a police detective.'

'You always had a thing for uniforms.'

'And handcuffs.'

Pippa laughed, rolling onto her back, running her hands through her long, brown hair, fanning it out around her, a medusa halo on the rug.

'You like him?'

Pippa pulled an ambivalent face and Uma didn't need to ask any more. *I take after Mum*, she'd said to Uma once. *Short attention span when it comes to men. At least I never marry them.* Pippa's mum divorced four husbands in twelve years.

'Have you heard from Aaron?' Uma asked.

'Not since he went trekking.'

'So you don't know if anything's happened with Jo-Jo.'

'There's no way that's going anywhere.'

'You reckon?'

'They're both terrified of commitment. It'll be over before it starts.'

Uma reached for a piece of cake and nibbled crumbs from the edges, playing with it more than eating it.

'And if it isn't over next time I see him,' said Pippa. 'I'll do my damnedest to convince him what a prick he's being.'

Uma laughed. 'You really hated her.'

'Now, hate is a *very* strong word, Uma,' Pippa said in mock-mother voice. 'But, yes, she wasn't exactly my favourite person.'

Uma continued laughing, nibbling cake, watching Pippa running her hands through her hair.

'I just don't like narcissists,' said Pippa, staring up into the forget-me-not-blue sky. 'I grew up with one remember, and I won't stand by and watch him be slowly consumed.'

'I think he can look after himself.'

'Well, you say that…'

Uma thought back to the time when Aaron got married, to the feeling she'd had as she looked down at the photo of him and Jo-Jo on that tropical beach. It had been a slow, insidious feeling that she couldn't shake. Like nostalgia, but for something that hadn't even happened.

'We were all so young,' she said, quietly, putting the last little piece of cake into her mouth.

'Maybe I'll seduce him,' said Pippa, turning her head in Uma's direction.

Uma forced a laugh. 'You've been there, done that.'

'We were kids, and I was so drunk I hardly remember it.'

Pippa returned to staring at the sky and Uma flopped backwards onto the rug, turning towards Holly who was picking raspberries.

'Distraction through seduction,' said Pippa.

'Just forget about Jo-Jo.'

'D'you think Aaron would go for it?'

'You're not serious?' said Uma.

'Why not?'

'But why would you? You've never had a thing for Aaron.'

'I've always had a soft spot for him. We've been friends forever. I like the guy. He doesn't seem to be able to find anyone for himself. *I* don't seem to be able to find anyone. Could be a match made in heaven.'

Uma's mind was scrabbling for something to put an end to Pippa's game playing.

'It's a bad idea.'

'Oh, I don't know.'

'It's not worth it.'

Uma thought about the clumsy way she had offered herself to Aaron on the evening of Daniel's wake. She didn't have to work hard to reignite those feelings of regret and mortification. It had seemed like such a good idea in that moment. More than that, it had seemed right, natural, good. But afterwards her whole being had churned with fear. Wasn't loss a just reward for greed? Hadn't fairy tales warned her of that? There would always be paths not taken, she had reprimanded herself repeatedly since that night – people not loved, opportunities unpursued. Surely that's just part of life? Surely everyone has a list of unlived possibilities. Did she really think she was different to everybody else? *You can't have everything*.

Pippa was laughing to herself, drawing her knees up and wrapping her arms around them.

'But it would make me happy.'

Uma didn't want to look at her. She knew what she'd see – Pippa's bright green eyes sparkling with excitement.

'Don't be daft, Pip.'

'I'm serious.'

'You're not.'

'I am.'

'Really,' said Uma, turning to look at her. 'Stop it.'
Pippa frowned.

'I couldn't bear it,' said Uma quietly, turning away.

There was a pause before Pippa spoke.

'I don't get it,' she said.

'No, you don't.'

Uma watched the clouds skittering across the sun.

'So tell me.'

It seemed strange that Pippa really didn't know. It had always seemed futile to hide her feelings from Pippa. But maybe when it came to her feelings for Aaron she'd been burying them for so long, watering them down whenever she could, that she really had fooled everyone, herself and Pippa included.

'*Uma*?'

'I was always slightly in love with him.'

It was astonishing to say the words, to hear them as actual sounds. She could almost see them drifting away on the warm air, lifting up and up to join the wispy clouds. *I was always slightly in love with him*. She felt relief settling through her body, as if everything might be okay if she could just continue to say things that were true. Like telling Mary about Millers. Like telling Anna about Daniel's affair. Perhaps this is how people did it, create the life they want by telling the truth to themselves and everybody else. It seemed suddenly so simple. She smiled, twisting her head to look sideways at Pippa; her friend's face had narrowed into something incredulous.

'You did this before.'

'Did what?' Uma asked, breathless and afraid.

'He doesn't *belong* to you.'

'I'm not saying–'

'You're fucking some guy from round the corner, Daniel's just died and I can't make a move on Aaron because you want *him* too?!'

Pippa made a show of laughing, sitting up, turning away to look around the garden for Holly.

Uma's mouth was dry with fear.

'I know it sounds a little…'

'It *does*, you're right.' Pippa was nodding her head. 'It does sound *a little*…'

'I can't help how I feel.'

'You can help what you do, what you say.'

'Pippa! You said you wanted me to tell you the truth. You're always telling me that I should talk to you more. You used to sing that Beautiful South song to me all the while remember? *You know your problem, you keep it all in…*'

Uma sang the words, imploring, thinking that Pippa would soften, but Pippa kept her gaze on the far end of the garden, almost imperceptibly shaking her head.

'What does that even mean? *Slightly* in love? Completely, *madly* in love? Have you been having an affair with him?'

'Of course not.'

'Why *of course not*? You say that as if it's obvious.'

'I wasn't having an affair with Aaron. I'm just telling you how I felt.'

'*Felt*? Or feel?'

Uma pushed herself up to sitting, pulled her knees up and wrapped her arms around them, lowering her head into the cocoon of her limbs, obscuring her face from Pippa's scrutiny.

'Feel,' she whispered, so quietly she wasn't sure if Pippa would even hear.

'How well do we know each other?' said Pippa, her tone all of a sudden phlegmatic.

Uma lifted her head and met Pippa's stolid gaze.

'I don't know what you mean.'

'For years I've thought of us as… I don't know… best friends. But sometimes I feel like I don't know you at all.'

'We are best friends. Of course you know me.'

'They're just words. Easy to say. What do they mean? How do I know you Uma? How?'

She was right. They *were* just words. Uma was saying things that ought to be true. But *were* they true?

'I felt like something was wrong,' Pippa continued. 'Ever since Daniel's accident. And I know what everyone would say – well of course it seemed like something was wrong.

161

Something *was* wrong. But I don't mean that. I mean, on top of that something was wrong.'

Pippa's voice was steady in a way that it was never steady. It was monotone. And Pippa didn't do monotone. There had always been a lilt and lift to Pippa's voice. No matter who she was speaking to, no matter the dullness of the subject, words came alive on her lips. But not now. Now she was suffocating every syllable as it formed in her mouth.

'*Are* you in love with Aaron?'

'I think so.'

'Have you always been?'

'I think so.'

'So why didn't you tell me?'

'We had that fight about it when I was leaving uni.'

'Because you slept with him a week after he slept with me.'

'I never slept with Aaron.'

'You spent two weeks together at your cottage when you both should have been in lectures. Are you still going to pretend you weren't sleeping together?'

'We weren't.'

Pippa laughed sardonically, looking away.

'I'd had a termination and got an infection. I was in intensive care and Aaron looked after me at home until I was well enough to be on my own.'

There was a pause, just long enough for both of them to take a breath.

'Whose baby?' Pippa's tone hadn't changed.

'Daniel's.'

'Did he know?'

Uma shook her head.

'But you told Aaron?'

'That actually kind of just happened. I didn't mean to tell him.'

Pippa raised a single eyebrow, an unimpressed arch that said it all.

'And why did you never tell me?'

Uma paused, thinking. *Because I never trusted you to keep it to yourself.*

'Because I was afraid of Daniel finding out. The less people who knew the better. I've never told anybody else, you know. Not a soul.'

'Why have I never been good enough for you?'

'Oh *Pippa*.'

'I've always felt your distance. The way you like to keep yourself to yourself. This aloofness. Only, I tried to tell myself you were the same with everyone, but you're not. Actually it's just me you don't confide in. Blabber-mouth Pippa.'

'Pip, don't.'

'When have I ever actually let you down?'

'You haven't. You haven't let me down. It's not how it seems.'

Uma's heart was pounding. She grasped for threads of the tapestry, hoping to pull it back together, to show Pippa the intricacy of the stitching and how all the little pieces joined together. Small parts of a larger whole.

Pippa was crying. Silently. Great tears falling from her eyes down her cheeks and wetting the pale pink of her silky shirt. Uma wanted to reach out for her, but knew better than to do that now. Pippa hated sympathy almost as much as Uma did.

'It's more complicated than it seems. I never wanted to hide things from you. I value our friendship so much and it's been harder than you know, having to keep everything to myself.'

Pippa laughed, wiping her cheeks furiously.

'This is what people do, you know. They create themselves a shitty situation and then feel sorry for themselves that their situation's shitty. Have you ever heard me complain about being single? And you know why? Because I know it's my own fault.'

'Okay.'

'And even now I know you're keeping something from me.'

Uma shook her head, her heart still hammering, collecting

the plates from the rug. Holly came running towards them, raspberries spilling from her cupped hands. Pippa kneeled up and took the berries from her.

'These look tasty. *Are* they tasty?'

Holly's mouth was smeared with red, and she nodded, eyeing Pippa suspiciously, glancing at Uma for reassurance.

'Are we going to the beach soon?' she asked.

'We'll go next time, darling. We're going to go home now.'

'But you said we were having a sleepover with Auntie Uma.'

'We've changed our minds and we're not doing that anymore.'

Holly looked back to Uma, her eyes watering, and Uma wanted to reach out and pick her up but Pippa was already walking her away, speaking to her brightly about collecting their things together.

Chapter Twelve

1999

Aunt Sylvia made cocktails with a sugar rim. Aunt Pamela was ferreting in the back of a drawer in search of a packet of miniature umbrellas, whilst Daniel rolled his eyes, apologising to his accumulating friends. Nobody else seemed to think it was embarrassing, and Uma wondered why Daniel didn't see how lucky he was.

'Twenty!' Mary said, voice loud, ruffling his hair, drunk already.

They knew how to throw a party. They turned the music up loud, kept the drinks topped up, pulled hot quiche lorraine from the oven at regular intervals, opened the doors to the garden despite spring being weeks away and lit a monstrous bonfire as darkness crept in around the edges of the evening.

The house – Aunt Sylvie's – was full to bursting. There wasn't a room on the ground floor that wasn't thronging by 10pm.

'Aaron still not here?' Uma asked.

'He had another party first,' said Daniel. 'He'll be here.'

'Of course he'll be here,' she said, as if she hadn't been doubting it.

Most of the party moved outside as the bonfire got going, throwing sparks high in the darkening sky. Uma was lost in it, alone briefly, after Pippa disappeared with the new boyfriend who she had brought with her from uni. They

165

couldn't keep their hands off one another and Uma presumed they had found themselves a quiet place to be alone by now. She wasn't thinking about that though when she felt him at her back, she was thinking about the year ahead and how it would stack up compared with the last. She had been deep in thought when his arm snaked around her midriff, his face in her hair. Immediately, she knew that it was Aaron, and yet something about his presence felt strange and she twisted towards him. He looked drunk, although Uma suspected it was more than that. He grinned at her, putting his hand to the side of her face, clutching her hair.

'Aaron, you look fucked.'

He stepped away from her, putting his hands behind his head as if stretching, pushing his chest out. 'Do I? Like, badly?' He grinned again. 'I feel fucking *great*.'

Uma had seen Aaron like this before. It had unsettled her the first couple of times, but it never amounted to whatever it was that she feared, something unpredictable and out of control. She didn't want to be his straight, square friend. She wanted to just let him be what he needed to be. Which is what he always did for her. She took the joint that he offered, putting it to her lips.

'What have you taken?' she asked.

He shrugged, tapping his nose.

'What really? It's a secret?' she challenged, laughing at him.

'I wouldn't want Aunt Sylvie to throw me out.'

Uma frowned, looking at him patiently.

'But I am ready for what I need to do. I'm like, so ready. Like, completely, just completely in the zone. On task.'

She laughed again, tipsy, and just a little bit stoned all of a sudden.

'What's the task?'

'It's fucking classified. You will be the first to know when... when my mission is complete. The first. Definitely the first to know.'

Uma felt a flutter of anxiety through her intoxication.

What the hell is he talking about? She took another drag on the joint, but didn't return it to Aaron, fully aware that he had had quite enough of everything.

'We should go and sit down,' she suggested. 'There's a bench at the bottom of the garden.'

He flung his arm around her, trapping her hair and hurting her.

'*Aaron.*'

He ignored her, encircling her in a rough bear hug.

'I need to go and find Daniel. But then I will be back. I'll come back here. I'll see you right here, or on the bench if you think.' He pulled up the sleeve of his coat as if to check the time. 'I definitely put my watch on. Do you have a watch? What time does it say? We should just agree to meet back here. In five minutes. Is that long enough…?'

'Aaron…' Uma stepped away from him. 'Stop being weird. I'll come with you to find Daniel.'

'No!' Aaron put his hand up in between them, his palm in Uma's face. She pushed it away. 'I will go alone. And then I will be back and I will tell you about my successful task.'

Uma watched him go, walking in a reasonably straight line up the garden. Part of her knew that she ought to be following him, but part of her really couldn't be bothered. She turned, contemplating their exchange, staring back into the fire, Mary appearing at her elbow after a moment or two. Uma slipped her arm through Mary's and the two women watched the fire together, content in its warmth and the blurring of everything around the edges and all the things they understood that didn't need vocalising.

After a while Uma left Mary and began walking back up to the house with the intention of finding Aaron. Pippa appeared beside her in the darkness, as if from nowhere, breathless, grabbing Uma's hand.

'They're fighting,' she said, turning and dragging Uma along, and Uma knew instinctively who she meant, partly because of the shock on her face, and partly because she offered no names, as if Uma would simple *know*. It must be them.

'Oh, God.'

They were out the front of the house, on the other side of the road, down the lane that snaked across a series of fields if you followed it far enough. But they weren't fighting anymore. Daniel was alone, sitting on a fallen tree, his head in his hands, his clothing muddy. Aaron was nowhere to be seen.

'Daniel…' said Uma as they drew close. He looked up. His face was smeared with blood, a gash across his eyebrow, his left eye puffy and swollen. The top button was missing from his shirt, the fabric ripped.

'Where's Aaron?' Pippa asked, and Daniel shrugged.

Uma knelt on the ground in front of him, looking at his face, assessing whether he might need medical attention or whether they could just clean him up.

'I'm going to find him,' said Pippa, walking back towards the house.

'He went along the road,' said Daniel, his voice uneven, croaky. Pippa looked at the two of them, then towards the road.

'Don't go after him Pippa,' said Uma. 'He could be anywhere and you're not dressed for the cold. Go inside and see if you can find a first aid kit, bring some cotton wool and water. And our coats.'

Pippa ran towards the house and Uma looked back at Daniel.

He touched his face, tentatively, with trembling fingertips and Uma reached out for his hand, pressing it in hers, wanting to make him feel better, wanting his hands to stop shaking because she just couldn't bear it.

'What happened?'

He shook his head, looking away from Uma's gaze.

'What did he say to you? Who started this?'

'I don't even know what this is. He was fucking wasted.'

'What did he say?'

'He was talking crap.'

Daniel started to cry, the tears mixing with the wet blood

on his face. Seeing him like this made Uma want to cry too. A tiny voice was warning her, that Aaron had been out of control and could have said anything. He might have broken his promise to her and told Daniel about the pregnancy. *He wouldn't*. But maybe he would. He was, as Daniel said, *fucking wasted*. She looked at the broken man in front of her and ached to know what his tears were about.

'Please tell me what happened,' she said softly.

He looked at her, his eyes brimming with tears. Anger at Aaron was welling in her chest. Whatever he had said or not said, he had caused this. He had turned up wasted with some kind of twisted plan, and this was the result. This should have been Daniel's day. She looked at the mess of his face. She touched his cheek with her fingertips, their eyes meeting. Her heart was full of concern and affection for him. She wanted to take him in her arms and wrap him up. He mirrored her, his trembling hand on the side of her face.

'Oh Daniel.'

Regret is a terrible feeling, so pointless, and so painful. Uma couldn't turn back the clock, but right now she wanted to make things right for this kind, generous, loyal friend who was broken and bleeding in front of her. She thought of Anna and Mary and all the other women of his family, those people he cared for so deeply, showing up for them every day. He had shared his family business with Uma, knowing it was what she needed, ever generous, never presumptuous despite his feelings for her. Uma knew – of course, Aaron had been right – that Daniel was in love with her. And maybe she would have been glad of his feelings, if it hadn't been for Aaron. But with Aaron, she was stuck in a place of longing. *We'll never be together*. There had been opportunities, it hadn't happened, and Uma couldn't explain it. Her mother would have told her to forget him. *You must learn to let go*. She had always been quick to remind Uma that *some things are just not to be*. She would have been matter-of-fact, encouraging Uma to be the same, with the shrug of a single shoulder, as if Uma really shouldn't trouble herself.

Uma leant forward and placed a slow, heart-felt kiss at the corner of Daniel's mouth. Their eyes locked and he smiled. He gently pulled her face towards his, kissing her full on the lips, Uma kissing him back, pulling away only when she heard footsteps behind them.

'Here.'

It was Pippa's voice, and then she was next to them, pushing coats at them and a first aid kit. She took a bottle of water out of her pocket and knelt on the ground beside Uma. Together, they cleaned up Daniel's face, wiping away the blood, inspecting the injuries and declaring them not as bad as the blood suggested.

'You still look like you've been fighting though,' said Uma, smiling. 'What will your mum say?'

'Fighting like girls they were,' said Pippa, laughing, making Daniel smile. 'On the floor, cat fighting.'

Uma looked to Pippa, imagining the scene.

'Were you with them?'

'I came for Aaron's gear. I'd seen them heading down here.'

'What was it all about?'

Pippa shrugged. 'As I said, fighting like girls by the time I got down here.' She stood up, collecting the blood stained cotton wool pieces, stuffing them into her pocket, taking the first aid box away.

'I'm going back. Tom doesn't know anybody.'

'I'll stay with Daniel for a bit,' said Uma, and watched as Pippa disappeared into the darkness, reappearing again in the lights of the house.

'*Fuck*,' said Daniel, touching his eyebrow.

'Don't touch it,' Uma said, taking hold of his hand, taking in his face, the features she knew as well as her own. He pulled her towards him and Uma surrendered – to the kiss, to Daniel, to the idea of them being together.

Chapter Thirteen

2015

The sound of tyres on the gravel outside nudged into Uma's dreams, leading her away from them, tugging her into a bleary consciousness. Her eyes flickered open and she glanced at the clock on the bedside table. 5.37am. She lay still, listening for some other sound of a car outside but hearing only birdsong and the blustery wind and the dog-rose scratching at the bedroom window. Sometimes it happened that a lost tourist would drive onto the road that led to the house, turning round on the gravel out front once they realised their mistake. It had happened in the middle of the night once, her heart pounding as she watched through a tiny slit in the curtains.

Rolling over, she told herself she had imagined the sound, hopeful of being able to return to a comfortable slumber. But a nagging doubt had her throwing back the covers. She padded barefoot to the little window and teased two fingers between the fabric of the curtains, parting them a little. There *was* a car, parked out the front of the house in the fog. She watched it, waiting for something to happen, wondering whether Mary might have taken it into her head to pay a visit – to barrage Uma further with her protestations and anxieties. *But that's not Mary's car. And who on earth would arrive so early in the morning?*

Uma turned away. She pulled on her clothes, picking them

one by one from the end of the bed where she had thrown them the night before. She put on a coat, more for a sense of protection than anything else and laced her feet into her boots. Unlocking the door she stepped out into the fresh, misty July morning. She walked across the veranda, down the steps and towards the car. The door opened and she registered a tanned face, a flash of blond hair, a collarless shirt. Her heart leapt at the shock of it.

'Aaron!'

He smiled and opened his arms, scooping her up when she embraced him. He squeezed her tight, holding her just long enough.

'You sound surprised,' he laughed, as he let her go.

'I am.'

'Didn't you get my message?'

'Oh. Well I'm sort of avoiding the phone at the moment.'

He looked at her questioningly, but she shrugged him off.

'I'll tell you later. Have you got stuff you want to bring in?'

He shook his head. 'It can wait.'

'Will you be staying?'

'Maybe a night.'

'How was the trip?' she asked.

'Amazing,' he said. 'So amazing. You and I should do something like it one day. Just walking and walking. Awesome scenery, beautiful cities. Met some great people.'

'I would love that,' said Uma. 'When did you get back? I wasn't sure how long it would take you.'

In truth, Uma hadn't known whether to expect Aaron to return to the UK at all. It wouldn't have been unlike him to send a message to say that he had returned to work – that he had a new contract somewhere on the other side of the world. That was how it had been for years. Sporadically flitting back and forth across the globe, in and out of their lives.

'I've literally just flown in. Drove straight here. I'd planned to have a kip in the car, wait until you were awake. Did I disturb you or were you up anyway?'

'I think the car woke me.'

'Sorry Moo. How's your sleeping been?'

'Better than it was.'

'That's good,' he said, running his hand through his hair, stifling a yawn.

'You must be shattered.'

'I am.'

'Do you want my bed for a bit?'

'No.'

He draped an arm round her shoulders and pulled her towards him. Something inside her relaxed as she realised that things were okay between them. This was normal. Aaron was being Aaron, letting her know from the outset that all was well. She presumed that at some point they would talk about what happened between them, what nearly happened, what she had wanted to happen. But for now everything was just as it had always been.

They went inside and Aaron took off his coat and hung it on the back of the door. He eased his boots from his feet, groaning, then followed Uma into the kitchen, took a glass from the draining board and helped himself to a long drink of water. Uma filled the kettle.

'Didn't think I would ever find you,' he said.

'How did you?'

'I got directions from Pippa. They were pretty good, but I must have taken a wrong turning at some point. Anyway, I kind of stumbled upon you in the end.'

'How was Pippa?'

'Not her usual self, although she said everything was fine. Has something happened?'

The memory of their fight was bright around all the edges as if Uma's mind had flagged it in some way. It would be filed, she was sure, eventually, in some special recess in her brain. *Handle with care*, perhaps. *Confidential*. Uma had glimpsed what honesty could do. It had been liberating, and terrifying. She imagined telling Aaron about the conversation in its entirety, how his name had spilled, scalding, from their mouths.

'Mmm. Kinda. Would you like tea?'

He nodded and she reached for the mugs.

'I told her about the termination all those years ago. She's upset that I never confided in her. And who can blame her really? She knows that I told you but kept it from Daniel.'

'Blimey. So, how the hell did that come up?'

'It just did. I never imagined it would.'

'At least-'

Aaron stopped himself mid-sentence, but Uma knew what he had been about to say.

'Was it wrong of me to never tell him?' she asked.

'Who gets to say what's right and wrong?'

'Oh, come on.'

'You did what was best at the time. That's all any of us can do.'

'That sounds very convenient.'

'No more convenient than a list of commandments. Thou shall. Thou shall not. As if life is so straightforward. If it was there wouldn't be so much conflict in the world. None of us can agree on anything. I mean, literally nothing.'

'I did do my best. I honestly, really, truly always did what I thought was best.'

He nodded, clearly, encouragingly, coming towards her.

'We all did. We all *do*,' he said.

'But then something like this happens with Pippa and I think – she's right! I treated her like she wasn't good enough. And I kept a secret from Daniel the whole of our marriage. I might have tried my best, but I made the wrong choices. My best wasn't good enough.'

It seemed too soon to be unwrapping these untouchable keepsakes in the middle of the kitchen. They'd hardly said a proper hello.

'Grief isn't what I thought it was going to be,' said Aaron.

'No,' she said, looking up into his face.

They regarded one another for a second or two, then Uma turned to the cupboards, gathering small plates and knives and a tin of vegetable fritters. Aaron looked around the kitchen, opening cupboard doors.

'Is this all your stuff?' he asked, nodding towards the jars of spices and packets of coconut, tamarind, curry leaves, the pestle and mortar, the tins balancing one on top of the other.

'I've been cooking crazy.'

'Nice.'

When the tea was ready they sat at the little table.

'I can't believe you're here. Just suddenly here,' she said, as she handed him a mug.

Lines divided his face when he smiled these days. He looked older than he was. But his eyes were the same as ever. Would she be here in forty years' time, looking into his face across a kitchen table, sipping tea, seeing the young man behind the changing exterior?

**

'This way,' said Uma, leading him into the woods. The mist hadn't lifted yet and all around the trees were silent ghosts stretching away from them. She held the branches so they didn't flick back into his face and after a moment or two they were on the path that Uma had created on her regular walks from the cottage to the beach.

'Listen,' she said, after another few minutes, stopping, putting her finger to her lips. 'This is where you start to hear the sea.' And as they listened, the sounds of it crept towards them through the rustling leaves and the warbling birds, the rhythmic breath of waves breaking in the distance.

They began walking again.

'So you come this way every morning?'

'To swim.'

'Even in the rain?'

'Especially in the rain.'

175

There was something about the rain on the water, being *in it,* surrounded by it, that gave Uma a rush of something she couldn't quite name. It was like being overwhelmed, but in a good way.

'So, no wetsuit?'

'Naked swimming.'

As soon as she said the words she felt a flush of embarrassment.

'The beach is deserted early mornings,' she clarified.

'The best time.'

'Come on, I'll race you.'

She broke into a run, desperate to throw off how she was feeling, not looking behind to see if he was following, but concentrating on pumping her legs and arms, jumping a trunk that lay across the path, hearing him behind her then, the building of a playful fear. There was a nausea too, but she kept running, the beach ahead of her in the mist. She made it to the beach before he caught up with her, her feet sinking into the softness, Aaron appearing at her elbow, catching her foot accidentally with his, sending them flailing down onto the sand. Uma rolled over onto her back, chest heaving, breath coming in short, fast bursts. They laughed in between their panting and he turned to look at her. She could feel him taking her in, could feel his breath on her face, but she kept her eyes on the thick, grey cloud above them.

'Are we going in?' he asked, peeling off his clothes, answering his own question.

It wouldn't be the first time they had stripped naked to swim. They had plunged into cold, wild waters in the Peak District on plenty of occasions. The four of them. Summer picnics. The river at Chatsworth. The crystal-clear waters of Lathkill Dale. A deep, flowing pool in the young Derwent river, the water brown with peat.

'Okay, then,' said Uma, looking up and down the deserted beach.

She unlaced and stepped out of her boots. She began peeling her clothes away, her skin flushing with goosebumps as it met with the fresh morning air – first her arms, then her legs, then her torso as she pulled off her t-shirt. Aaron was doing the same, half turned away from her. She unhooked her bra and let it slither off her arm to the ground. She took a deep breath, pulled her knickers down and added them to the pile, racing off as quickly as possible into the mist.

She entered the water as she did every morning, throwing herself into the water before she could change her mind. She surfaced a few seconds later, brushing her hair away from her face, turning to Aaron.

'Just dive!' she called. 'Get it over with!'

Her breath came in short, uncontrollable gasps. She ignored it and began to swim, front crawl, for twenty metres or so, treading water then for a moment, feeling the bottom brushing her toes, turning to look for Aaron. He was just behind her.

'*Fuck*!'

She laughed at him, her body trembling.

'Cold?'

'I can't believe you do this every day.'

'I'll miss it so much.'

'I need to get moving.' His teeth were chattering.

'Parallel to the shore,' she said.

They were swimming close to one another, their limbs knocking occasionally, but Uma concentrated on cutting the water with her arms, kicking her legs, warming and tiring herself, knowing that later in the day she would trade this exertion for exhilaration as she ate her breakfast – her skin cold to the touch, her mind zinging with life – and, much later, for sleep. That most gilded of gifts.

She slowed, stopping after a few moments, looking towards him.

'How you doing?'

'Fantastic,' he replied, grinning at her. And they laughed

together, treading water, rising and falling with the undulating swell.

They struggled to pull their clothes over their wet limbs – laughing at the tangled mess they found themselves in – and walked back to the cottage discussing the Sultan Trail and marvelling at their stinging-cold skin. He talked her through the hike – Austria, Slovakia, Hungary, Croatia, Serbia, Romania, Bulgaria, Greece and Turkey. *I never knew it was possible to become so obsessed with the state of my feet,* he said. And she admitted her envy, her desire to get away and do something completely different.

They ate toast beneath blankets on the little sofa, Uma thinking about the things they hadn't talked about yet – Daniel and Alex, Jo-Jo and Richard, and what happened between them after the wake. She thought about how sorry she was for trying to kiss him. *Forgive me for that won't you? It was stupid. Don't think badly of me.* She thought about Jo-Jo and imagined shaking Aaron until he listened properly. *You can't be with Jo-Jo! She's not right for you.* Uma thought how much she wanted Aaron to be happy. She thought about Richard and felt a heaviness in the pit of her stomach.

It was later, after a long game of scrabble and several pots of tea that Uma told Aaron about Daniel. *He was seeing somebody*, is how she put it.

'*Seeing* somebody?'

Uma nodded, putting her plate onto the floor and hugging her knees to her chest. Aaron was shaking his head, looking confused.

'I wondered if you knew,' said Uma. She had been dreading this question, fearful of his answer, knowing, however hypocritical it was, that Aaron keeping a secret for Daniel would have felt like a betrayal.

'He'd have never told me something like that.'

She had pulled it apart with her thinking already, but she thought about it again.

'No, I suppose he wouldn't.'

'So, who is she?'

'A woman called Alex he met in Devon. She did some graphic design work for us.'

'How long have you known?'

Uma told him the story from the beginning. She described listening to Alex's message to Daniel, her struggle to navigate those first few weeks, her desire at times to share the information with everyone, her wish to vilify him and her wish to protect him, or, at least, to protect their marriage, or, if not their marriage as such, then the image of their marriage. And she told him about her escape to the cottage, the opportunity to think. And to *not* think. Just to be.

'And then she turns up at the house. Mary found her peering into the windows.'

'So Mary knows.'

'God, no. It'd break her heart. Anna knows. And I told Eva, that's how I found out about who she was.'

'Fuck.'

'I've said I want to meet but she won't.'

'I'm not surprised.'

'I know where she works though. I'm going to go.'

'Is that a good idea?'

'I want one conversation, that's all.'

Aaron looked unconvinced.

'It's not a fight I want.'

'What *do* you want?'

'I suppose I wonder if he hated me.'

Aaron shook his head, a look on his face that said *of course he didn't hate you*.

'Maybe not hate,' she said, searching for the right word, trying to clarify it in her own mind. 'Whether he resented me.'

'Why would he, though?'

'Deep down. Beneath the good person that he was.'

'*Uma…*'

'There was lots we didn't talk about. It can feel better at the time to leave things unsaid. But give it time and it isn't better at all.'

Did we punish each other? Uma thought about her refusal to have children, his refusal to travel. And she thought about the duplicity – her secret at the start of their marriage, eliding with his at the end.

'You're focusing on all the negative parts,' said Aaron. 'I know you two better than anyone else. I understand what you're saying, but I also know how great you were to each other. It was what it was.'

'*It was what it was*?' She laughed. 'Typical Aaron understatement.'

He leaned forward and grabbed her hand, looking her right in the eye.

'It *was* what it was. It's not an understatement.'

'And I'm trying to understand it.'

'And that's fine. But don't swing from pretending that everything was fine to telling yourself that everything was just one big worthless lie.'

She smiled begrudgingly.

'*Okay*. But I still want to talk to Alex.'

'But if she doesn't want to see you…'

'I've got to start trusting my intuition. My intuition says *go*.'

'Then let me come with you.'

Uma shook her head.

'I don't need you to,' she said.

She told him how she wanted to go alone. How much she knew she would appreciate the silence of the journey. How she had found the comfort of solitude in this dilapidated cottage, remembering actually how she had always needed it, and how she had forgotten the fact over the years. *It's like coming home*, she said.

They talked more about Daniel, and Uma, and all the years they had spent together, creating Millers, this admirable thing. *And now it feels like a big heavy coat in the summer.*

'Are you angry with him?' Aaron asked, after several long moments of silence.

'Not anymore. It wouldn't be fair, would it? To be angry with him when I know now I never loved him properly.'

'You *did* love him though, all those years.'

But never like I loved you.

'I didn't love him enough.'

'You loved him best you could. And he chose that. He must have known how things were. At some level.'

Uma shrugged.

'And anyway,' Aaron said, 'surely there's no such thing as loving someone properly.'

She thought about it. Wasn't there though?

'I think we love people differently,' he said. 'That's all.'

And I've loved you always. Deeply. Like part of me is missing when you're not here.

**

Somehow he persuaded her to go out into the nearest town that evening.

'You can't stay cooped up here all the time,' he said dismissively when she began to protest.

'You sound like Mary,' she joked.

'Mary's probably got your best interests at heart.'

'She thinks she has.'

'Well I think I have too. We're going out.'

'Two drinks somewhere quiet.'

'Three drinks wherever I choose.'

**

The pub was busy. Teenagers littered the stone steps outside, smoking and jostling one another, prodding and jibing. Aaron and she struggled through to the bar, queuing, trying to talk above the sound of the band playing in the back room – Irish

181

jigs that could have tumbled in from across the sea. They drank whisky, and too much of it.

Later, after being told about a late bus that would drop them just a mile from the cottage, they queued for chips and took them down onto the beach. They sat on the rocks in the near-dark and unwrapped their paper packages. Uma's stomach growled at the smell and they ate, looking out at the dark shadow of the sea, sharp vinegar on the greasy potatoes, gritty salt, tiny crispy pieces left at the end. She screwed the paper and sucked her fingers one by one, relaxing, satiated.

He insisted they stop at the car on the way to the bus stop and he rummaged – he said for a toothbrush – in a big holdall in the boot.

'Aaron, come on, it's a long walk to the bus stop, we'll miss it if we don't go now. You can use mine.'

'Just a moment. Nearly... *there,*' he said.

He slammed the boot shut and grabbed her hand. 'C'mon then.' They strode up the long hill to the bus stop, a deserted wooden shelter on a country road just out of town.

Once they were there he turned towards her.

'Here,' he said, 'I've got something for you.'

And he held a clenched fist in her direction.

She offered him an upturned palm and he carefully released eight tiny little stones out of his hand into hers. 'Sultan's stones,' he said. 'One from each country. Although I can't remember which is which.'

None of them were bigger than her smallest fingernail, impressively uniform in size although varying in shape and colour. She smiled, looking up at him briefly and then back down at the stones.

'I love that you still do this,' she said, putting an arm around him and leaning her head against his chest for a moment. There was something about the fact he never forgot, that he hadn't tired of it over the years, that it seemed to matter more as time went by, rather than less. He wrapped his arms around her and they breathed in unison, Uma closing her eyes.

At a quarter past midnight they realised that they had probably missed the bus.

'We'll have to sleep in the car or something,' said Aaron. 'Drive back when we've sobered up.'

But by the time they had walked back down the hill, they had decided to take Aaron's sleeping bag down onto the beach as a makeshift mattress.

'Let's add a few layers,' he said, pulling long-sleeved tops and a fleece out of his holdall. Uma pulled something over her head and took a pair of socks that he was holding out to her. Laughing at their predicament they found an area of sandy beach that was declared *good enough*. They unzipped his sleeping bag and spread it out. Aaron had brought two towels and he folded them into pillows.

'Will it do?' he asked, and Uma lay down, testing it out, nodding.

'It'll have to,' she said.

He lowered himself onto the sleeping bag next to her and lay back, resting his head on the folded towel, crossing his arms over his chest. She mirrored him on her side of the sleeping bag and experimented with closing her eyes, testing how tired she felt, what chance there was of drifting off out here on the beach.

'Will you be able to sleep?' she asked him, without opening her eyes.

'Probably. I can pretty much sleep anywhere.'

They fell into a comfortable silence, looking up at the stars.

'So, what about you and Jo-Jo?' Uma said, after a while.

'Not happening.'

'How come?'

Aaron took a deep breath, exhaling slowly before replying.

'When I told her about Jo-Jo, Pippa asked me why I always choose relationships that won't last.'

'That sounds like Pippa. What did you tell her?'

'I couldn't explain myself. Or didn't want to. And then Donny, the guy I was trekking with, pretty much asked me the same thing. I suppose it got me thinking.'

'And?'

'They're right. I *do* do that.'

'Pippa said it wouldn't last with Jo-Jo because you're terrified of commitment.'

'Well, Pippa's not right about everything.'

Uma waited for him to say more, both of them staring up at the stars still, but he didn't. After a silence that was so long Uma wondered if he'd fallen asleep, she said 'I've been seeing someone.'

'So quickly?'

'Just someone I met here. It's nothing serious.'

He turned to look at her, and she didn't look away. Her head was swimming from the whisky.

'I think it's time for us to start doing whatever makes us happy. Don't you think?' he said.

Uma looked away, swallowing the fear in her throat.

'I suppose so. But…'

'But what?'

'Sometimes I'm not sure what'll make me happy.'

There was a pause.

'I've decided to pack in working abroad,' he said.

'But didn't *that* make you happy?'

'Of course. But it's lonely work, making new friends all the time. I've always thought of everything here as home, but the longer I stay away the more tenuous it feels.'

They went back to staring at the stars in silence.

'There's a poem in one of the books at the cottage,' said Uma. 'It's called Hokusai Says. I wish I could remember all of it, but there's this one line that sticks in my head. *Keep changing – you just become more who you really are*. I love that so much. At the moment I'm going round in circles with regret, feeling as if I've wasted my life, as if I haven't been on track in some way. But maybe being on track isn't what we think it's going to be. Maybe I've been completely on track without knowing it.'

'Keep changing,' he said, repeating the words. 'You just become more who you really are.'

**

Uma wasn't sure how long she had been asleep, but she woke shivering, the sound of waves close by, the clouds low and dark in the sky. Her body felt stiff as she began to move, pushing herself up to sitting, glancing at Aaron who was sleeping still, breathing evenly and deeply. She reached out and touched his shoulder, giving him a little shake. He didn't stir and she shook him again, leaning down towards him, saying his name. His eyes flickered open and stared straight into hers. She could almost see his mind making sense of the situation and he smiled.

'Morning,' he said, stretching and rubbing his eyes. 'Now that was a comfortable night's sleep.'

Uma laughed.

'Did you sleep?'

'Kind of, I think, a little bit!'

She stood.

'I'm meeting Richard to go fishing this morning. I need to get back.'

'Fishing? What the fuck?'

Uma shrugged. 'He wanted to take me out in his boat. What can I say?'

'I thought you said it was just a sex thing.'

'Did I say that?'

'Didn't you?'

'I said it wasn't serious. I didn't say it was just a sex thing.'

'Is it a romance thing?'

'Definitely not.'

'And do you have sex?'

'Yes.'

'Then it's just a sex thing.'

'I don't know why we're having this conversation.'

'But you don't go fishing when it's just a sex thing.'

'Well apparently you do.'

'I'm telling you, you don't.'

'We're fishing for mackerel and cooking it on the beach.'

He raised his eyebrows and got to his feet, turning to grab hold of his sleeping bag, rolling it up and tucking it beneath his arm. Uma had picked up the towels and he held out his hand for them.

'It's okay, I'll carry them,' she said, taking a quick look at the sea before heading up the beach in the direction of the car.

'Cooking fish on a beach is romantic,' he said.

They fell into an awkward silence on the way home. Uma rested her head on the window and closed her eyes, feigning sleep. And once they were back at the cottage, Aaron asked whether he could use her bed for a few hours while she was out.

'Of course,' said Uma. 'Just let me grab some stuff and it's all yours.'

She rummaged in the wardrobe drawer for some jeans and some tops to layer, and grabbed a thick jumper from the end of her bed.

'There,' she said, passing him in the doorway. She headed for the bathroom and heard him close bedroom door.

Her face flushed when she heard the sound of Richard's motorbike, and something heavy turned in the pit of her stomach. He was revving his engine to announce his arrival and Uma hoped that Aaron was asleep. She had left him a note on the table saying she'd only be gone for the morning and would see him sometime just after lunch.

She went outside, giving Richard a quick wave before turning to lock the door. He lifted his visor as she got close and twisted to retrieve the spare helmet and leather jacket that were strapped to the back of his bike. She took the things he proffered, noticing that her hands were trembling, heart fluttering. She shook the feeling away, eased on the leather jacket and zipped it up. The sooner they left, the sooner she'd be back.

'You put your feet here,' he said, pointing. 'And when we round a corner just go with it, relax and you'll lean with the bike. Don't *try* to lean, and don't resist it, okay?'

She nodded.

'Great,' he said, grinning at her. 'Then let's go.'

She pulled the helmet over her head and flicked the visor shut, lifting her leg across the seat and easing onto the bike behind Richard. It was all shiny red and silver chrome. It growled, reverberating through her, and he revved the engine more than was probably necessary, pulling out onto the main road, picking up speed.

She did as she was told, relaxing into it, letting herself lean with the bike. The cold air rushed into her neck, vibrating through her jacket. She tried to conjure what she knew she would have felt a week ago, her torso pressed up against his back, her arms around his waist. She tried to feel it. But her minded drifted to Aaron back at the cottage. She imagined him sleeping in her bed. She remembered his words as they had been leaving the beach – the disgruntled tone of them.

After about half an hour they reached a small village with pebble-dash houses and grey slate pathways. The road down to the beach was peppered with touristy shops selling handmade chocolate and fudge, pottery seals, dolphins, wind chimes and gem stones. There were a couple of pubs and a fish and chip shop.

Richard pulled in to a little car park, driving to the far side, bringing the bike to a stop. He turned to speak to Uma, lifting his visor, checking that she was okay. She smiled at him, thinking about the sea and how good it would be to catch fish and cook them. She had brought little packages of spice and her phone to take photographs. *It will be nice.*

Uma dismounted, moving gingerly, waiting for the blood to return to her legs.

'Your trousers aren't thick enough, you must be cold,' he said, appraising her jeans.

'I'll warm up as soon as we're moving,' she said.

They gathered their things and headed down to the beach and onto a little jetty with scores of boats tethered to great wooden stumps.

'It's this one,' said Richard, indicating one of the boats – a sturdy looking thing, painted white, an engine at one end. He threw his stuff into it, stepping down afterwards, watching Uma do the same. He fished a key from his pocket and turned the engine over. The engine complained at being roused from its long slumber but eventually, with a relieved smile at her, he got it going. Just as they began to move away from the jetty into the waves the boat seemed to have a change of heart and chugged to a silent standstill. Richard tried to get it going again, turning it over and over but coaxing nothing from it but a sorry spluttering. With a quiet sigh, he pulled out a couple of oars and rowed the few metres back to the jetty.

'Sorry about this,' he said, tethering the boat to its moorings.

After a few minutes fiddling with the engine, checking fuel levels and making a couple of phone calls, Richard suggested that Uma go for a walk along the beach while he waited for a mate to come and help.

'It does this occasionally when it's not been used for a while.'

I don't want to be here. She looked at Richard's face, pinched with concentration and was shocked at how easily her feelings could change. *I don't want this anymore.*

'I don't mind waiting,' is what she said, forcing a bleak smile, but he shooed her away. 'There's a lovely little café on the beach that way,' he said. 'Go get yourself a cup of tea. Stay warm.'

She didn't go to the café, but walked along the shingly beach, picking up little stones and shells and putting them into her pockets, thinking of Aaron. She watched purple clouds gathering in the distance, noticing the gusts picking up, wondering whether today was a good day to be going out to sea at all. It was cold, blustery, more like autumn than July. Perhaps it was serendipity that the boat's engine had failed. The clouds were darkening and all she wanted now was to be back in front of the fire playing scrabble with Aaron, waiting for the storm to sweep overhead.

She went for a cup of tea in the end, sitting at a wooden table, looking out of a grubby window. She still needed to talk to Aaron about the night of Daniel's funeral. And she needed to tell him how she felt. She needed to tell him that all these years she had carried him around like a polished stone in her pocket. That no matter how far away he had been, it had always felt like no distance at all. And that for so many of those years she had been relieved that he was on the other side of the world.

Richard came to fetch her once the boat was fixed, and she felt a flash of disappointment.

'Shouldn't we listen to the forecast?' she asked him as they made their way across the beach.

'I have. It's going to be fine.'

'But it looks like a storm's coming.'

'It's not coming this far. It's miles away.'

It didn't *look* miles away.

Uma zipped up her jacket and thrust her hands into the pockets. They set off into the choppy waves, the boat rising and dipping as Richard headed straight out to sea.

'How far do we need to go?' asked Uma, glancing at the darkening sky.

'Not far,' he said, raising his voice above the rasping engine.

Waves slapped against the side of the boat, jostling them, spraying their faces with water. Uma eyed the life jackets shoved down the sides of the engine, wondering whether to ask for one or whether that would send the wrong message. *I'm not feeling safe. I don't trust your judgement.*

'They feed just out there,' he said, pointing some distance away where the sea looked less choppy. He glanced at her, reaching over, grabbing her knee, shaking it.

'Stop worrying.'

Once they were there Richard switched off the engine. She smiled at him. *Concentrate on the moment*. She watched him putting the rods together. He attached the lures and showed Uma how to drop the line, letting the weight fall, leaving it for a few seconds before reeling it in. She did her best to ignore the darkness that seemed to be gathering around them, the lack of other boats out with them on the sea, the heavy slap of choppy waves against the side of the boat. She focused on dropping the line and reeling it back. He had been so confident that they would catch something. *Nothing is easier to catch than mackerel*, he had said. *A four year old can do it*.

They let the lures plummet into the depths below, then pulled them up, repeating and repeating. Each time Uma reeled in the line she was sure there would be something on the hooks, flapping silver in the water. *Please let us catch something because then we can go*. Each time the hooks came up empty she threw them out again, her hands beginning to stiffen in the cold.

'We might have to try another spot,' said Richard after a while.

The wind was getting stronger, and Uma saw the storm clouds gathering overhead, moving closer.

'Perhaps we should head back,' said Uma, feeling the patter of rain on her face. But Richard was busy throwing out his lures.

'I'm not going back without mackerel,' he said. 'Although we might not want to cook it on the beach. I reckon if we head out just a little more…'

'I don't want to go further.'

'Just another hundred metres. We need to try a different feeding area.'

Uma paused for just a second or two, long enough for Richard to start the engine and point the boat towards his desired destination. *This is stupid*. The engine sounded dodgy and the wind was picking up by the minute.

'Richard,' she said, reaching out and placing her hand on his arm. 'I think we should go back.'

He looked at her, relaxing the throttle, slowing the boat.

'It'll be fine,' he said. 'Trust me.'

Uma shook her head, overriding him. It began to rain. A sudden, heavy downpour – great huge drops that turned the sea to boiling. The weather was proving her right and he knew it.

'Okay,' he said, turning the boat, and speeding them as fast as possible towards the shore. She supposed he was annoyed by her lack of confidence, her lack of *joie de vivre*, but she didn't care.

They tethered the boat and gathered their things, all in the pouring rain. They half ran, half walked across the beach and into the nearest pub. Uma headed to the toilet to dry herself as best she could with paper towels. She checked her watch and thought of Aaron back at the cottage, and her promise of being home just after lunch. It was lunchtime already. *I shouldn't be here*. It was time to go.

Richard was waiting at the bar by the time she came out.

'It'll be a chilly ride back,' he said.

Uma pulled a resolute face. 'We'll survive.'

'I've ordered food,' he said, pointing at the specials board. *Seared mackerel with beetroot and horseradish*. Uma felt that tight knot in her stomach again. She could hardly bear to smile, but forced herself, rousing as best she could some gratitude for his kindness.

'A consolation,' he said.

They found a table to sit at, pulling out stools opposite one another.

'Thanks for the idea of today,' she said. 'I know it didn't exactly work out.'

'Hey,' he said, reaching out and drawing his fingertips across her arm. 'What's wrong?'

Uma tried to shake off his concern, arranging her face into something buoyant. But he wasn't fooled.

'What's changed?'

She smiled at that, looking him in the eye, holding his gaze, reaching out for his hand.

'Everything's changed. And nothing.'

'You're leaving.'

'I've been leaving for ages.'

'You're leaving *me*.'

He cupped her hand in his.

'We knew it was temporary,' she said.

'This is true.'

She tried to gauge his feelings.

'I'm a big boy,' he said, keeping hold of her hand.

'It's not like…'

He shook his head, dismissing her explanation. They had talked about it at the beginning. No strings.

The waitress brought their food to the table, handing them cutlery, checking they had everything they needed.

'This looks good,' said Uma, glancing down at her plate and then at Richard. They began to eat, hardly speaking.

He took her hand as they walked back up the road to the car park. They stood at the bike, pulling on their leathers and helmets. At least it wasn't raining now.

'Do you want to go anywhere else? Do anything?'

She looked at him through his visor.

'Why don't you just drop me home?' she said.

They were damp still, and Uma was tired and cold, and maybe Richard was too because he didn't say anything more to try and persuade her. He smiled a small, gentle smile and gave a tiny nod of agreement. She sensed something that might have been sadness and didn't know what to make of it.

In view of the cottage Uma wondered whether they were being watched. She dismounted, and removed the helmet and the leather jacket, passing them to him so he could attach them to the rack on the back of the bike. He removed his helmet and drew Uma into a hug. She rested her head on his shoulder, and when she pulled away he kissed her briefly on the mouth.

'Go,' he said.

And Uma walked away, turning at the door, raising a hand in farewell.

**

The note she had left on the kitchen table for Aaron had been turned over and he had written her a message on the other side. *Decided to head off to my folks. Was more than great to see you. Take care xxx* And then, underneath, in tiny writing, he had written out the complete poem, *Hokusai Says*:

Hokusai says look carefully.
He says pay attention, notice.
He says keep looking, stay curious.
He says there is no end to seeing
He says look forward to getting old.
He says keep changing,
you just get more who you really are.
He says get stuck, accept it, repeat
yourself as long as it is interesting.
He says keep doing what you love.

He says keep praying.
He says every one of us is a child,
every one of us is ancient
every one of us has a body.
He says every one of us is frightened.
He says every one of us has to find
a way to live with fear.
He says everything is alive —
shells, buildings, people, fish,

mountains, trees, wood is alive.
Water is alive.
Everything has its own life.
Everything lives inside us.
He says live with the world inside you.
He says it doesn't matter if you draw,
or write books. It doesn't matter
if you saw wood, or catch fish.
It doesn't matter if you sit at home
and stare at the ants on your veranda
or the shadows of the trees
and grasses in your garden.
It matters that you care.
It matters that you feel.
It matters that you notice.
It matters that life lives through you.
Contentment is life living through you.
Joy is life living through you.
Satisfaction and strength is life living through you.
Peace is life living through you.
He says don't be afraid.
Don't be afraid.
Look, feel, let life take you by the hand.
Let life live through you.

Roger Keyes

Uma read through the poem, folded the piece of paper into a small square and left it on the table. She ran a bath, knowing it would be neither hot enough nor deep enough to offer the comfort she needed.

**

The next morning she headed to the beach just as it was getting light. It was one of those beautifully still days, fabulously clear, the birds singing and the finches chasing one another in and out of the trees. The crocosmia were in blood-red bloom and the hydrangea were bursting with colour. The garden was never the same from one day to the next. It liked to surprise.

The way to the beach was obvious now, easy to follow, even if a stranger were to stumble upon it. Uma had worn a path through the woods and it felt strange to think that when she left in a week or so that it would succumb to the rampant vegetation again, disappearing, just like she was going to disappear.

She had reassured herself with promises to return, but she also knew that it would never be the same again. Her time here had been somehow without bounds. She had not known when it would end. She kept thinking it would end and it kept continuing. Just when it seemed urgent that she return to her old life something had shown up to keep her here. It had stretched ahead of her and behind her, and all around. It was sometimes all she felt certain of. This place, the water, the trees. The moon and the stars that shone so brightly. The birds that woke her at dawn. The damp-earth smell in the woods. The most essential people showing up, or calling on the telephone occasionally, anchoring her somehow, just enough.

How could she ever return here in the future and expect it to be the same? She knew if she came that she would have to prepare herself for disappointment. She remembered what Aaron said about grief not being what he expected it to be. *Isn't it the same with everything?* Nothing ever seemed to be what she expected it to be.

She had joined the main path down to the beach when she noticed a scattering of unusual, flat stones – stones that seemed to have appeared since she was last here the day before yesterday. There were more of them as she looked ahead, placed in a meandering line, like stepping stones. They increased in number as she got closer to the beach, each stone almost touching its neighbour – a small, thin pathway. Uma frowned, perplexed, looking behind her at the new almost-cobble-stoned path stretching back the way she had come, and stretching ahead of her too, down onto the sand. She followed it, stepping on to it in places. As she came down through the dunes and reeds onto the beach, the stones led her, as deftly as if they had taken her by the hand, to a message on the sand. A heart made of stones and rocks and shells. A heart several metres across. A tremendous heart. Perfectly formed. Impossible. A message of love.

Chapter Fourteen

1999

Uma watched Daniel at the water's edge, lifting Anna high into the air over the breaking waves.

'It's coming, it's coming, it's *coming!*' he taunted his little sister. Anna was squealing, kicking her legs. She clapped her hands each time Daniel put her back onto the sand.

'Good father material, that boy,' said Mary, nonchalant, running her hands over her tanned arms, clasping her large pendant in her right hand, making a fist of it.

'Shut up Mum. Ignore her, Uma,' said Ruth, not looking up from her text book.

Mary rummaged in her large basket bag, fishing out a packet of toffees and holding them in Uma's direction.

'Good husband material too.'

Ruth gasped, slapping her mother's leg. 'Don't embarrass her.'

'*Are* you embarrassed?' Mary challenged, looking at Uma, a familiar mischievousness twitching in her face.

'I think I'm used to you by now.'

Mary pulled a face of mock-outrage, twisting to look at Ruth.

'What does she mean?'

'You know exactly what she means,' said Ruth.

'All I was saying is that my son would make a good husband. A good father too.'

'And what are we basing that on, Mum?'

'He's hard working. Loyal. Loves kids.'

'He *is* a kid,' said Ruth.

'You're practically the same age, miss high and mighty.'

'Boys take longer to grow up,' said Ruth, stretching out her legs, putting her book down in the sand, pushing her glasses up onto her head.

Anna let out a shriek and the three women turned to see the small child slipping from Daniel's grasp, landing on her back, legs flailing in the shallow water. Daniel lifted her, scooping her, soothing her cries and Ruth looked at Mary with her eyebrows raised.

Daniel began walking up the sand with Anna wriggling in his arms, her cries audible from high up the beach where the three women were sitting. She sounded furious and was twisting to be free. Daniel put her down onto the sand and she ran towards them, hardly getting anywhere in the soft sand, Daniel lolloping alongside her as she did her best to leave him behind. He had grown tall in the last few months, as if his father's death had catapulted him into adulthood. He was lean, a small triangle of hair in the centre of his chest.

'He looks so like Clive,' said Mary, matter of fact, and the three women watched him walking towards them. 'Minus the grey hair and beer belly.'

'And Dad hated the sand,' said Ruth to Uma. 'He stayed fully clothed on the beach. Shoes and everything.'

Mary held her hands to her chest as she laughed. 'He was stubborn when he wanted to be. Soft as a kitten the rest of the time, but there were certain things – you couldn't budge him.'

Anna threw herself onto Uma, pressing her wet face into Uma's chest, unabashed.

'Mooma, Mooma.'

Her chubby toddler limbs were cold and Uma reached for a towel, wrapping it round her and pulling her onto her knee.

'Ahhh,' she soothed, pressing her lips to Anna's hair, breathing her in.

'Mooma,' said Anna again, making everyone laugh with her mispronunciation.

'Good mother material, that girlfriend of yours,' said Mary, looking at Daniel as he cast a shadow over them, dripping cold sea water onto Uma's hot skin. The three women leaned into one another, laughing at the shared joke. Inwardly, though, Uma felt a shard of discomfort at the memories she hoped would have seemed further away by now.

'Let's go get lunch,' Daniel said, holding his hand out to Uma, pulling her up off the sand. He wrapped his arm around her, pulling her to him, his body cold from the sea. She shivered, her instinct to pull away, but she leaned into him instead, Mary watching them, smiling.

They walked along the rocky beach, bending to collect the occasional shell or unusual rock.

'There's a fossil in this one,' Uma said, showing Daniel the jagged line around the middle of the rock. 'We could crack it at home with a hammer and chisel.'

'Are you sure?' Daniel asked, turning the grey, unremarkable rock over in his hands.

'My dad used to fossil hunt. Runswick Bay was his favourite place. And early in the morning is the time to come, when the tide is going out in the winter. When the sea is rough the waves churn everything up and that's when you find them. It's an ammonite.'

Daniel threw it back onto the ground, but Uma snatched it up.

'Let's keep it. I can show you when we get back.'

They walked in silence for a while.

'Your mum was saying that your dad hated the beach.'

Daniel shrugged.

He hardly talked about his dad. He especially didn't like any talk of what happened the day he died. Uma had discussed it more with complete strangers than she had with Daniel. Customers had called an ambulance and a woman who'd been a regular for years had given him the kiss of life, pummelling his chest as she'd learned decades before on a St John's ambulance first aid training. *But I'm a florist*, she'd told Uma at the funeral. *And they're always changing what you're supposed to do. Twelve compressions and five breaths. Five compressions and two breaths. I didn't know what I was doing, but there was no one else.*

You did your best, Uma had tried to assure her, thinking to herself that it probably wouldn't have made any difference. That's what she'd heard.

Each attempt to get Daniel talking about his dad was a cul-de-sac of stilted conversation. But he would sometimes take her hand and give it a little squeeze and when she talked about her own dead parents he would get tears in his eyes. Only slightly, a vague watering, but Uma noticed and she would lean her head against him and he would wrap his arm around her shoulders. Barely twenty, with three dead parents between them.

They wandered back with parcels of fish and chips warming their hands. The five of them ate, barely speaking apart from mutterings of appreciation. The chips were crispy and soft all at once and the fish fell apart as Uma picked it up. The sound of the sea, creeping up the sand towards them and the sun beating down was all that Uma needed to get that burst of happiness in her chest. She always noticed it when it happened, knowing not to take it for granted. Maybe Daniel felt it too because he caught her eye and beamed at her, and held her gaze for just a moment longer than necessary before they carried on shovelling salty chips into their mouths.

In the afternoon Daniel's two aunts arrived, their seven children hurtling across the rocks and sand, strawberry blond hair flying. The children were a tumbling, shrieking pack of wolf cubs. Bony in that way that some children are, ribs showing, elbows sharp. Mischievous, rarely bored, goading one another on with dares and accusations.

**

Back at Daniel's house that evening Uma asked if he had a chisel. It took him a while to find one, coming several times, proffering different screwdrivers. Mary kept insisting that Clive definitely had chisels. *Get back out there and look with your eyes*, she told him. Eventually Uma had what she needed and she took them out onto the patio, showing Anna the rock with the crack round the middle. Anna was tired, grizzly and distracted, but Uma kept promising it would be good, speaking in a certain voice to keep Anna's attention. 'Look,' she told her. 'Keep looking, Anna.' Uma balanced the stone on its edge and nestled the chisel into the thin, jagged crack. Two or three taps of the hammer and the rock split in two, revealing a corkscrew spiral, in-laid with sparkling white crystal.

Daniel took a sharp breath, reaching out and snatching one half of the ammonite to have a closer look. Anna's eyes were wide, looking at Uma, then back at the other half of the ammonite lying between them on the ground.

'She thinks you're magic now,' said Mary, one hand on her hip.

Anna soon bored of the jewel-fossil that Uma had conjured and Mary took her to bed.

'I'm going to go home,' said Uma, aching and tired after their day at the seaside. She liked the feeling, her face glowing from the sun and wind. Her bed would be deliciously cool when she slipped between the sheets.

Daniel was still marvelling at the ammonite, fitting the pieces back together, opening them up. He held it out to her as she began picking up her bag, her cardigan, her car keys.

'You keep it,' she said.

He came towards her, splitting it, looking down at the pieces.

'Why don't you take this half?' he suggested, holding out one of the pieces to her. 'And I'll keep this one.'

She reached out for it slowly. 'Okay,' she said, looking up at him and smiling.

He leaned forward and kissed her gently on the mouth.

'Thank you,' he said. 'For a perfect day.'

Chapter Fifteen

2015

Uma couldn't remember the last time she felt so scared. Receiving news of his death, attending his funeral – those events had been full of dread, but mainly a strange unreality that kept her submerged in a dream-like fug. *This,* on the other hand, was fear. Her heart fluttered at her throat, weak and skittish. Her light summer shirt clung damply to her back, and her foot trembled on the clutch as she parked the car. She wiped perspiration from her top lip and opened the car door, looking across the road to TK Designs.

She imagined Alex, ignorant of Uma's imminent arrival, getting on with her work, or enjoying an early lunch. Perhaps she was having a good day. Or perhaps she was having one of the inevitable not-so-good days. Had grief been what *Alex* had expected it to be? Uma took a deep breath and forced her legs to walk her across the road. It was the same tactic she employed to get herself into the cold, cold sea. *You're just going to do it. Don't think.*

Uma was lifting her hand to the door when she happened to glance down the street. At the other end, a flush of bright red hair, springing out in all directions, back-lit by the sun. Alex. It had to be. Uma clutched the door handle, waiting. The figure slowed, faltering, recognition hitting, perhaps. Before Uma could do anything to change things Alex was there. Right there in front of her.

She was neither princess, nor dragon. Skin the colour of

milk. Eyes a bright, light blue. Unremarkable features, other than her hair which was wild, forced into submission across the front of her head with a silk scarf.

'The Lavender Lounge, Duke Street, ten minutes,' said Alex, pulling open the door, ignoring Uma's hand on the handle, although careful not to touch it.

Uma stepped backwards, stumbling off the curb, turning and heading towards the car. She shut herself in and turned on the sat nav, starting the engine, bringing up a map. Her mouth was dry. She reached for her water bottle and took a few deep swallows.

**

She pushed open the door with its little bell, stepping into the warm, fragrant atmosphere. The tearoom was busy. Scanning the place, she saw Alex at a table in the corner, and she thought *that's where I would have chosen too*. Out of the way. As hidden as they could be.

Her hands trembled as she took her cappuccino to the table. She positioned it carefully between them. Taking off her coat, she hung it round the back of the chair, placing her bag carefully beneath the table, all the time silent, not deliberately or cruelly, just out of fear, delaying the moment when she finally sat down.

It wasn't so bad when she did – Alex taking the initiative.

'So, here we are.'

'Yes.'

Uma wondered if she ought to apologise for forcing the issue. For turning up despite Alex's refusals to meet. There was a pause as they drank from their cups.

'I don't remember seeing you at the funeral,' Uma said, knowing from Father Michael that Alex had kept herself out of the way.

'I stayed at the back and didn't come to the wake,' said Alex flatly.

Uma had been thinking about this, wondering what it must have been like to be so invisible in a crowd of mourners, to have felt so strongly, and to have been forced to hide the depth of that grief. Uma could remember, on the day of the funeral, being glad at the thought of his *other woman* being set apart – not one of the mourners at the front of the church. She had been territorial in her bitterness. But more recently she had imagined the two of them, Alex and she, strangely connected on that day by an invisible thread, grieving in parallel worlds. A kind of parity between them. They had loved him in different ways. But both of them had loved him.

'I've tried to think what it must have been like for you,' said Uma.

'I'd lost the man I'd fallen in love with. We were making plans. I saw my future with him. I was grieving him in every way you can imagine.'

'You sat with his coffin through the night.'

'I couldn't bear to think of him being alone. And then later surrounded by all of you – no space for him and me. I needed that time with him. Those last hours.'

A single, fat tear beaded on her lower eye lid, trembling as she spoke, falling onto the table as she looked down at her coffee. Uma's throat tightened at the thought of what Alex had said, her strength of feeling, and the knowledge that this emotion had been reciprocated by Daniel. *He loved you.*

'When was he going to tell me?'

'He was plucking up the courage.'

'Had he been putting it off for a long time?'

'Not really. We weren't sure for a while. It was a big step. But we'd made the decision.'

He was going. She thought about it, knowing it was true.

At the beginning it had seemed impossible that Uma hadn't known. But she hadn't. There had been no alteration in how Uma and Daniel were together. No indication from him that things were different. It would be easy to blame that on the skill of his duplicity. *Can you imagine? Just carrying on at home exactly as before?* But his affair with Alex hadn't deprived Uma of anything. If their life together had been full of passion then perhaps she would have noticed. Perhaps there would have been less passion for her. If sharing their innermost thoughts had been a habit of theirs then maybe she would have seen the lies in his eyes. Perhaps some barrier would have erected itself between them and Uma would have noticed it. Things may have felt off kilter, out of balance. But none of that had happened.

'I'm sorry the two of you didn't get a chance to be together.'

Alex looked wrong-footed. Perhaps she had been expecting a fight of some kind. And six months ago, perhaps that would have happened.

'And I'm sorry we deceived you,' she said.

Uma shook her head. 'You didn't. Not really.' A flash of something – pride perhaps – rose up. Her equanimity was not entirely smooth. 'We'd been deceiving each other, and ourselves, for years.'

You didn't do this, she was tempted to say. *The demise of our marriage had nothing to do with you. Don't you see?* Uma tried to shake off the thin veil of indignation. Why should there be indignation at all when her own heart had been somewhere else for so long?

'I wouldn't blame you for hating me,' said Alex.

'Maybe I did, early on.' Uma stirred her coffee. 'But not for the obvious reasons. Mainly, I think, because you just took what you wanted. Daniel too. In the end, he found something he wanted and he took it.'

She thought of her father and his advice about sticking with decisions, seeing things through. She saw the benefits of his philosophy – it had, after all, shored up her determination to make Millers a success and strengthened the commitment to her marriage. It got things done. But it left other things undone. It left no space for a change of heart. For mistakes to be made. *Keep changing. You just become more who you really are.*

'I think that's what's been most difficult,' Uma said. 'This feeling, although I hadn't thought it through at the time, that I'd stuck with everything out of some sense of doing the right thing, being dutiful, being *part* of something – his family, Millers and the success of all that. It was the only meaning I'd carved out for myself over the years. I'd chosen that above other kinds of happiness. And perhaps, without thinking about it very consciously I presumed that he had done the same, that we were sticking with the choices we'd made.'

Alex was staring down at her coffee.

'That seems like a waste,' she said, looking up, something hard about her expression all of a sudden.

'Does it? I've thought so much that perhaps Daniel and I should never have been together. I've picked it over, thinking how did one thing lead to another thing and then suddenly there we were? But who knows? I haven't been miserable over the years. And I don't think he was either. We rubbed along okay, isn't that worth something? And we were great together in some ways. Not everyone can work with their spouse. Day in, day out. He was my *friend*. He'd always been my friend...'

Alex was nodding. 'He said the same. I know he loved you. He felt terrible.'

Uma tried to imagine Daniel opening up to Alex.

'He didn't talk much about how he was feeling,' said Uma.

'Not left to his own devices. But if I asked him directly...'

Uma took a mouthful of coffee.

'He never talked badly of you,' Alex said.

'So he never told you his wife didn't understand him.' It was an attempt at a joke.

'He said you... didn't... *fit*.'

Why, when it was what she felt herself, did it hurt to know he'd said this to Alex. Surely, it should be some comfort to know that he had felt the same – that she hadn't just imagined how things had been?

'It's a relief to know he didn't blame me,' said Uma, thinking how easy it would be for Daniel to have resented her for the fraying fabric of their marriage, to blame her for not stitching it all together a little tighter over the years, for letting it, instead, come apart at the seams. Perhaps he understood that he must have been part of that too.

Chapter Sixteen

2015

It was strange to be back. Sitting in the car after a long drive from Devon. Uma looked up at the house. It looked so big. She took a deep breath. It had been so long. She swallowed, closing her eyes, asking her mother's many Gods for the strength she needed. *It won't be as bad as you think.*

She climbed the steps to the open porch, just like she had thousands of times before. The key was already in her hand and she opened the door. The house smelt strange, unfamiliar. She walked down the hall and into the kitchen, the last of the evening sun was creeping low through the large patio doors. Everywhere was bright and clean. *All this space.* Once upon a time she might have thought that she couldn't possibly live with less. Now she knew differently.

She opened a bottle of wine she found in the fridge and poured a glass. It had been a long day – leaving the cottage before it was even light, hoping to be in Devon by lunchtime. It had taken seven hours to get home to Derbyshire, Uma barely concentrating on the road in the end, staying sandwiched between lorries on the inside lane. Her exhausted mind had shuffled Alex's words with images of Daniel, and Aaron, and the cottage, and the beautiful heart left behind on the beach.

She sipped her wine, taking it with her as she wandered

round the house. She walked from room to room, remembering the time before she left for the cottage, the whorl of feelings that she just couldn't straighten out.

She opened Daniel's office door, standing on the threshold for a moment before walking in. She went to his desk and ran her fingers across its surface, taking in the photos of herself and Anna and Aaron. There was one of Mary and Clive. A Christmas picture of all the family, giddy in paper hats.

She sat in his chair and leaned back, the soft leather seat easing backwards with the gentle pressure. Uma closed her eyes, breathing deep breaths, thinking about Daniel, trying to conjure him up.

'I wish you were here,' she said.

She reached for a jumper of his that was in a small pile on the other chair. She half expected a flurry of moths. Lifting it to her face she was relieved when it smelled of nothing. Pulling it on, she wrapped herself in its softness.

She wondered what she would exchange for the chance to spend one more day with him. What would she give if the Gods could be bargained with? When she realised that she would give the house gladly, the money in the bank, most of her friends and acquaintances with only a few exceptions, she changed the question. What *wouldn't* she exchange for the chance to speak to him just one last time?

**

Pippa's hands were full. A bottle of something in one and several packets of chewy sweets in another.

'Vodka and gummy bears,' she said.

Uma laughed, stepping back from the door to let her in, reaching out her fingers so they brushed Pippa's chiffon-covered arm as she passed.

'Come here, you,' she said once the door was closed, pulling Pippa into a hug, holding her there.

'That's nice,' Pippa whispered into Uma's dark curls.

'Sure is,' said Uma, feeling the relief of it, the comfort. 'I'm so glad you're here.'

'I'm glad I'm here too.'

They stepped away.

'You could have brought her, you know.'

'I wanted to come on my own. My neighbour's baby-sitting.'

Pippa followed her down the hallway. Uma reached for glasses from the cupboard, and orange juice from the fridge. She slid the things across the counter top and watched her friend pour them both a drink.

'I can't believe you brought gummy bears.'

'Old school.'

'Listen Pip. I'm so sorry about-'

'No,' said Pippa. '*I'm* sorry. I overreacted.'

'But I'd have been pissed off if I were you. I've not thought enough about it from your perspective. Not really.'

'It's silly when I say it out loud. I just think I always had this thing about being left out. A lot of the time it felt like you three and me.'

Uma shook her head.

'It was never like that. In fact, I suppose I always felt that *you and Aaron* had a connection. Doing drugs, being at Uni together.'

'Only because you *left* Uni. I'm sure Aaron was at Manchester in the first place because that's where you said you wanted to go. And Daniel only ever had eyes for you. No one else got a look in.'

'You were the cool one Pip. The crazy, *just say yes* girl! You were so integral to the four of us. It was always the *four of us*.'

'Oh my God! Do you remember *just say yes* days?'

Uma laughed and Pippa passed her a vodka and orange. She opened one of the sweet packets, held them out and Uma took a handful, looking down at the colours. She sighed.

'And I was just so ashamed about the termination. Aaron

211

only found out because I collapsed on the train and needed someone with a car to come and get me. If I'd known how ill I was I'd have called for an ambulance. But I just thought it was pain. I had no idea what it meant.'

'I wish you'd felt able to tell me.'

'I know. I wish that too, of course I do. I was just petrified of Daniel finding out what I'd done and it causing a rift between us all.'

Pippa was spreading the gummy bears out on the counter top, arranging them into piles according to colour, posting one occasionally into her mouth.

'How did you never tell him? I'm not judging you, but just *how*?'

Uma shrugged. 'Once you get used to it, a secret isn't that difficult to keep.'

'I'm no good with secrets. It's like they burn through me and escape. I'd rather have everything out in the open.'

'Well, maybe *that's* why I didn't tell you.'

It was a risk, and Uma knew it, but Pippa laughed.

'I actually need to tell you something else,' said Uma, taking a swig of vodka. 'A secret of sorts.'

'You don't have to tell me anything you don't want to.'

'This is a new start okay? I want things to be different.'

Pippa reached for Uma's hand across the counter top.

'I love you Moo.'

'I love you too.'

Pippa let go of Uma's hand and took a sip from her glass.

'Daniel was having an affair.'

Pippa looked shocked.

'I met her today, down in Devon. That's where I've been.'

'Oh my God.'

Uma paused, waiting a moment for the news to sink in.

'How long for?'

'About a year. It sounds like it was pretty serious.'

'Serious how?'

'He was planning to leave.'

212

Uma described everything she knew, the best way she knew how. The story had become a familiar shape in her mind. She knew its curves and ragged edges by now, and offered all the segments that made up the whole. They talked for hours, finishing the gummy bears, drinking vodka. By the time the sky was black, the moon the barest sliver, they weren't talking about Daniel anymore – they were talking about Uma, her future, and they were talking about Aaron. Pippa offered Uma memories and moments, suspicions and suggestions. Their past was a path leading right up to this moment now. By the time they had finished it was like an old mosaic. Patterned. Intricate. With little pieces missing here and there.

'Can I borrow something?' Pippa asked, looking up at the coats hanging on the hooks by the door. The clear summer night was cold, the air rushing in, a flurry of goosebumps prickling Uma's arms.

'Take this,' said Uma, reaching for her long woollen coat.

Pippa slipped it on, covering her bright summer clothes with black wool, pulling it about herself, turning away.

She had told Pippa so much that evening. But she hadn't told her about the coat, and the memory she liked to keep just for herself at the very back of her mind. The memory she had reached for every so often over the years, taking it out, just to look at it, like a piece of jewellery from a safe. She conjured it now, watching Pippa disappear round the corner at the end of the street. She could almost feel the soft warmth of the wool, the fingers that fumbled at the buttons.

It had been Christmas 2008. Daniel and Mary had left Ruth's Christmas Eve party for midnight mass. Aaron and Uma had walked the tiny distance home, every breath a fug of condensed air, their skin lit orange from the streetlamps. Uma was wrapped in her long woollen coat, and was laughing, clumsily tripping up the steps to the house, Aaron eventually searching her pockets for the keys when he had tired of her unsuccessfully looking for them herself. She could clearly remember the moment they had stepped into the dark hallway together, how they were suddenly quiet, neither of them reaching for the light switch.

'Let me,' Aaron had said, moving closer, taking her top button between his fingers, his eyes on hers, never wavering. It was as if she sobered suddenly, woken by the moment unfolding and the sense of wanting to be right inside of it, to make it last and last. Perhaps he felt the same because he seemed to be taking his time, one slow button after another. He pushed the coat from her shoulders and Uma shook it from her arms. He put his hands to her waist, pulling her towards him almost imperceptibly, uncommitted, as if the action wasn't an action at all, but only a thought.

She was aware of every part of them that touched and Uma, even intoxicated, could feel the push-pull of their desire, the subtle dipping and rising of something that held them there for an excruciating minute. He stooped and lifted her into his arms, taking her up the stairs, across the landing, kicking open her bedroom door. Unceremoniously, he had tipped her onto the bed, laughing at her indignant cry. He lent over her, his face close to hers, tracing her face with his fingertips. The moment seemed to stretch on and on, and Uma felt the weight of it, the line they were about to cross. *We can't though, can we?* She hadn't known how to answer. He had brushed a kiss against the side of her mouth, lingering there, waiting perhaps for one of them to make the decision. And then he had lifted himself away, dissolving into the darkness of the room, towards the light of the hall.

'*Aaron!*'

She had wanted to tell him that *yes, we can. Actually we can.*

'I'm going to stay at Ruth's,' he shouted from the stairs.

'But you were staying here.'

'I *was*.'

'Aaron!'

Uma stumbled from the bed, making for the door, tripping

214

over the rug and landing with a painful thump on her left hip and elbow. She had listened to the door slam shut and had lay down on the floor, hip throbbing, elbow grazed. She hadn't moved and had slept eventually where she lay, pulling down the duvet sometime in the night when she must have been cold. She had woken in the morning, pulsing with pain, shame, regret. Bruises had flourished down the side of her body and had lasted for weeks – a sickly reminder of that moment, and of how, when he walked away from her, desperation had risen like bile in her throat.

Pippa gone, Uma found herself pulling books, one by one, from the bookshelves in the front room. She was looking for something she hadn't laid her eyes on for years. She'd excavated a blurry memory of slipping what she was looking for between the pages of a fat old book with a fabric cover. She was sure it had been a complete works of Shakespeare, or something similarly literary, something they might own but not have actually read. She had already located that particular book on the shelves in Daniel's office, but there had been nothing inside.

It must be here somewhere. She worked her way through the books one at a time. She had discounted all the smaller paperbacks – unless her memory was failing her completely the card, covered in petals that she had meticulously dried and pressed, was too large to fit between the pages of a standard-sized paperback, hundreds of which now surrounded her, strewn across the floor.

She found what she was looking for eventually in an old Oxford Dictionary. She had almost given up hope and her heart leapt when the thin piece of card slithered from between the tissue-thin pages. She let the dictionary slip from her grasp and reached for what she had been looking for. The petals were in remarkably good condition – pressed flat, carefully preserved all these years. She smiled, remembering Aaron giving them to her. He'd invited her for a day out with his parents walking in the Peak District, but Uma had been unable to go. *We'll do it another time*, he had promised her. *Bring me something back*, she'd said, off-hand, the kind of thing she might have said to her parents if they had been going somewhere without her. He'd returned with hundreds of petals in a brown paper bag. *One from every flower I saw on the way.* Uma shook her head to think of it now. It couldn't have been more revealing, and yet somehow it had seemed quite natural that Aaron might bring her a bag of petals. *No flowers were harmed in the creation of this gift*, he had joked.

Uma had pressed them between pieces of tissue and heavy books. Patiently for months, forcing herself to forget about them until they were perfectly dry. And then, one day, alone in her parents' empty cottage she had glued them carefully, meticulously, spiralling from the centre in order of colour, into one single flower. It had taken her hours. Fearful of it getting damaged she had kept it pressed, hidden, between the pages of the book.

It had hardly faded with the passing years. She gazed at it in wonder and took it through into the kitchen. She took a pen from the dresser and sat at the table. After staring at the empty fruit bowl for ten whole minutes she picked up the pen and began to write inside the card she had made nearly two decades earlier:

What does it mean that once upon a time you picked a petal from every flower you came across? What does it mean that I pressed and preserved every one? Was it your heart I found on the beach? Hadn't we better go back for it?

She found an envelope, addressed it to Aaron at his parents' house, not knowing for certain whether he was even there still. She thought about texting him to check, explaining that she wanted to send him something, but decided against it. She had a feeling that her message would make its way to him safely. Just as his message had made its way to her.

It was 2.30am but still Uma went out of the house to post the letter, fearful that by the morning she might have found a reason to change her mind. She let the envelope hover in the mouth of the post-box, her fingertips gripping it, reciting what she had written, checking that it sounded okay, that it wasn't too presumptuous, that it wasn't too vague – still anxious that she might have got it wrong, that he might choose fear over her. That it might not have been *his* heart of stones after all. She let the envelope go, heard it land with a soft *fflltt,* and made her way home to bed.

Chapter Seventeen

2000

By the time she opened her eyes on her wedding day Uma knew that it was too late. If she was going to tell Daniel what she had done then she should have done it by now. She couldn't tell him on the day they were getting married. And how could she tell him afterwards? Her terminated pregnancy now somehow felt as if it had been *their* pregnancy, rather than hers alone. *I should have told him.* He was to be her husband, and she was bringing a secret to that union. The shame of it was like a worm in the pit of her belly. Sometimes it lay still but never for long.

Once Uma had realised, many months ago, that she and Daniel would be together it had seemed to her that she owed him the truth. Aaron had not, after all, relinquished Uma's secret to Daniel on the night of his birthday party. She had never got to the bottom of what their fight had been about. Neither of them would tell her, or, as they claimed, neither of them could possibly tell her because they didn't know themselves – both of them blaming a mutual intoxication. Uma hadn't been sure that she really believed them. There was something she couldn't quite determine that made her think they were lying to her. She tried to tell herself that if Daniel was keeping things from her then it didn't matter that *she* was keeping things from him. There was a parity between them in their holding back of the truth. It was a slippery argument and she knew it.

It was a small affair. Uma had fought for that, resisting all attempts to let things roll out and gather momentum. A small church wedding. Daniel's family and a small gaggle of close friends made thirty guests.

Mary had offered to walk Uma up the aisle, and although she wondered whether she really needed walking up the aisle at all, it had seemed churlish to refuse. She had grown close to her mother-in-law over the last eighteen months. Their relationship had blossomed even before Uma and Daniel's. Uma had found herself looking for excuses to call Mary, and it wasn't long before their conversation was peppered with confidences so that Mary knew most of what was happening in Uma's life and vice versa. *Most*, but never all. Uma's Sunday planning meetings with Daniel about the embryonic business became an excuse to also help Mary in the kitchen, making puddings under Mary's watchful eye, bringing her own recipes in the end too, persuading Mary to try something new. They bustled together in the warm fug of the kitchen and Uma had felt something inside of her settling.

On the morning of the wedding Uma stood in the cold porch of the church. The guests had gathered and were waiting inside. Anna was excited, skipping across the tiled floor, spinning round like a ballerina, gleeful at her princess-skirt puffing out and rising up. Mary passed Uma the hand-tied bouquet of yellow roses, and Uma pricked her finger on an unseen thorn. It hurt in a deep, throbbing way and blood beaded repeatedly, Uma sucking at the small, but persistent wound.

'I'm so sorry,' said Mary, fishing in her bag for tissues, dabbing Uma's finger. 'I was so careful to remove them all.'

The roses had come from her garden, from a bush that Clive had loved for its brave, persistent winter flushes of flower. *There's nothing like a winter bloom to lift the spirits*.

The organ started up inside the church and Uma felt a rush of panic, her heart beginning to pound. The panic had been coming in waves the last few weeks. After months free of the

219

attacks they had returned with a vengeance. She had tried not to think too much about the wedding as it made her anxiety worse, concentrating instead on Millers, the flourishing new lines, the taking on of staff, the commissioning of adverts in glossy magazines. It had gone from strength to strength, and it had been easy to distract herself.

Standing in the cold church porch Uma took deep breaths. *Everyone gets cold feet* she reassured herself, thinking of her parents, reminding herself how proud they would have been of her. But it was no good. Still she wanted to run away, and, as if Mary could read her mind, she turned to Uma and took her narrow shoulders in her hands, looking her in the eye.

'Try and *relax*,' she said. 'It'll be over before you know it.'

It seemed a strange thing to say, as if, like having a tooth extracted, getting married wouldn't be so bad after all. *Did she know?* Uma felt the horror flood through her, but Mary had turned away and was getting ready to enter the church. *She didn't mean that*. She meant – *relax and enjoy it, it'll be over so quickly you'll miss it*. Make the most of it, is what she meant. Pin pricks of light burst in front of her eyes and Uma waited for them to pass, aware only vaguely of Anna bouncing round the two of them, oblivious to everything in her glorious three-year-old way.

'Ready?' Mary asked Uma, glancing at her only briefly, offering her arm.

'I just need a minute,' she said, pulling away and walking to the church doors, standing on the threshold, gulping in the fresh, winter air. The sky was beautifully clear, contrails the only blemishes.

'Just thinking about my parents,' she lied, when she sensed Mary's presence behind her.

'Take your time. I can tell the vicar you need a few minutes.'

Uma took a deep breath, pushing away the darker thoughts that pulled at her like an impatient child, replacing them with something else. *I love him*, she told herself. *I love him enough*. But what flashed into her mind wasn't an image of Daniel at all, it was an image of Anna, thumb hanging from her mouth, asleep on Uma's lap, and Mary in the kitchen on a Sunday afternoon, the conspiratorial aunts, Ruth plying Uma with rum and coke on a Saturday evening. And, *of course*, then Daniel too. In amongst them all, she loved him enough.

'No,' she said, turning back towards Mary and the church and all the people waiting the other side of the double doors. 'I'm ready now.'

She was wearing her mother's tunic, the one with hummingbirds on it, taken in so it fitted her properly. White trousers underneath. A long linen scarf around her neck and hanging down behind her back. As they entered the church Uma felt something like relief. It was happening now, and, just as Mary said, it would be over before she knew it. She looked at Daniel as she walked towards him, holding his gaze, his face full of love. It made her smile and relax just a little. *I love him enough*.

Aaron flanked him, a tall, blond sentinel, matching him in grey, roses in their buttonholes. Uma saw all that with the briefest of glances, but didn't look at Aaron again. They spoke their parts and Aaron passed the rings. It was only then that Uma noticed her finger was faintly sticky with a smearing of blood. It was too late to do anything about it, but it was all she could think about as Daniel gave her *this ring as a sign of our marriage*.

Outside the church, everything was cold and bright. *Everything will be okay now*. Mary and her sisters were full of smiles – confetti, cameras, hats clutched in their hands. Daniel's arm was wrapped around her, holding her firmly at the waist and Uma leaned into him, raising her face to him, relaxing into every kiss he placed on her mouth. *My husband*. And he would be a *good* husband. Uma never doubted it.

They gathered their thirty guests at a local restaurant for a meal. The champagne was poured. Warm nibbles of food were passed round before the starters arrived and Uma realised how hungry she was. Yesterday she had hardly eaten. After putting some food and champagne inside her she was able to let herself be absorbed into the evening properly, to stop being on the outside looking in, as was her habit.

Daniel spoke briefly to thank everyone for being there, to thank Uma for doing him the honour of marrying him. And then, to cheers and table-thumping, Aaron stood to deliver his best man's speech. Eventually, once everyone had quietened enough for Aaron to be heard he smiled, bowed his head briefly to look at the table and took a breath. Then he lifted his eyes to the expectant faces around the table and, with no notes to refer to, began to describe how Daniel and he had been the very best of friends since the first day of primary school. He made fun of Daniel in the usual best-man way, retelling stories of scrapes they had got themselves into as young boys.

'He's been the brother I never had,' he said after a while, becoming serious. 'And most of you will know that he also saved my life one winter when I was a stupid eleven year old messing around on a frozen lake and I'd fallen through the ice. There's no other way to describe what he did, other than heroic. I wouldn't be here now if he had chosen to do anything but exactly what he did.'

Daniel and Aaron exchanged glances, warm smiles, and the room erupted into cheering and applause.

'Obviously that makes Daniel an amazing person. But it's especially relevant today because for lots of years he reminded me that I owed him my life, and what the hell was I ever going to do to repay him?'

Laughter rippled round the table.

'Well then... five years later, he calls in the debt. It's a few days into the start of sixth form and he tells me excitedly about this new girl called... you've guessed it...'

'Uma...' the room chorused, erupting again into cheering and applause.

'And Daniel said to me *she's going to be mine so stay away! I'm calling in the debt.*'

The room erupted into laughter and Uma felt something slipping away. The chair beneath her, the room itself, everybody around her. Everything was fading, becoming remote and unimportant. Aaron was smiling, but Uma saw how his amusement was forced around the edges, and she saw what he was telling her as he looked straight into her face, recounting the story. *I had no choice* he was saying. He was opposite her on the large round table, and she wondered if he had chosen that place deliberately, looking at her and Daniel directly, smiling gamely at the rest of the guests in between directing his speech at them.

'He knew as soon as he met her that he wanted her to be his wife.'

It was the punchline and Uma looked around at the beaming faces, wondering why it seemed like such a lovely story to them, when it felt so awful to her.

Once he was seated again and the whole table was engaged in chatting and laughter, eating and drinking, Uma sneaked a glance across the table at Aaron. He was deep in conversation with Tim, one of Daniel's cousins. She drained her glass of wine in one gulp, knowing that soon she would be too drunk to care that everything now felt wrong. She was fighting a rising anger at her new husband – dutiful, loyal, lovely, but somehow also a cheat. So what that Daniel had pulled him from a frozen lake? It wasn't Daniel's right to demand a particular loyalty. *How ridiculous.* At some point in their lives Aaron would have given something freely, something that would have repaid Daniel for the risk he took, for loving Aaron in the way he must to have crawled across the ice on his belly.

She didn't want to look at her husband now. It was as if he had tricked her out of something that should have been hers. *You can't blame Daniel. You chose to be with him. He didn't force you.* Uma sighed gently, clenching her fists beneath the table, trying to pull herself together. If she had been clearer with both of them then things would have been different. *What have I done?*

If she could have talked about it with Pippa then she would have, but she couldn't trust Pippa with this. And who else was there? She thought of Mary and Ruth and almost cried over-emotional, drunken tears at her wedding table. Instead, she plastered a big smile onto her face and went outside for some fresh air. The good thing about not wearing a wedding dress was that she didn't look like a bride. She could stand on the street and nobody paid her any attention, and right now that was just what she needed.

Anonymous, thinking about her parents, about Aaron, about Daniel and his family she burst into tears. She covered her face with her hands. The air was freezing and, although the street was busy, nobody seemed to notice her. She felt invisible. Blissfully invisible.

Chapter Eighteen

2015

She took a long drink of water, threw her bag onto the bed and made her way straight to the beach. *One last weekend.* She spared the time to glance around the garden, noticing how long the grass was after only a week and how the peony blooms had collapsed and faded, browning round the edges. Soon, rotting petals would carpet the ground beneath the plants. They had been magnificent the day that Uma left – pale pink, tinged with red, tightly packed ruffles falling open, their stems arching gently with the weight of their offerings. They had been almost too beautiful to leave.

Her path through the woods had been partially reclaimed, just as she had known it would be. Nature marches on so briskly. She had to pluck swaying, wayward brambles between her thumb and forefinger, lifting them out of her way.

The trees were alive with birdsong and the thrumming of woodpeckers. How familiar that sound had been and how good it was to hear it again. Uma stopped to listen to the short, quiet bursts of drumming, looking up into the thick canopy for a flash of black and white, a small smile turning the corners of her mouth. She gave up after a while, remembering the water, feeling that pull towards it, the urgency that had been building ever since she got into her car that morning and left the city behind.

She half ran, half walked the rest of the way to the beach,

something inside of her leaping when she caught sight of the flat pebbles on the pathway, creating her a trail to follow, leading her down onto the sand and to the heart of stones that was still there. There were fresh footsteps coming down out of the woods, and Uma allowed herself to briefly imagine that they belonged to Aaron, that he'd received her message and had understood, that he'd made his way here, that it *had* been his heart laid out here on the beach. She had texted him yesterday to say she was coming to the cottage for the weekend, although she hadn't gone as far as inviting him. *Whatever will be*, she kept telling herself.

The sun was high in the cloudless sky. Groups of people, children, dogs, were scattered the length of the beach. Summer holidays. She had never seen it so busy, although, by the afternoons there had always been a scattering of people here and there, walking in the shoreline, bending for shells or stones, throwing something for a dog to chase. It had only ever been in the early morning, when the light was ethereal and tentative, that Uma could hope to have the beach entirely to herself.

She stood in the middle of the heart, turning a full circle, marvelling at its perfect edges, the care with which the stones had been chosen – darker towards the outer edges, lighter, paler, smaller stones towards the centre. She had expected to return and find it scattered somehow, but here it was, as perfect as she remembered it.

She stepped away, turning to face the sea, walking towards it, slipping a finger beneath the tight strap of her swimming costume where it was biting into her shoulder, rubbing at the skin there to sooth it. She stopped momentarily, bent to remove her sandals and carried them with hooked fingers towards the shoreline. The shallow waves licked her toes, ankles, heels. She bent in greeting, offering her hand for the waves to break against.

She walked back onto the sand, high enough for her things to be out of the way of the lapping waves and undressed down to her swimming costume.

She began the same as always, purposeful strides into waist-high water and then one smooth dive, breast-stroke arms until she surfaced, front-crawl after that, out far enough to feel she was away from the shore and all its familiarity. When her arms began to tire she surrendered, floating on her back, eyes closed.

She hadn't expected anything from it when she had thrown herself into the biting water that first April afternoon. The wind had roused the sea into something frightening. The waves had been as angry as she had been. They had met one another defiantly, keen to see who would turn away first. It had been a fight, but now she couldn't imagine such a thing. Now, even when the wind and swell were up, even when the sea tossed her like a play-thing, testing her resolve, forcing its salty self into her eyes, her mouth – even then she felt safe, her heart at ease, content. Perhaps it was foolish, but she had found her faith. And she gave herself to it willingly, like people give themselves to God. *Then sings my soul – how great thou art!*

Back on dry land, in the heat of the sun, warming herself, Uma lay back on the sand until her skin was dry. Then she sat up and pulled on her clothes, one by one, slowly, taking her time, remembering what it meant to be here, with so little to do and the lists of jobs so short.

Walking back up the sand towards the woods, Uma looked up and noticed, between the reeds and the dunes, a figure, standing at the place where the stone heart was laid out. If she had known for sure that Aaron had created that heart then perhaps she would have indulged some territorial jealousy. Get away from there! Be careful! But she knew no such thing and, looking around at the scattering of people enjoying the beach, she realised that although she had always felt that the beach was hers – at dawn, in spring at least – there must be hundreds of other people who feel the same. *You don't have to own it, for goodness sake.*

It was only as she drew closer that Uma's heart lurched at

the sight of the figure between the reeds and dunes. He was standing on the heart of stones. Right on top of it, looking down the beach towards her, waiting. She watched him as she continued to walk, recognition hitting her like a wall of water, crashing down on top of her, threatening to wash her back down the beach and into the sea. She was slowing, realising what this meant – that the heart really *had* been for her. She imagined the effort of it, how long it must have taken to collect all those stones, to separate them into darker shades and lighter, to arrange them into something beautiful, to make the edges all so neat and even.

She imagined he was smiling although she was still too far away to know for sure. She stopped momentarily, grinning, her hands coming to her face, staring at him through splayed fingers that tasted of salt. She laughed, her head tipping backwards. And then she continued, walking towards him, grinning, feeling silly, trying a more insouciant smile, something a little more demure. But her laughter persisted, bubbling out between her lips.

The sand was warm, shards of dry seaweed scratched the bottom of her feet and she stubbed her toes against unseen stones. The wind was coming in off the sea behind her, lifting her hair so it fell every so often in front of her eyes and she had to push it back, doing her best to hook it behind her ears. When she was close enough, she noticed that he was smiling too, watching her, shaking his head slightly as if it was amazing that they should find themselves there together. When she reached the pile of stones she hesitated, looking down at them.

'Did you do this?' she said, smiling, looking up into his face, knowing the answer.

Aaron nodded, and held out a hand to her. She stepped forward, onto the stones, grasping his hand in hers, closing the small gap between them. They looked at one another and laughed afresh, clutching each other's arms, anchoring themselves, grinning in between laughing.

'I'm so sorry,' she said, her spare hand coming to cover her mouth. He shook his head, shrugging her apology away. 'I'm just feeling very weird.'

He pulled her against him and she rested her head on his chest to calm herself, wrapping her arms around his back, breathing him in. They stood, encircling each other, the wind picking up and dying down. Picking up and dying down. He moved a hand into her hair and closed his fist around a clump of damp curls. Easing her head away from his chest, he tilted it so he could look down into her face. A tear fell from one of her eyes, taking her by surprise, and he caught it with his lips, finding its saltiness with his tongue. After the worst kind of longing there was finally *this*. And Uma knew that he was luxuriating in it as much as she was.

'Is this happening?' he asked.

'This is definitely happening,' she whispered.

He lowered his face onto hers and they kissed. A long, slow, meaningful kiss. The easiest thing in the world.

**

Aaron continued sleeping as the dog-rose scratched at the window. He slept as Uma said his name again and again, softly, beneath her breath, curious to try the syllables afresh, to see how they sounded now. And still, he continued to sleep as she untangled her limbs from his. She was tired from a sleepless night, but happy to be awake, to wander barefoot in the brand new world, full of him, to feel unbreakable.

She had appreciated the cottage before, it had given so much more than she could possibly have expected when she had first arrived. But now it was perfect. The mossy terracotta pots, cracked and crumbling, were perfect. The bare window frames, dusty with peeling paint, were perfect. The overgrown grass. The woody lavender. The slate tiles slipping from the roof.

She collected her things from the kitchen cupboards and

229

put them into a cardboard box, her heart no longer heavy at the thought of returning home. Once the box was full, her job done, she took a bowl for her breakfast and filled it with roasted plums from the tin on the top of the cooker. She and Aaron had picked them from the tree in the garden yesterday, taking the few remaining that weren't alive with wasps, risking being stung every time they reached their arms into the branches, dropping the fruit whenever they felt the tremor of wings against their skin. Uma had mixed tamarind with honey, coating the fruit before roasting them. They had eaten them hot from the oven, burning their lips and mouths, laughing at their greed.

She took her bowl outside and sat on the wooden bench, looking at the garden beginning to fade, the reddening leaves. Summer was dying, but autumn would be there to break its fall. The syrupy plums slid down her throat, and everything was just as it was meant to be. There was no uncertainty, no tremor in her heart, no skipping of her pulse. This wasn't the heady excitement she had felt with Richard, bursting with not knowing. This was belonging. This was the same world, suddenly changed.

Uma hardly noticed the car until it was grumbling on the gravel. She twisted to see, half standing, craning her neck. *Mary*. It couldn't be. Why on earth had Mary come all this way? It made Uma think of disaster, catastrophe, more bad news. She went to meet her, opening the car door as Mary put her glasses into their case.

'*Mary*. Why are you here?' said Uma, stepping away to allow her mother-in-law to manoeuvre out.

'For you. Why are *you* here? You'd only just come home.'

Mary had heaved herself out and was clinging on to the car door, looking earnestly into Uma's eyes.

'You said you were going back to work on Tuesday,' said Mary.

'I said I had meetings on Tuesday. With the CEOs. The accountant.'

'Then why are you here?'

'Because it's Sunday and I came to get the rest of my things.'

'The rest of your things?'

'Let me make you a cup of tea.'

'So, you're not staying?'

'I'm not staying.'

'That's what you said last time.'

'I'm done here. I'd left a few things behind in case-'

'In case what?'

Uma searched for the words.

'In case I just couldn't be at home.'

Mary ran her hand through her hair, scrutinising Uma.

'But you *can* bear to be? It was okay, wasn't it? You seemed okay on Thursday.'

Uma nodded, smiling.

'You just need to get back to things…' said Mary.

These words had become Mary's mantra. *You just need to get back to things*. And Uma wanted to respond with *keep changing, you just become more who you really are*. A movement caught their attention and they turned towards the cottage, towards Aaron, bare-chested in the dark doorway, Uma's heart leaping at the sight of him. She grappled with the various words she should offer Mary right now.

'*Oh*,' said Mary, looking to Uma, then back to Aaron. '*You two*.'

Aaron disappeared into the cottage but reappeared almost immediately, pulling a shirt over his head. He was coming towards them, trying a smile but letting it fall when he saw the expression on Mary's face.

'That's why you're here.'

'*No*.'

'I couldn't understand why you had come back so soon…' said Mary.

'I need to show you something,' said Uma, taking Mary's arm, walking her into the cottage and into the kitchen.

'Look here,' she said, pulling open the flaps of the card-

231

board box. 'All my spices and kitchen things. I deliberately didn't bring everything home. I left clothes in the wardrobe, I could show you those too. I came back for my things. I'm coming home.'

'But... *you two*?' Mary said again, swivelling to look at Aaron who was stood in the cottage doorway.

Uma didn't want to deny it. They had denied one another for so long. But what to say? Aaron seemed to be calculating the same equations. Mary seized on their hesitancy, adding it up into something it wasn't.

'This is why,' she said.

'This is why what?'

'You were here so long, hidden away.'

'No. Aaron and me... this is... this is new. Only just.'

Mary was stepping away, shaking her head.

'All these months,' she said, but clearly to herself, not expecting an answer.

'Mary, you're making something up that isn't real,' said Aaron.

'Aaron's been away, remember? He was trekking, he wasn't here.'

'And now I suppose you'll be traipsing her all over the world with you?'

'That's not the plan.'

'Right,' said Mary, turning, her face empty of expression. 'Well, anyway...'

'I'm making tea. Let's go and sit in the garden for a while,' said Uma.

'Come out with me,' said Aaron, beckoning Mary, turning away, seemingly trusting that she would follow. She did, and Uma made the tea, wondering how her perfect morning had changed so swiftly into something else entirely. She scooped the plums into bowls and took them outside, putting one down in front of Mary without asking if she wanted any. She went back for the tea, taking all three mugs at once.

The swallows and swifts were circling, banking and diving,

feeding on the wing. The three of them watched the birds for long moments at a time – respite from their stilted conversation. Uma and Aaron said things that sounded like sense. They said that *this whole thing* had taken them by surprise. They said there would have been no hiding it. They said there was no shame in loving one another. Aaron even ventured his belief that Daniel would have been happy for the two of them.

Mary ate her plums and watched the swallows, saying very little, as if her opinions had deserted her. Uma knew that wasn't possible. She knew that her mother-in-law had simply packed her opinions away, along with all the parts of herself that were now unavailable.

Chapter Nineteen

2015

Ruth's house smelt of lavender. The girls were round the table, cutting squares of material, passing the scissors, holding up their half-sewn fabric pockets for Uma to see. She took their offerings, inspecting them enthusiastically, kissing their warm heads in turn.

The lavender had been crumbled into a large bowl in the centre of the table. Uma plunged her fingers into it, squeezing a handful, grinning at her nieces, bringing her empty, fragranced hand to her face, inhaling. She turned to Ruth who was emptying the dishwasher.

'I was hoping Mary might be here. She's not returning my calls.'

Ruth rolled her eyes. 'It's just change. You know what she's like.'

'I also think she's got the wrong end of the stick. About Aaron and me. She was acting as if she thinks it's being going on for months. As if we were hiding away at the cottage together. Maybe she even thinks it was going on before.'

'She doesn't. It's not that. She's just afraid of everything changing.'

'Everything's bound to change. How can it not?'

'Exactly. We can't put our lives on hold to spare her worry.'

'I've always thought of her as so resilient. She's one of the strongest people I know.'

'She just likes to be sure of things. Don't confuse certainty with strength.'

Uma remembered what Mary had said about *traipsing around the world*. She remembered her dismissiveness. The way she had hardly looked at them for an answer to her question.

Ruth closed the dishwasher door and stood, rearranging the loose, summery linen that was draped around her neck.

'I've been looking up psalms,' she said, reaching for her phone. 'Isaiah 43, 19. *See, I am doing a new thing! Now it springs up; do you not perceive it? I am making a way in the wilderness and streams in the wasteland.*'

'I'm not sure we should quote the scriptures at Mary.'

'Or *then I saw a new heaven and a new earth, for the first heaven and the first earth had passed away, and the sea was no more.*'

'Let's leave that to Father Michael, I'm sure she'll be bending his ear.'

**

Because there was no answer at Mary's house, Uma went through into the garden, hesitant at first, this thing she had done thousands of times before seeming, suddenly, like trespassing. She made sure to call Mary's name, then to knock before trying the back door, only then peering in through the patio windows, cupping her hands around her face against the glass.

The church was empty too. Sometimes Mary stayed after the daily mass, to help with arranging flowers or changing candles, scraping wax from the floor, or cleaning the few windows she could reach with the wooden ladders that Daniel had complained would one day be the death of her.

Uma walked the short distance to the cemetery, thinking she might find Mary there. She entered through the western gate, going the long way round to Daniel's grave, knowing that Mary, if she was there, would have stopped at Clive's grave first. This was a regular routine for Mary. Mass, followed by helping out in church, and then the cemetery. Uma read the headstones as she went, prolonging her walk, not sure she wanted to find Mary in amongst the lime trees. *In loving Memory. Much loved. Never forgotten.* Green granite, grey granite, India red. Portland Limestone. Nabresina. It wasn't possible to bury someone you love without falling into cliché. They had all this to come, when the soil had settled.

As she passed the church on her way home Uma saw Father Michael in the grounds, sweeping confetti from the path that wound its way down onto the road. Perhaps he felt her watching him, for he looked up in her direction, straightening, taking steps towards her, half-raising his hand. Uma gave a quick wave, looked away and kept on walking, not sure exactly why she was so keen to get away, to *not* talk, to just be home.

They must have been in all the same places but at different times, because there was Mary on Uma's voicemail by the time she arrived home. She had been to church and the cemetery, she said. And was planning a Sunday roast. *Daughters only.* She had checked with Anna already. *I'll believe it when I see it, but she says she's coming.*

**

Uma arrived to the smell of roasting meat, the kitchen full of steam.

'You might need that knife,' said Anna from the back door, gesturing with her head, busy rolling a cigarette. Uma looked to the carving knife ready on the work surface. 'To cut your way through the atmosphere.'

Mary said nothing, but heaved a great, heavy sigh, lifted the beef from the roasting tin and wrapped it in foil. She scraped at the roasting tin with a spoon, turning eventually to Uma.

'*This* one,' she said, pointing the greasy spoon at Anna. 'Has dropped out of university.'

'*Ah*,' said Uma, looking towards Anna, wondering how much more of her new life she had revealed – the new band, the older lover. Anna put the cigarette between her lips, lit it, and took a single step outside.

'All those fees down the drain, thousands of pounds.'

'*One* year's worth of fees. Better that than *three* years' worth of fees.'

'But you'd have a degree!' Mary threw her hands up in the air.

'That I'd never use!' Anna mimicked Mary's arm gesture.

'You don't know that. You have to look to the future, think ahead. It might not seem of value now because you're young and hedonistic.'

Anna laughed.

'You're only ever thinking a day ahead,' said Mary, pointing at Anna again.

'Exactly. Living for now,' said Anna, dragging on her cigarette, tipping her head back and blowing the smoke towards the skies.

'All that money,' said Mary.

'That's now a debt. *My* debt. Not yours.'

Mary was making gravy, stirring the contents of the roasting dish over the flame. Ruth was behind them all, laying the table with a crocheted tablecloth that had belonged to Mary's mother, the willow pattern plates that had been Clive's mothers, and the same cutlery set that Mary had had since her wedding day.

'Mary,' said Uma, fixing her with a warm smile. 'What can I do?'

'Oh, okay, yes, you could get the Yorkshire puddings out of the oven. And the roast potatoes.'

Between them they got the food onto the table, fetched

drinks and sat. Mary said grace, while Ruth, Anna and Uma eyed one another from beneath their lashes.

'Your hair is even shorter,' said Uma to Anna, as they helped themselves to roast potatoes and freshly podded garden peas.

Anna ran her hand over her closely shaved scalp.

'And you look well,' said Ruth.

'I *am* well,' said Anna.

The dark rings had disappeared from beneath her eyes. She'd put on weight and lost her skeletal look.

'What's with the earring?' Mary asked, indicating the large crucifix that dangled from Anna's lobe.

'Nothing's with it.'

'You've no time for Jesus, you said that years ago.'

'Jesus was a dude.'

'I thought you didn't believe in him.'

'He's not Father Christmas, of course I believe in him. I'm pretty certain he existed in some form.'

'In *some form*? He was the son of God.'

'Well…'

'You have Jesus in your ear and these ridiculous great skulls on your fingers and *that* thing there.' Mary motioned to the large, colourful tattoo on Anna's shoulder.

'*That thing there* is Artemis,' said Anna. 'She was a dude too.'

'It all seems very confused to me. As if you're not quite able to make up your mind.'

'But that's the beauty. I don't have to make up my mind.'

'She's obviously slightly more committed to Artemis,' said Uma.

Anna laughed and Ruth joined in and Mary grumbled something to herself that Uma didn't quite hear.

She couldn't help wonder if all this was intentional on Anna's part – whether she was deliberately provoking Mary to deflect attention from whatever it was they had all been gathered for. There had been no mention of it yet, but Uma was sure that it was coming. Whatever it was she would have to wait, as Mary chewed her beef, one small mouthful at a time.

When their plates were empty Mary offered the bowls around again and helped herself to more of everything. They talked about the girls and school and where Ruth and James were thinking of going on holiday in the October half term. They talked about autumn and the change in the weather, and how they all love this time of year with its falling leaves and bonfires and candles. And they talked of Daniel, of how they wished he was with them, how nothing was the same without him, and how they must decide what words would best memorialise him. They talked about stone. And they talked about flowers.

'Bulbs would be nice,' said Mary. 'Because they'd be flowering around the anniversary. And they'd be something bright in the bleakness of March. And they don't mind the frost and snow. And we could plant all different types so we have a nice long run of them.'

Uma thought that this talk of Daniel might be Mary's catalyst, that the conversation might lead seamlessly into some accusation of betrayal. But just as Uma was expecting Mary to breathe fire into her words Mary reached across the table for her daughter-in-law's hand, covering it with her own for a brief moment. Uma was shocked by that one, small action. It made her think that perhaps they hadn't been summoned at all. *Summoned* is how she had described it to Aaron as they had lay in bed that morning. But perhaps she'd been wrong. Perhaps there was to be no forced humiliation. No request for Uma to explain herself.

They ate pudding – a lemon meringue pie, and a tarte tatin because Ruth didn't like meringue. The conversation meandered, between mouthfuls of sweetness with cream. And afterwards they cleaned the kitchen together. Ruth did the clearing away while Mary did the washing up, her arms elbow-deep in soapy bubbles. Uma took things from the draining board, dried them and put them away. And Anna smoked at the door, looking out, staring off into the distance.

'Father Michael said something that's made me think,' said Mary.

This is how it began.

'What did he say?'

'He said that perhaps Daniel had been the one wanting to sell Millers.'

'He said that?'

Mary looked askance at Uma.

'There's no need to protect me,' said Mary.

'I'm not protecting you.'

'*Was* Daniel thinking of selling before he died.'

Uma shook her head. 'We hadn't talked about that. What did Father Michael say exactly?'

Mary turned back to the sink and the washing up.

'He was vague in the way that somebody is when they don't want to betray a confidence. But he was very clear that Daniel was preparing for some big change he was nervous about.'

Uma thought about it. He would have been nervous, of course. He would have feared judgement about his decision to divorce. He would have worried about breaking his wedding vows, those promises made partly to Uma, but partly also to God.

'I think there'd been something going on, something on his mind, but we'd been so busy, to be honest, we never really had a chance to discuss it. We'd planned to talk but it didn't happen.'

Every word she said was true. Perhaps Father Michael had done the same. Uma kept herself from looking at Anna.

'It got me thinking, anyway,' said Mary.

'That…?'

'If he'd wanted to sell Millers I wouldn't have liked it, but I'd have accepted it. In the end, whatever choices he made,

I would have accepted them eventually. And it's made me think that you need to do what you want with your life now he's gone.'

'Oh, Mary.'

Mary turned towards her and Uma saw that her eyes were watering.

'I just don't want you to disappear.' Her voice cracked and a tear fell from each of her eyes. 'I just couldn't bear it if you went too.'

Uma shook her head. 'I'll not be disappearing.'

'You'll be off round the world if you and Aaron make a go of things-'

'*Mum*,' said Ruth.

'Okay, okay,' said Mary, turning back to the sink.

After a moment, Ruth spoke.

'Father Michael also said a few things about change, didn't he?'

Mary scrubbed at a plate, lifting it onto the draining board, making a small sound of agreement.

'What did he say?' asked Uma.

Mary was scrubbing at another plate.

'He said that change is part of life's mystery,' said Ruth. 'But Jesus is the same yesterday, today and forever.'

Ruth was smiling, seemingly satisfied that Father Michael had done a good job, talking Mary down from her place of fear and judgement. Uma felt something inside of her softening, suddenly regretting dismissing him the other afternoon as he had been sweeping confetti from the path. She thought about the power of the right words at the right time. How a few sentences could dampen a fire, or fan its flames. That the choice had been his.

'So, let's just take things a day at a time and see what happens,' said Ruth. 'What Uma does now, what Anna does next… Let's just wait for things to unfold shall we? You have three daughters. Perhaps we won't *all* be here, *all* the time. But that's not so terrible is it?'

Mary seemed to think about it for a minute, scrubbing hard at the roasting tin in the soapy water.

'Oh, *you girls,*' she whispered eventually, almost to herself.

Chapter Twenty

2015

It was the autumn equinox. Singular leaves, crisped at the edges, fell from the city trees. Soon, they would scatter the air like flakes of snow, rushing to gather in the curbs and drift against the garden walls.

'We'll be here until it's done,' said Ruth, depositing a stack of flattened boxes onto the kitchen table. Mary, Anna, Pippa and Aaron were gathered too. A retinue of helpers. They started with tea and cake. Uma had made an orange and polenta cake and she eased it from its tin onto a large plate where it oozed its honey topping, waiting to be sliced. While they drank their tea Uma sat in front of the wood burner with Aaron, their feet, bundled in thick woolly socks, rested against one another, conversation happening behind them at the table.

Daniel and Uma's house had gone on the market a few days ago. There had been no viewings yet and Uma was relieved. She hadn't seen the point of postponing it, but she had wanted, she realised, to finish the task of sorting out Daniel's things before showing people round. It wouldn't make any difference to anybody else – but it mattered to her for some reason that she couldn't quite explain.

'We should start,' said Mary at last, pushing herself up from the table.

'We should,' Uma agreed, easing herself reluctantly from the sofa.

They started in Uma's bedroom first, going through his clothes, deciding amongst themselves whether items should go to charity or whether anybody wanted anything in particular. Anna took a couple of his jumpers and Uma could imagine her in them, snuggled up on the sofa watching a film, wrapped in the soft woollen security of her big brother.

With the help of Anna, Pippa and Aaron, Uma surreptitiously put together a bag of things for Alex. She used the nice, leather holdall that had come back from the car after his accident and picked out the jumper he had been wearing that week. Uma imagined that Alex might recognise it. She gathered a few photos together – a couple of recent ones, but a picture of him as a teenager and one of him as a small child too. Mary had hundreds, she wouldn't miss a couple.

They ate sandwiches for lunch in the kitchen, talking about other things, all of them keen to keep the emotion at bay. Dispersing his belongings was more excruciating than preparing to bury him. They'd had no choice but to do something with his body. But months later, throwing away things that mattered to him was a choice. They didn't *have* to do it. They could choose to cherish everything, to keep it all. But instead they were choosing *this*. They were sending his things out into the world without him. *It feels terrible*, they kept saying to themselves, to each other. *I hate seeing his things like this.*

As the afternoon wore on and they sorted through his office, the boxes in the hallway downstairs became a small mountain, provoking tears from Uma when she saw them suddenly for what they were. She stood looking at them, her hand over her mouth, shocked at the sight of his life all boxed up and ready to be taken away. *All these things that mattered.* Aaron almost collided with her as he came back from the kitchen, and his face crumpled too when he saw that she was crying. They stood, leaning against one another, wetting each other's faces with tears. When they pulled apart he wiped her face with the palms of his hands.

'I can move them,' he said. 'I'll take the stuff for Oxfam.'

Uma helped him move some of the boxes into the back of his car, watching him drive away.

In the hallway she noticed Daniel's coats and jackets still hanging from the hooks on the wall. She reached out and ran her hand over them, stroking them gently as if they needed her comfort. Slowly, one by one, she unhooked them, folding them over her arm and taking them into the living room, sitting down with them on the sofa. She held them in turn, remembering him wearing them, slipping her hand into their pockets in search of forgotten objects, some little part of Daniel's life that he had left behind. When she found all of them empty, she folded them into two neat piles and fetched a box from the kitchen, put them inside and sealed it with parcel tape, labelling it after she had moved it to the hallway.

She followed the voices to his office, meeting Ruth and Anna coming out with bags in their hands.

'We're nearly done, I think,' said Anna.

Uma stepped inside, watching Pippa and Mary stacking books in the corner. She looked around at the emptied shelves, the scattering of photos that were being left. It was hard to believe he'd never be here again.

'Thank you so much,' she said, to no one in particular.

Mary stood, twisting to look in Uma's direction, shaking her head, dismissing Uma's appreciation. Her eyes were red rimmed from regular crying throughout the day.

'We're in this together,' said Mary.

Uma nodded, feeling her own tears starting all over again.

'I think it's gin and tonic time,' said Pippa, lifting the box that she had just taped shut. 'Come on, everyone. Downstairs.'

'We should wait for Aaron,' said Mary, but Pippa waved away the suggestion.

'We'll have a quick one and make it look like we're just starting when he walks in.'

'You all go down, I'll be there in a minute,' said Uma.

She turned towards the window, aware of everyone

leaving the room behind her, suddenly needing a few minutes of solitude. She stood, looking out at the fading day, the rain blowing against the glass, the leaves swirling in the crepuscular light.

As she was closing the blind, fiddling with the cord, she noticed something behind some photographs on a shelf – something that she recognised immediately, but something she hadn't seen for years. She reached in and grasped the ammonite in her hand. It was the same size as her palm, both pieces locked together, masquerading as just any old grey, speckled rock.

She took hold of the top piece and lifted it, opening the ammonite and revealing its complicated interior, re-membering cracking it open all those years ago when Anna was just a tiny child and Uma and Daniel had been on the cusp of their life together. She remembered Daniel holding the newly separated pieces and offering her one to take away. Standing in his office, all these years later, she hefted its two halves, one in each hand, bringing the pieces together again, feeling a resistance as she twisted them subtly, looking for that one, singular angle where all their intricate, jagged edges sunk into one another. *A perfect fit.*

She brought it to her lips and kissed it, liking the coldness of it against her skin. Daniel and she hadn't been a perfect fit at all. But it didn't matter. They had been something different. Something that for lots of years had been good enough.

She took the ammonite out of the room, to the window ledge in the hallway. She heard laughter from the kitchen, and the sound of Aaron returning home. She put the pieces on the window ledge, nestled amongst the other stones – the two halves opened out, exposing their whorls of crystal, and spirals of seemingly infinite edges.

Acknowledgements

I would like to thank everyone at Legend Press for their commitment to this book, especially my editor Lauren Parsons, Imogen Harris and Ditte Løkkegaard.

I am indebted to my wonderful agent, Ella Kahn, for her hard work, guidance and warmth.

I am grateful to everyone who read and commented on the manuscript, including Rebecca Bonner Wallace, Karen Dunn, Sophie Hunter, Sue Hepworth and Jamie Voce. And to Rachel Skinner-O'Neill, for peppering the years with advice.

Special thanks to Sarah Dadswell for advising me about Uma's dual Indian-English heritage, sharing with me stories, insights and observations, and, later on, finding the time in your busy life to read the manuscript and advise me on errors and necessary adjustments.

To Christine Poulson, writing companion, wise friend, you have been a constant source of guidance and encouragement; I am so grateful.

Heartfelt gratitude to all my friends for keeping my spirits up with cups of tea, words of encouragement, film watching and game playing.

To Cora Greenhill, Christine Kelly, and River Wolton, thank you for being there, and inspiring me to live creatively. And to Angus Mcleod, full of creative passion and joy, thank you for all your support and for being your own marvellous self.

To my parents, for teaching me that anything is possible: thank you.

Love, love, love to Schuyler and Elfie for your laughter, enthusiasm, and for doing without me when I am trapped in my writing world.

Deepest, loving thanks to Lance, for everything.

Come visit us at

www.legendpress.co.uk

Follow us

@Legend_Press